IN AND OUT OF TIME:
lesbian feminist fiction

edited by Patricia Duncker

Published by Onlywomen Press, Ltd.
Radical Feminist and Lesbian publishers,
38 Mount Pleasant, London WC1X 0AP.

Copyright © this collection, Patricia Duncker, 1990.
Copyright © each author, 1990.

All rights reserved. No part of this book may be reproduced in any form or by any method without the written permission of Onlywomen Press, Limited.

Printed and bound in Denmark by Nørhaven.
Typeset by Columns, Reading, Berks, UK.

Cover illustration copyright © Geraldine Walsh.
Cover photo of Patricia Duncker © Porcher: Mansle.

"The Great Tropical Hardwood Walkout" first appeared in a slightly different version in *Horticulture Week*, December 20–27, 1985 and also in *Everywoman*, December, 1986.

"Diwali Muburak" first appeared in *Bazaar Magazine*, March, 1990.

"Saccharin Cyanide" appears in the collection of short stories by the same title, Onlywomen Press, London, 1990.

British Library Cataloguing in Publication Data
In and out of time.
 1. Short stories in English, 1945– . Special subjects: Lesbianism – Anthologies
 I. Duncker, Patricia, 1951–
 823.0108353

ISBN 0-906500-37-0

*To all the Lesbians who wrote and produced
'In and Out of Time'*

CONTENTS

Gypsophila Claire Macquet 1

Diwali Mubarak Daljit Kaur 15

Naomi Tina Kendall 23

Penelope Is No Longer Waiting Cherry Potts 30

The Wedding Stone Caroline Halliday 33

The Lizard Barks At One Valerie Potter...................38

**Dope Smoking Lesbians Can Never Be
   Good Teachers** Berta R. Freistadt..........................40

You Can't Say That Rebecca O'Rourke 58

In And Out Of Time Shameem Kabir......................61

Another Garden Aspen...86

The Secret Of Chantal Grey Margaret Melvin 100

Below Zero Alison Ward..107

The Runners Char March..119

**The Great Tropical Hardwood
   Walkout** Frances Gapper......................................129

Someone In Some Future Time
   Shelley Anderson 136

Saccharin Cyanide Anna Livia 156

Scarlett O'Hara Mary Dorcey 175

Suit, Goodbye Helen Smith 217

Afterword: The Word And The World
  Patricia Duncker 224

Contributors' Notes 235

GYPSOPHILA

Claire Macquet

Perhaps I hate gypsophila. It is here in a room lit in part from the leak of light through the door but largely by a great constellation of gypsophila.

In the day there were tiny white flowers threaded with green; tonight only hundreds of points of brightness. They merge here into a Milky Way; there, on the edges, lonely stars are turning.

How strange associations are, things yoked together by one private history. Or even by a non-history, by something that, in Johannesburg's winter more than twenty years ago, didn't happen.

I hadn't even meant to bring her gypsophila. A bottle of wine would have been more appropriate, certainly more useful to me, already stiff with nerves. But although I had thought about the evening all week, nothing practical had presented itself, nothing so sensible as: would I take her champagne, a book, chocolates, flowers (proper flowers, not something that was only just not a weed).

She hadn't given much of a lead, come to think of it. She had barely described the way to her flat after "Come and have a bite to eat at my place, say, next Wednesday, about eight." I didn't hear what she was saying at first, there was such a din in the bar, such a din in my head.

It was Johannesburg's only regular gay bar in those days, and not even a proper gay bar. Called The Pro, it was a slit of a place in a drab modern hotel where actors hung out after the theatre. Since the law excluded women from real bars, drinks were poured behind a curtain and it rated as a lounge. Since apartheid was a fact of life, only the ponciest of screaming African queens, only the butchest of Indian dykes — non-citizens acceptable so long as they were no more than bedding material — could appear, namelessly. They brought the total numbers to about 20. Perhaps it wouldn't have been thought of as a gay bar at all had it not been for Beatrice, a huge Boer well into his fifties. He came in every night at about ten, with carrots in a little wicker basket, to sing dirty songs in a cracked falsetto until closing.

I was also there every night. To feed this habit, I had taken a flat around the corner. I was 21 and alone. I had had a lover at school and later languished after various stony-hearted women, but I wasn't looking for a lover, though I thought constantly of love. I was looking, I suppose, for meaning. I was certainly looking.

Sometimes women came in, mostly in twos, and, whatever I was looking for, I would look at them. They had bleached short hair, lacquered into unyielding DAs, masses of lilac or green shadow around eyes ringed with black, no lipstick. They didn't say much to Beatrice or the queens or me, but perched with straight legs on stools, intermittently talking to each other.

Some spoke in English, conversations easy to follow in their confident colonial tones about who was cheating on whom, what BMs were secretly camp, and who had got off with the most gorgeous doll at any of their hundreds of parties.

From other groups I unravelled threads of darker-toned talk, in Afrikaans. Occasionally, these close women would break out to twit Beatrice (fellow-Afrikaner, fellow-pervert, but further down the line) in nervy music-hall English. Sometimes, as they got drunker, voices and fists would rise in fury against the world. Sometimes one or two of them would be loaded into taxis by the management and a wave of relief (or perhaps self-satisfaction) would roll through the bar.

There was Evonnie of the powerful musculature who, after a few drinks, would challenge the men to arm-wrestling and lose with very bad grace. Sarie and Sannie would arrive incensed at their boss and leave incensed with each other. Petronella displayed jagged lines on her wrists, carved, she said, with shards of milk bottles.

"We, the Lord's Chosen People," Beatrice would say, "We are not couth."

Perhaps for that reason, I was drawn not to the English paper-dolls but these women whose stories were engraved on their faces. Discretion is not an option for Daughters of the Volk guilty of the only unnameable vice of an ethic obsessed with vice. I was also repelled by them, and for the same reason. It was many years and many failures later that I learned not to be shocked by people who wore, ribboned on their chests, their medals of defeat.

Months passed; there were for me no friendships made. In the lavatory sometimes a word was exchanged, but though these were my people, I was not yet theirs. Their clammed unhappy world was mine, when I would claim my place. I felt like a child sitting on the edge of a swimming pool, choosing her moment to plunge in.

Then one night the moment chose itself. Diana came in with three dykes – two bleached DAs, one delicate-featured Indian woman. They all had the same tight pants and short boots, they sat in the same huddle. But Diana's eyes, great pools of grey, wandered quizzically round the bar, and encountered mine. She held my gaze for a second, then, with a nod, turned back to her friends.

I stared after her and, champion eavesdropper that I was, soon picked up their conversation. Her talk was laced with all the slang I was still learning to push past my lips, but she was not twitting anybody, she was not muttering about what mine magnate's wife was secretly sleeping with what butch, she was complaining in a measured public voice about the working conditions of African actors. She was embarrassing the solitary African there, a pretty young man wearing a coral necklace, perhaps ruining for him a few hours of fantasy, reminding him that the oppressed have a duty to be angry. She wasn't saying anything clever or witty. She had no suggestions about what anyone could do about it. She said nothing that I hadn't heard before. But it brought together all the excitement I had felt at anything said in the bar. I wanted to meet her. I wanted to look through those clear grey eyes that could see our own ghetto with its spider encrusted wires; other people's iron ghettos; see beyond.

I didn't have the boldness to break in to her talk (which at her table was being met with yawning indifference). I just sat there and willed her to do something.

She did. She went up to the bar. I emptied my glass at a gulp and followed.

She ordered; I ordered; she half-turned towards me: "You're not from Johannesburg." I nodded.

"Ghastly place."

I was suddenly shy. Perhaps I grinned.

"You're from?"

"The country. Natal. Sugar belt."

There was a pause. She would soon nod and move off. I had watched too long; my tongue was tangled in my thoughts. I trawled for it. Out gushed, in an awful tweetie-pie voice: "Sugar cane cutters have even worse working conditions."

"I'm sure they do."

Her eyes wandered to my table, took in the plastic handbag and grubby white nylon gloves, then settled beyond, on the Tretchikov print, the one then to be found in every public place and living room, of a rose flung down beside a dustbin. She sighed.

"You shouldn't be drinking brandy and water alone," she said. "Come and join us."

Beatrice, beside us at the bar, had been watching this scene with raised eyebrows, perhaps put out of countenance that Diana had paid no court to him. He seized my hand and pushed a carrot into it. "Don't do it darling," he cried, "You're only a virgin lover once; go for a higher bidder."

I was startled, I was to Beatrice a stranger.

"Thanks Beatrice my angel," Diana took up the challenge, "We'll call you when the bill's due."

"You're on, so long as I can watch." Beatrice bowed as for an audience, but there was none. Groups at tables were preoccupied with themselves, and Diana was leading me to hers.

I don't remember what she said, what I said, what the dykes said. Only that everything she said was, of course, wise and subtle and funny, that her eyes drank in the world, that in the centre of their grey deepening to black hovered something unfathomable. She was certainly nice to me, bending from the neck to ask if I wanted a cigarette, if I had a job, if I missed my mother, if I lodged nearby, if there were poisonous snakes in the sugar-cane fields. I said yes to all these things.

Then, "Have a bite at my place", to which I also said yes.

They pulled on their leather jackets and left before closing time, roaring off on two Lambrettas, one of the dykes with her arms tight around Diana's ribs — into the cold neon-pointed night — Christmas tree gypsophila.

In the seven intervening deserts of nights, she didn't come into the bar. Beatrice's interest in me blossomed. "Come sit on my knee, girlie," he would say, "and hear auntie's warning about the slings and arrows of outrageous fortune. Beware, my lovely, beware of brickies."

The two outsiders now in huddle as exclusive as anybody's, he told me how, in the early hours, he would be haunting the metal halls of the railway station in search of brickies. I don't know if he offered them carrots. He usually found one or two; sometimes he chose badly — or perhaps too accurately — and ended up in hospital. He occasionally picked up a policeman by mistake, the other difference being that then he'd have to call the ambulance himself. "Let auntie's ruined complexion," he would say, "be a lesson to you of the perils of crawling outside the laager," and his crumpled face, brandy-scented sweat and grease oozing from its open pores, would bear down on mine. "You, little girl, you still have a choice. Let Mama pick you a husband and buckle down to it. Do as auntie Beatrice says and you'll get a garden with a swimming pool in it. You can spend your days there, dreaming about lesbian ladies over your G&T."

And again: "Mama must make it one of those men who grows fat when he gives up rugby; an army chappie say, thick as two short planks, a bloke who talks in grunts. He won't pry into your soul; he won't notice if you do your nails while he's screwing you."

Beatrice's two great hands, nails earthstained as hooves, would cradle mine. Sometimes he tutted over my nails, bitten to the quick. "Oh poor little claws. Why do women destroy their few weapons? Sharpen them, my angel, like a cat. Then you can teach your soldier to be a good boy. But first Mama must choose right. Tell her auntie Beatrice will advise."

The thought of Beatrice and my mother talking, even being in the same room, was so shocking that I laughed hard for minutes.

Beatrice, who had so recently seemed repulsive to me, whom I had feared because I could never tell when he was sending me up, became, in those seven nights, my best friend. He poured his accumulated despair into my ears. He came to my flat, and we slept in the one bed chaste as nuns. I was clearly not much cop as a brickie. We bumped across town to his smallholding to see neat rows of winter vegetables and the filthy shack in which he cooked and occasionally washed, and bedded his brickies.

We drank a lot of brandy together, and I found the sensation of workdays wobbly with hangover disturbingly pleasurable: they distanced me from the granite edifice of work. I grew able to treat the heap of papers on my desk with indifference. Faces at work which used to burn into my consciousness faded to ashes. I didn't eat much, though I had an endless supply of carrots, but got through a pack and a half of untipped Lucky Strike every day. And the dark and dangerous world he sketched and which I now found myself entering became increasingly fascinating. If I had read Genet, I would have been able to define this excitement. Definitionless, I poured all those feelings into the image of a woman with quizzical grey eyes.

I devoured every scrap of information about Diana. She came from Cape Town. She believed in God and tore strips off people who mocked her for it. She was a theatre manager. The three women with her were freelances, employed by her for one production, a musical based on *Cry the Beloved Country* by Alan Paton. She read thrillers. Her lover had gone off to Nyasaland with a liquor-shop owner. She designed her shirts and had them made up by an Indian tailor. She had a 125cc Lambretta. She lived alone in Doringbos, an area freshly whitened by the Group Areas Act. It was now largely occupied by white railway workers, the State having given them first option to buy there, to beat down the prices asked by the evicted coloured families. Beatrice didn't much like Diana. "She's cold, sweetheart, and a snob like all cold women."

All this, even the horrible place she lived, increased her glamour. That her one mind could command so easily the world of The Pro (which was to me the gay world) and the granite edifice beyond seemed miraculous. *She* had asked me to dinner. She could unseal the doors of a mind. Well before that Wednesday dawned, I was obsessed.

Beatrice, enticingly discouraging, bid me a lugubrious farewell on Tuesday night. He warned me that Diana tended to go on about things; if she did, I was to launch into song with "You ain't nothing but a hound Dog", since Diana loathed pop music. He was sure Diana wasn't the sort who would ask vulgar questions about butch or femme, but if the subject came up, I was to say that I was absolutely brilliant at both. Then he advised Listerine for the breath and silk knickers for the ass and gave me a bunch of carrots to take as an offering.

I didn't take the hint. Wednesday was so crammed with deciding what socks, what opening remarks (and how to get from them to an exploration of psyches), what to do if she fed me soft eggs or bloody steak (things that turn my stomach over), that I didn't think of Beatrice's carrots rotting in the sink. I didn't question, either, what I knew I wanted to do: to go to Doringbos on foot – not a great distance, in fact, but absolutely not to be done in a city where every night the streets were emptied of citizens by the pass laws.

It was only when I set out across the tsotsi-infested streets of Hillbrow – nerving myself to pass from there through the unlit pool of Berea to Doringbos where there might still be children playing rounders among the parked cars – that it came to me. I had no offering. Between a beer hall and a filling station huddled a little flower shop, its frontage a mist of gypsophila. The night was cold, and the wet streaks that ran from the flower buckets to the gutter glistened with the threat of ice. The smell of vegetation mingled with hops and petrol. I would bring to Diana that musky greenness, armfuls of flowers over which her eyes could wander. Inside, there were roses, red, pink and yellow; there were bold, theatrical strelitzias; yard-long gladioli and canna lilies; there were grey and purple proteas – rolled-up hedgehogs, the national flower. Outside, in the cold, gypsophila stars trembled.

I went in. "How much is the gypsophila?"

His voice was tense: "The baby's-breath? This stuff? This was left over from a First Communion at that Roman place up the road. Hell Dametjie, I wouldn't lie to you: it was a First Communion for a bunch of kaffirs. Really, man, all dressed up in white, carrying prayer books and candles!"

Oh, my countrymen; depression familiar as sin clouded the pretty little shop.

"You don't want them, no? Well, they have been aired. Say 20 cents a bunch."

Not possible; they were too cheap.

He misread my hesitation. "Ag man, just take the lot."

No need to panic. No need to run. The shop was no more awful than the rest of the world. I looked round for alternatives. Roses – too intimate; strelitzias – ugly; gladioli – common; what? I picked up a protea, two, three. Perhaps they were all right. No scent, no velvet texture, no glow, but they were handsome. And she came from the Cape. And they were suitably expensive. They would do. On the way out, I paused again at the gypsophila. Why not? I helped myself to as much as I could carry, and made up an unlikely bouquet of delicate white points with the three woody desert heads in the centre.

No inconspicuous passage through Berea was now possible; I was lit by candelabra of gypsophila. One kerb-crawler I escaped by dropping into the vestibule of some flats; another followed for several blocks, leaning out of his window to whistle, but fortunately not getting out of his car. The third didn't proposition but drove behind at walking pace, hissing insults about low white women. He seemed to be on his way to Doringbos. Perhaps his daughters were just then playing rounders in the street.

I walked fast, stopping only to answer the greeting of two black streetboys strumming a guitar made from a paraffin can. They admired the flowers. They were protection for a few minutes, and they didn't find it odd that there should be a lone white woman on the street after dark. I gave them a few cents which they rolled up in tattered handkerchiefs and stuffed into their shorts. Perhaps that night, if the police didn't pick them up, they would sleep curled round central heating vents.

In Doringbos, there were smells of frying boerewors and the yells of children fighting inside the carcasses of wrecked cars. I found Diana's place, a tall, dark house with sash windows pressed against the cliff which separated Doringbos from Highlands. Years later, I saw houses like that in Muswell Hill, and found them as forbidding even though they were on top of the cliff.

I checked my watch. Arrived early, and safe. I shouldn't have walked of course. I should have confessed that I had no scooter and asked Diana to pick me up. Would I ask her to drive me back? Would I have to go back? Perhaps we would talk for hours about this city, about this country, and perhaps she would say it could be saved. But perhaps she would be irritated that I had been silly enough to walk, perhaps she would want to lecture me and tie me down to the granite edifice. If she did, could I say that one tried to make something right by acting as if it were? To Beatrice, to whom nothing and everything was ludicrous, I could have said that I wanted to strip down, come dressed only in my soul. Could I approximate, say to Diana that I had wanted to do something dangerous, endure some foolish ordeal, because perhaps there was nothing that was real that was not plucked from the jaws of a shark? If I had known it, perhaps I could have said that like our mother Eve, like all her daughters, I was seeking knowledge of good and evil. Not the dessicated wisdom of the Catechism but of the living tree, living serpent. Or that I, like so many of Eve's daughters, like Eve herself who had lured her baby-faced Adam into the adventure, lacked courage to pluck the apple alone and wanted Diana to lead me by the hand. Safest to let her think I had taken a taxi.

The gypsophila bundle half behind my back, I rang the bell. After a long time, the peephole darkened, and the door opened on a black woman hauling on a dressing gown.

"You're for Diana?" She had recognised me as a lesbian as quickly as I had realised she was living in the house illegally. Diana would have collaborated in this. The woman had taken a risk in opening the door.

I ventured a smile, "Good evening".

"The flat round the back," she gestured.

"Thank you very much. Thank you very . . . ." The door had shut.

With a light heart, I trotted round past the dustbins, stopping to note the reflection of the big African moon from the gypsophila. The coloured woman didn't look like a theatre person; she was tight-lipped, even arrogant; could she be a member of Umkhonto we Siswe in hiding? Might I, who could walk the streets of Johannesburg at night, become a runner for them? Would this be one of the things Diana would initiate me into?

Even in winter, when it doesn't rain for months, the place, overhung as it was by the cliff, smelled damp, vegetable, tumescent with new life. I felt my way for the last few steps, till helped by a light from somewhere inside. The door was open.

"Hello." I carried the flowers high before me. "Hello, hello, Diana." A white-painted hall, a living room crammed with books and one of those new tape recorders, a glimpse of a neat bedroom with a Basuto blanket serving as counterpane. A beautiful place in the midst of all that awfulness. "Diana?"

In the kitchen, an African maid was ironing shirts. "The Missus is working," she said in a tired voice. "It's the dress rehearsal tomorrow."

"She's expecting me."

"You want to wait?"

I did. I sat on soft chairs and hard chairs. I explored the flat. I looked at my watch. I walked to the road. The curtains were drawn upstairs. The children had gone. I walked back. I searched the shelves in vain for banned books. I looked at my watch again. It hadn't stopped. I tried not to think it peculiar that a revolutionary should have a maid who called her "Missus". I examined the tape recorder but didn't dare to try it. I walked back to the road. I listened to iron bumping. I helped myself to a glass of water. I failed to get a conversation going with the maid.

At nine she said she was going and wanted to lock up. "That's okay," I said. I put the flowers in the butler's sink, fluffing out the gypsophila. "Goodnight," I said, and went.

Her keys jangled. How did she get home, or did she, too, squat illegally on the premises? I walked, itching to put my fist through the gob of every kerb-crawler.

But I didn't go home. I went to The Pro. I went up

and put my arms round Beatrice. "Oh, you appalling creature," he cried, "What on earth are you doing here? You've just ruined my best fantasy this week. It was taking cream-cakes to you and Diana in bed." I had my face flat against Beatrice's egg-stained shirt and was sobbing.

"Oh sweetheart," he said, dropping cigarette ash in my hair, "If you only knew how much I love women who can still cry. Now I'm crying too, and it's utterly delicious. In my next life, I'll ask them to make me a lesbian." I don't know how I got home. I was certainly very drunk.

I didn't go to the bar the next evening. If I was too sick to go to work, I was too sick for that. I cleaned the flat. There was no way out. Diana had forgotten. My odyssey was a very small show when there were dress rehearsals. I looked at myself in the mirror and saw one of twenty million bodies bred in a poisoned soil. If I could be allowed no inner life, perhaps at least I could pledge this body to freedom, fight and follow the leaders – Mandela, Sisulu, Mbeki, Goldberg – afollow them to prison. I had lived two decades and done nothing to change the ugliness. I hadn't even thought about it except as a reflection of my own discontent. Perhaps the revolution would not be too proud to accept a lesbian. I looked at my mirror image again: I had thought Diana might have liked that little triangle of dark hair. I ran my fingers through it, and it sprang back into curls, so gutsy, even on me, someone with head hair as straight and lifeless as nylon thread. I looked harder still at the mirror and tears welled up in pity for a vain and idle daydreamer who so craved to be part of something great.

The door bell rang. The peephole showed Diana. I scrubbed my face and ran for some clothes.

"Beatrice sent me." She came in grumpily. "Why did you rush off like that last night? Couldn't you wait a few minutes? There was a lot of traffic." She stood with her hands in her pockets. Her eyes were fixed on the blackened window. She did not bow, elegantly, from the neck. Her leather jacket was buttoned tight across her chest.

We were on her scooter charging through Hillbrow, Berea; we flashed past the two streetboys; we swung round the cliff to Doringbos. We were parked half up under the hedge, the Lambretta hidden from the attentions of children. We felt our way round to the back. She was banging pans in the kitchen, throwing together a meal. It was probable that I would sleep that night under the Basuto blanket.

She kept breaking off to answer the phone; people wanting changes made to the backdrop, a door to hang the other way, different lighting at the end of the overture. Nothing about Umkhonto.

I didn't take any phone messages; I didn't lift pans starting to burn in the kitchen. I was feeling the rugged sepals of the proteas, thrust into a thick brown earthenware jug. They hadn't opened any further, but then they unravel very slowly. Proteas last for weeks – for ever, if you like dried flowers. There was no sign of the gypsophila.

Perhaps the seeds of this brilliant constellation were scattered in the same Big Bang that made the other, older galaxy I thought, as I stood in the doorway of a room in London, looking at gypsophila, more than twenty years later.

Many things have scattered. London jostles with exiles, among them Diana, among them me. I hope the young man in the coral necklace found a better refuge than the Pro, but I fear he did not. Beatrice didn't escape; nor, I suppose, did the Afrikaans dykes. Perhaps they still drink at a descendant of The Pro, whispering fearfully of what will follow the brutal and now doomed order which gave them, and me, a gangster protection. They were not on an ascending curve: perhaps they live with ferocious dogs behind high walls; perhaps they are old and ill, or mad; perhaps they are dead.

Certainly many things have died. But there is still the Roman Church where gypsophila flowered at First Communion ceremonies. The white people have abandoned it for their exclusive chapels in the suburbs and all the prayer books there are held in black hands. Would Diana remember that church? Would she remember if I asked her what became of that other First Communion gypsophila, if she gave it to the maid?

Note: Umkhonto We Siswe [Spear of the Nation], a group within the African National Congress, set up a programme, using first persuasion, then, if that failed, industrial action, then sabotage, then armed struggle to bring an end to apartheid. Its leaders were Nelson Mandela and Walter Sisulu.

DIWALI MUBARAK

Daljit Kaur

VISIT:
Indian sweetcentre.
The Co-op.

Shopping List:
Pakoras
Samosas
Gulabjuman
Rasmali
Chicken Wings (2lbs)
Basmati Rice
Chicken Legs (4)
veg curry ??
Roti Flour (brown)
Mango Chutney
Whisky, coca-cola, etc.

The kitchen in the small council flat was painted white, with dark green woodwork. Dusty plants littered the two window ledges and the cupboard tops. Most were in desperate need of water. In one corner of the kitchen, at the small work surface next to the sink, stood a tall woman. She appeared to be about twenty-five years old. Her face was smeared with grease and sweat, and her shoulder length hair had fallen loose from the elastic band that held it. The hair now hung limply into her face and she automatically pushed back the strands as she chopped onions. Pausing to remove her glasses, she pulled a tissue from the pocket of her jeans, and wiped her eyes. The tears made it impossible to continue with the onions; and so, picking up the chopping board, Shabnam turned to the cooker.

"This is slave labour!" she muttered to herself as she dumped the chopped onions into the sizzling oil. "... And it's always the same. I go through this elaborate ritual of shopping, cooking and cleaning — yet they still manage to find fault. Why do I bother?" Shabnam reached for her watch, which lay surrounded by garlic and chillies on the work surface, and realised with horror that her guests would be arriving in just over an hour. "... And of course they're always on time," she snarled, opening her not very well-thumbed copy of *Mrs Singh's Punjabi Cooking for Beginners*. She paused to read the inscription on the front page: "To Shabnam from Mummy and Daddy," and smiled as she remembered how her parents had hesitantly presented the book to her as a "...late Diwali gift..." the previous year.

Turning to the recipe she had chosen, she read aloud: "'Fry the onions till they're golden brown, add 2 medium sized chillies — finely chopped — and continue to stir.' It's all very well for Mrs Singh," Shabnam cursed the onions, which were rapidly turning from 'golden brown' to black, "...I don't suppose her glasses get steamed up and she's probably got nothing better to do than sit around all day 'finely chopping' bloody chillies."

Cooking did not bring out the best in Shabnam. When she had lived at home her mother had continuously complained that she was the only girl in Southall who didn't "... know the difference between a curry and a casserole."

"More onions to fry! Mrs Singh must have shares in the bloody onion business!" Shabnam was rapidly losing all control. "It's too late now, they'll have to have plain rice, I haven't even started the chicken curry...." A shudder ran down her vegetarian spine as she caught sight of the pale lumps of fat chicken which sat mocking her on the draining board. Summoning up all her courage, Shabnam grabbed the chicken pieces and threw them on to the burnt remains of the onions. Discarding 'Mrs Singh', she added a liberal helping of "Bols all-purpose curry powder", turned down the heat and left the kitchen, confiding in the "Black Women Writers" poster in the hallway: "Chicken Massala! No problem sisters! Don't know what all the fuss is about...."

Shabnam entered the newly-tidied bedroom and began to feel pleased with herself. Tonight was going to be a nightmare but she was running ahead of schedule, and the meal was clearly going to be more successful than it had been last Diwali, when her guests had discovered (after their first mouthful of food), that Shabnam had somehow confused the quantity of onions with the quantity of chillies, and put a pound of chillies in the biriani sauce. (Luckily the papads had grilled perfectly, thus ensuring – along with "Patak's Original Tropical Fruit and Nut Chutney" – that the guests had not starved that evening.)

The memory of last Diwali unsettled Shabnam again, and she decided to allow herself a quick cigarette before dragging out the dreaded salwar kameez. Fumbling in the pocket of her jeans, she found the crumpled Rizlas and tobacco and sat down on the bed to roll herself the last cigarette of the evening. As she pulled the tobacco from its pouch, Shabnam noticed a piece of white fatty chicken skin lodged contentedly between her thumb and forefinger. Dropping the tobacco, she ran to the bathroom, and thrust her hand under the hot tap, spraying suds and water over the newly polished lino as she scrubbed furiously.

Grabbing a sock from the top of the "carefully stuffed" laundry basket, Shabnam mopped up the floor, cursing the chicken and the men who insisted on eating it with every meal. She mimicked her father: "Men must have their meat...." Suddenly she remembered the tobacco on the bedroom floor. "My God!

That's the first place they'll go snooping..." she muttered. Flinging the wet sock into the bathroom cabinet, she grabbed the dustpan and brush from under the sink and headed for the bedroom. Panic was rapidly returning.

The tobacco was quickly swept away, and discarding all thoughts of that "last cigarette", Shabnam began the search for the elusive salwar kameez. Clothes flew through the air from drawers and cupboards as she desperately tried to recall where she had hidden the suit after its last "outing". "Shit! I should have looked for this last night when Chris was still here ..." she muttered to herself, "...Now keep calm Shabnam, and think!" Sitting down amidst the scattered assortment of jumpers, knickers and jeans, she concentrated her mind on locating the salwar kameez. With a flash of inspiration she ran to the bathroom and grabbing the laundry basket, tipped it upside down and began rummaging through the contents. "A-ha!" she cried, holding the crumpled suit aloft triumphantly, "...now to find the iron!" In the spare room, where all traces of the other half of Shabnam's life had been carefully hidden the previous evening, she now stood in her bra and knickers, ironing out the creases in the salwar kameez. As the iron glided over the cotton print, Shabnam's mind drifted over the morning's events.... Chris had been making tea as she had entered the kitchen and, reluctant to face the inevitable argument, Shabnam had stood undetected in the doorway watching her lover in a detached way. Chris was not tall but had an attractive face and red hair that suggested the Irish parents which her strong Yorkshire accent might otherwise have concealed. After a number of minutes Chris had become aware of Shabnam's presence, and turning towards her smiled hesitantly, saying, "I've just made a fresh pot, would you like some?"

Drinking her tea in silence, Shabnam had felt the strained atmosphere and was at last compelled to re-introduce the subject that had already caused so much bitterness between them.

"I'm sorry Chris, but it's only once a year, they

only come to inspect me, and what I'm doing . . . see if I've got a man hidden away or something." Chris remained silent and so, somewhat self-consciously, Shabnam continued:

"It's not right just yet. . . I'm not leaving you out of my life, but I'm not ready to introduce you either. I honestly don't think they would take it very well. It seems pointless. . . ." Shabnam hesitated; it was difficult continuing a conversation when her lover was in the "silent mood". She drew a deep breath: "Look, this has to be discussed. . . ."

Chris looked up, "Tell me Shabnam, what is so awful about me? Why are you so sure they couldn't cope with me?" Tears were beginning to appear in Chris' eyes.

"Well for a start, you're not a Sikh, you're not Indian, shall I go on. . .?"

They both laughed, and the tension was eased slightly. Chris held Shabnam's hand, "Look love . . . I don't want to put any pressure on you. . . ."

"But you are," Shabnam replied, withdrawing her hand. She poured some more tea and continued, ". . .And don't try to tell me that I'm ashamed of you. We've been to Southall . . . my cousin's wedding . . . my nephew's birthday party, I haven't hidden you away. . . ."

Both of them were crying. Chris began to shout, "What the hell do you think you're doing now? Hiding me away. This has happened twice now and I'm sorry but I'm not prepared to go through with it again. . . . YOU shouldn't be prepared to put me through it. You keep telling me we've made a commitment to each other. . . ."

"Oh and what's the alternative then Chris? You stay here and we present ourselves as the ideal couple?"

"We could say I was your flatmate. . . ."

"No. That would be worse. I don't want to have to lie about you."

"So you ask me to disappear instead? Just to make you feel more comfortable?"

Shabnam's thoughts about the morning's events

were interrupted by the sound of the telephone. Pausing to unplug the iron and pull on a T-shirt, she ran down the stairs and into the hallway to answer the phone.

It was Chris – had Shabnam reached a decision yet? Would she tell her parents?

Suddenly Shabnam remembered the chicken curry. Hanging up the phone, she rushed into the kitchen. It had just begun to stick to the bottom of the pan and she quickly mixed the burnt bits in with the rest and turned off the gas. After checking to see if everything was in place, she once again climbed the stairs to finish dressing.

In the bathroom, Shabnam took off her glasses and washed her face, hoping the cold water would refresh her enough to endure the evening which lay ahead. Whilst wiping her face dry, she pondered on whether to wear any make-up – it would please her mother – but decided against it, realising she didn't own any. The clock in the hallway chimed, startling her.

"Damn! Seven o'clock! That only leaves me half an hour before they arrive."

Rushing into the spare room she hurriedly pulled the salwar kameez over her angular six foot frame and turned to where the mirror hung. "Where have I left those glasses?" she cursed. (This was nothing new – whenever Shabnam took off her glasses she had a problem finding them again.) She continued cursing as she hunted for them in the spare room, then in the bedroom and finally in the bathroom. The problem was that she needed her glasses to look for her glasses; without them everything was a blur. Eventually they were found and putting them on, Shabnam felt as if she had rejoined the world – not that she particularly wanted to; she hadn't decided what, if anything, she was going to say to her parents. At least she could now see what she looked like in the mirror.

The cotton print of the salwar kameez was in her favourite colours, pink and blue; even though the suit was quite old and dated it was still Shabnam's favourite. Glancing at the tall, skinny reflection of herself, Shabnam's thoughts wandered back to the shopping expedition she and her mother had undertaken in order to buy the suit. Reluctant to endure the pain of choosing the material, picking a design, and then the long fitting sessions conducted by giggling ladies who did not have a tape long enough to measure "Mrs Sahota's extraordinarily tall daughter", Shabnam had insisted on visiting the new trendy "off-the-peg" Indian boutique in Southall. This in itself had been a trial; most of the kameez barely covered her bottom. The few salwars that she could manage to squeeze her size 8 feet into, had hung sadly on her thin legs, ending somewhere around mid-calf and resembling the plus-four trousers favoured by English 'gentlemen' in the 1920's. Her mother had become increasingly agitated. She and the shop assistants appeared to be under the impression that Shabnam had deliberately grown to this size, in order to make life awkward for them.

"Don't worry. We pride ourselves on having styles to suit ALL types," the exasperated owner had said in a sympathetic voice to Shabnam's mother, as he brought her a sweet tea and two digestive biscuits. He tutted. Poor woman. Such a difficult child. . . .

Eventually a suit was found.

"Well? How does it look?" Shabnam had asked her mother. Discarded salwar kameez and chunnis lay on every available surface in the shop. Mrs Sahota looked up from her tea at her youngest daughter, who stood before her with dishevelled hair, sweaty face and the loathsome "Doc Martens" that she insisted on wearing (no matter how inappropriate the occasion). Shabnam's mother drew a deep breath, "Well. . . Mmm. . . At least take off those 'Gandhi' glasses. You look more normal without them."

"Normal? But I can't see without them! Aren't Asian women allowed to have bad eyesight?"

Shabnam stopped day-dreaming. Her parents would be arriving in less than half an hour and she still had a dozen things to do. The bedroom looked in order and ". . .if they go round snooping they deserve the shock they get," she thought. Shabnam went into the spare room to tidy her clothes and put away the ironing board, while her mind wandered back to the phone call from Chris.

"...There's no way, no matter what I do, that I can win! Chris wants me to tell my parents about her – and they're probably coming to talk to me about marriage...."

It was slowly becoming clear to Shabnam that in order not to lose Christine, she must tell her parents. It was unfair to expect her to hide away whilst they visited. The worst thing her parents could do was disown her – or hit her. Chris's father had beaten her when she had told him she was a lesbian. Shabnam laughed ironically, "At least I'm bigger than my dad."

The fear of telling them made her feel physically sick. Sitting down in the easy chair beside the window that overlooked the play area, she contemplated their reaction to her news. Shabnam practised saying the words:
"...Hello mummy ... daddy, Happy Diwali. I've got some news for you...." No. That didn't sound right.

"...Happy Diwali, I'm a lesbian...."

It suddenly struck her – would they know what it was?

Shabnam could hear her mother: "Acha Beti, is that your new job?"

A child's scream from the play area brought Shabnam back to reality. Instinctively knowing that it must be time for them to arrive, she walked slowly across the room, switched off the light and began to descend the stairs. Her mind was made up. The door bell rang. Shabnam glanced at her watch; they were five minutes early. "How typical..." she mumbled under her breath as she opened the door.

NAOMI

Tina Kendall

First, I wish to remain anonymous, the reasons for this may or may not become clear in the course of this discussion. However, if this omission is in any way problematic for you, please feel free to create. You can, if you wish, assign me with any name you care to. Go ahead. A certain percentage of you may, unwittingly, hit on the right one, but that I am powerless to do anything about. You see, to me, and you may feel exactly the opposite, names mean everything. Give away your name and you give away yourself, lay yourself open to any number of forms of attack. A name renders us so much more tangible, vulnerable to those who do not know us. But anyway, anonymity is part of my history, part of me.

Tonight I waited. Waited for the moon, all gunged in cloud like a child on the brink of birth waiting to ooze through the layers, to cast some of her light down on me. Watching in the silence of a country village late at night. I could, of course, name the village, but I won't. Suffice to say that it is one without modern developments and where a sense of tradition, of history, of repeated human activity through centuries, lies heavy, lies strong. I came here to burrow into my soul, discover unsuspected strengths and unexplored terrain from which to plot a move forward.

You see, I cannot pretend to be satisfied with my life. I am already in my late thirties – I shall be as precise about my age as the rest – and this is a time of great upheaval for me, a major crossroads. I thought a little distance might help.

Tonight I waited. Feeling good to be in the country again, filling my lungs with a lighter air and at last, some space to breathe. So now I write from the cosy comfort of my hotel room. There is a primrose print bedspread, and flowers, reddish, purple and blue, of a variety unknown to me, on a polished dark oak table. Long petals, no fragrance. But earlier this evening, I went down and spent a good two hours in the lounge bar of this country hotel, which, low-season, works out remarkably cheap, primrose bedspread, oak-table and all. There were about eight or nine of us in there, me, another woman, and all the rest, elderly men. I sat sipping the thick, dark beer, reflecting and observing. A couple of the guys were playing cards, another couple were involved for a time in a darts competition and another small group huddled in conversation at the bar with the barman. They sat perched on tall wooden stools and I watched them from my corner by the fire. The backs of their heads, from time to time, bobbed up and down as they poured the drink into their bodies. The woman among them was in her late forties and on one occasion, when she turned round, I saw a thick layer of orange lipstick smudged across her teeth. She emitted, throughout the evening, shrill, narrow peals of laughter, which disturbed me, though I cannot say why.

Perhaps it is the gentle calm of the country that makes the philosopher in me come rushing to the surface. As Pauline, one of my close friends back in Philly, always says of me, "You are an instinctive Buddhist." Perhaps. Harmony and tranquility are two of my key-words, this is true, which allows me to justify my self-indulgent trips to the countryside from time to time. But being Black, I can't say I am too turned on by the concept of nothingness, which, from what I understand, is fairly central in Buddhist thought. We Black people have been made to equate with zero for too long. I prefer to take in the whole, a circle of entirety, ambitious as this may sound.

I can imagine you sitting there reading this with just a touch of impatience. Just what is this woman driving at, you ask yourselves. Where is she taking us to?

The answer is not very far. I have a short tale to tell. An incident which took place late one night in London, but one which echoes on and on inside of me, stirring up new thoughts, unearthing new layers of me, of my collective past. I hope that it will speak to you accordingly. If not immediately, then at some unnamed future moment.

The tale opens at a time before I had made the decision to settle permanently in Britain and I was over on vacation for three months visiting an Englishman. This was back in my heterosexual days so I will spare myself and you the gruesome details of that particular relationship. Let us simply say that power was a central issue between us – and for whatever reason – I had none. However, the relationship with him served as a stepping stone. One that sent me thankfully flying off in a completely new direction. For if I had never met him, I might never have been walking out late one night in London....

We had been to a pub and then on to a jazz club. The music had been rather disappointing and the club unbearably crowded. It had been a relatively pleasant evening but neither of us had felt any particular desire to prolong it until the early hours. No, we thought we would save on exorbitant taxi fares and aim to get the last tube home, home being a fifteen minute walk from a station quite far out on the Jubilee Line. But we had hesitated just a little too long before making up our minds, so that, by the time we reached the station, we had missed the last tube to the end of the line and were obliged to take one that only did half the run.

Familiar places and people change their form slightly late at night and this is an alteration that pleases me. Different aspects of people and places and things intrigue me. Take my young English companion, for example. He became gentler and more considerate after midnight and several pints of beer. I cannot say for certain, but if other occasions are anything to go by, it seems likely that our short tube trip would have given him sufficient scope to place a hand on my knee or over my shoulder, showing, in short, that he cared for me. This would no doubt have set me glowing with happiness at the time. Bursts of recognition were something I was regularly in need of.

Picture then, if you will, a fairly cosy couple riding home late on a tube train, apparently not madly in love but satisfactory together. The train arrives briskly at its final stop, a guard calls, "All change please. This train terminates here." Sleepily, reluctantly, the passengers descend and topple into the lift, then out into the cool night air and form a queue for taxis. There are ten or twelve people in front of us. Next to us, behind us, I notice another Black woman. I am facing my Englishman, with my back to the people in front of us, so I can see the woman clearly. She looks younger than me, her hair is flattened in medium-sized braids which go from the front to the back of her head. I cannot quite explain why, but I feel particularly drawn to her. She is not strikingly beautiful, so that is not the reason. I glance from my friend to her repeatedly — he is talking about some political teachers' group to which he belongs. I nod and smile absently, my thoughts are elsewhere and his words barely register. My attention keeps pulling itself towards the woman standing behind him. She is skinny, not very tall and there is some kind of hostile timidity about the eyes. Or perhaps it is to do with her hair being flattened, her braids woven into a young girl's style. She has the air of a librarian, say, or a first school teacher, and noticing my glances, she begins to survey me in a slow, deliberate fashion. All the while this looking is going on, we are gradually advancing in our line for a taxi home. When we are finally at the front of the queue, my friend, still elaborating on the implications of some aspect of Marxism for education, and a taxi draws to a halt, I suddenly feel a touch upon my sleeve, no, it is summer, upon my skin. It is as light and as hesitant as a moth flying into your face at night. I turn and smile into the eyes of the woman.

She looks at me and I wait, expecting her to speak, to say something, to explain. My smile eventually stiffens for the woman does not say a word but keeps looking steadily into my eyes. What on earth does she want? Sure of having captivated my attention, she takes a tube map out of her bag and indicates questioningly a tube station three stops up from ours and then accompanies her gesture with three low bleating sounds. This all takes time. My friend is already seated in the taxi and asks me what the matter is. At the moment, give her a name, any name taken at random, say Naomi. The woman Naomi is dumb, is probably deaf and dumb. For a second, I flounder. "Do you want to share a taxi with us?" I say, making my lips move as clearly as possible. She nods and a sudden wing of smile flits across her face. "And you want to go to Kingsbury?" I ask again. It is the name of the district she has pointed to on the map. Again a nod. "Well, of course you can share our taxi. We're going as far as Dollis Hill."

It is a big, black cab and there is room on the back seat for all three of us. My lover and I are both struck silent in the face of this woman's speechlessness. But heavy thoughts swim round in my head.

Who is this woman, I think. What is her life? How does she spend her days, her evenings? Where is she coming from now? A meal with friends, the cinema, the pub? I provide imaginary answers, pad out situations, and then, before I know it, want it, the taxi is pulling up at our house, a large one that my friend shares with five other teachers. We pay up and I explain that the young woman wants to go to Kingsbury. "What address?" the taxi driver asks mechanically. The taxi light has been switched on to facilitate transactions. "What address?" I ask Naomi. She opens a bag and pulls out one of those plasticised library cards, on which is written a name and an address, let's make it 24, Hillside Court, for simplicity. I read it out, in what seems an abnormally loud voice, my voice feels to be banging against the sides of my throat as I speak, and the taxi driver mutters, "Right you are."

Then I follow my friend out of the car and before I slam the door shut, I look at Naomi and say, "Goodnight, then." There is a noise in return which is something between a gasp and a groan, she gives a brief smile and then the car's gone and I am in the middle of the road. Then my friend, with a heavy arm on my shoulder, steers me away from my vision.

That's it. That is the essence of my story, a snatched moment when two lives entwine, a story which I have clumsily told, since it deals with action which occurs deep down inside of us, largely beyond the scope of words.

I could not sleep that night. I remember I refused my friend's advances, the first time ever, I believe. Anyway, they only lasted a couple of moments before alcohol drew him into sleep. Men are like bears and I was in no mood for entering into some nonsensical union with him, while inside my mind and body all was churning. In fact, if I recall correctly, I got up and walked barefoot over the green carpet, went downstairs and sat in the dark of the living-room. Just thinking.

Initially it was fear for the woman herself that took hold of me. Fear that she could be an easy victim of attack with no access to sounds that could forewarn her and unable to signal an attack by screaming and shouting.

That wore off as I realized that would-be assailants do not usually go checking their potential victims for disabilities beforehand. So from that point of view, she was in as much or as little danger as the rest of us. Eventually a sort of admiration came over me. This woman, let's call her Naomi, was going out and about and living her life. It seemed an incredibly strong, forceful thing to do. I imagined that in similar circumstances I would only be capable of folding inwards, not out on the town on a Saturday night on my own. Perhaps this was fanciful, but in the darkness of that North London sitting-room, Naomi came to equal a celebration of life in its fullest sense.

The vision went on chipping away inside of me. The vision, the revelation, I see it as such, went on working on me long past that night. In fact, I am sure I have not felt the last of the tremors.

****

So here I am in a tiny village hotel sharing one of the central anecdotes of my life with you, while at the same time trying to come to a decision or waiting for a decision to come. Taking some time to sit back, relax and reflect.

You see we Black women have been deafened for centuries by the insults, the hatred of others. Words have been used to destroy us, so you end up closing your ears to all language to shut out the pain. We Black women have, for so long, been denied a voice, we have grown hoarse, we have grown mute through the effort of speaking to unhearing ears, and having our words spat back at us, forced down our throats.

So our language turned inwards, our listening turned inwards. In the eyes of the rest of the world we were deaf and dumb. We ceased to respond to their language, and unable to make ourselves heard, we withdrew, were ignored, grew invisible. For the eyes of the rest of the world could not see that we walked in a quiet place and the language we used with each other – sometimes we did not so much as move our lips, a look could say it all – was poetry, fresh, springwater to heal our cuts and bruises. We were singing and dancing and chanting together. Creating our world in our movements and song.

It is late. I have talked for so long. Things are still and resting and waiting. I will roll into my primrose-covered bed in a few moments. But tonight I waited. Waited, while the moonlight splashed down, while the worries, futile little worries about everyday life things, were hushed away, while the drums in my head beat real slow, for those rights words to come.

PENELOPE IS NO LONGER WAITING

Cherry Potts

Penelope is no longer waiting. Her husband has been gone nearly ten years. Silently she agrees with the suitors who say he must surely be dead, secretly she hopes it is true, but knows that if anyone can take ten years coming home, if anyone can survive all the pitfalls of the anger of the goddess he has roused, he can. Publicly she denies his death and does not put on the mourning gown she made with her own hands these twelve years gone, in readiness.

Publicly she says that Odysseus will return to meet his nearly grown son, to claim his crown and to take back as his own his still beautiful wife.

Until then, her silence and the tilt of her head say: *I rule here*. As regent, certainly, but with pride and skill; and with a consort.

Daily she sits at her loom, weaving the beautiful, careful tale of her life.

Nightly, she rips it gleefully apart, each beautiful skillful lie.

Daily she rules with sense and courage the doubtful, restless people of Ithaca.

Nightly she lies in the arms of her lover and wills her husband to the arms of the Siren, or the jaws of the Scilla, or the wiles of her sister Circe.

She thinks of how it will only be a few more years, and then her son will be old enough to rule. Then no one will want to marry her, and the endless stream of seemingly tireless suitors will fade away, leaving her to enjoy her retirement with the woman she loves. If only they can keep up the pretense those few years longer, if only Odysseus does not ever return.

Then one day a beggar comes to the door. Penelope looks him up and down suspiciously, she has been waiting for this. She recognises the ingratiating whine the man affects, she has heard it often enough before. She draws away from him, pretending disgust at his filth, straightens the crown on her noble brow. The blood pounds in her ears as she considers the puzzle before her. Her heart races with excitement and a little fear. She turns over the thought of poisoning the broth given him by the old woman who nursed him as a child. Knowing that she too will recognise him, she resists temptation.

She waits, and watches him, as he slithers through her hall for a day and a night, sowing the seeds of discontent, setting one suitor on another, dripping his own subtle poison in each and every ear.

She sits motionless at her loom for hours, waiting, now, for a different moment. She reaches out a tentative hand and runs a finger along the dark thread she wove last, not yet ripped from the frame.

Odysseus will not be using *this* winding sheet after all.

She knows that soon he will declare himself, and she holds herself in readiness. On the second evening, she sees him rise to his feet, and she motions swiftly to the waiting servant. Odysseus straightens his back and cries aloud to the assembled throng that he is King of Ithaca, come home at last. A soft murmur of amusement runs through those dining at the Queen's table. He hesitates only a second, before holding up for all to see, a ring. Is this not the ring with which Penelope encircled the finger of Odysseus when he went away to war? Indeed it is, but who but Penelope would recognise it after all these years?

She smiles to herself, a small, pitying smile, and stands.

Can this humble, ugly, dirty creature be her

husband returned? She asks those at her table. Would the great Odysseus creep into his own hall and not make himself known to his own wife for two whole days? Her voice shakes with anger. No, she says, he would not. Her husband, she cries, would sweep in with the night wind behind him, carrying the booty of his ten years journey and place it at her feet. This is nothing but a madman, a cruel charlatan, playing on the tolerance of their Queen and she will have none of him, nor his tawdry ring. Then she orders him whipped from the City like so many previous pretenders to the crown she wears.

A paid assassin follows him, and later that night the ring he tried to give her as a token that he spoke truth is brought to her, stained with blood. She washes it tenderly, for her mother gave her the ring when she was married to Odysseus. When she goes to bed that night, she gives the ring to her lover to wear on her finger as a token of the love between them, that will never now be disturbed.

Penelope is no longer waiting.

THE WEDDING STONE

Caroline Halliday

Daddy had said Toby was very suitable.
Only too...! her sister Rosemary said.
Only too what? she demanded.
Forget it, Rosie said, eating fruit with her cereal, her mouth bulging.
Just too, too suitable for you, darling, mother said.

Marion wants to stalk away like that woman, hands in pockets, striding towards the long path over to the right. It's funny pausing in the grey limousine, in the middle of woods. She feels all alone, and then corrects herself. Alone, except for Toby, of course.

He is clutching his gloves, the corner of his bow-tie visible as he leans against the car, smoking with the driver. She feels like a character in a film. The bride. And in the corner of the screen a figure, walking away.

They're awaiting Daddy. Before she can get out of the car, Daddy has to arrive.

Marion giggles. Stalking, in this cascade of silk! The figure is getting smaller and smaller and is hidden among the trees.

They await the photographer also. With the black cloth over his head and his moustache and coat tails.

Marion clutches the yellow and pink and white flowers. *Come on, Daddy*. Where has the other car got to.

The walker treads the path to the right, her usual route, across the down and over the ridges of stones and birches. Down to the base of the woods, where the big trees rise and birds call.

There are many paths. Some along ridges, some steeply down into the hollows. Paths rippling in grey and black and tan coloured stones, rounded and sculpted by the sea thousands of years before, and now humped up and carved again in these woods just south of London. Stones that have shifted and ground smooth and round under the force of waves throwing them back and again back against each other, in some motion, some shape of shore, that formed them oval, round, a few almost perfectly round. All of them smooth and curved, except those split into half circles, or shattered off at one end.

The walker comes to the fallen tree, pausing to notice some branches are dying, others green. The silver birch fallen, still graceful, grey and white and black. It lies across a path, which winds down through the trees, and along a narrow cleft in the earth, where a stream might run in winter.

The walker follows the beginnings of a new path, footmarks in the dark brown leaf mould, round the tree, down through speckly leaves, splashes of sunlight. Cool. Deep woods smell, leaves and growing things, and things slipping away into earth.

She sniffs the smell. She bends to pick up a stone from the thousands cascading the path. Stones down ridges and up slopes, and hundreds of sizes. She bends, always looking for another round one. She picks up a grey one, oval and large enough to grip in the palm of her hand. A comforter; a sensuous companion warm in her grip. A weapon against the unexpected, cracking against a skull. A toy to throw and catch into light and air.

I'm going to stretch my legs, Marion says, unexpectedly. Toby pushes his head through the car window. He has been listening to the driver's analysis of the traffic from Purley to Addiscombe.

Marion, he says. Sweetheart. You can't. Your father. . . .

Oh, alright. She wriggles on the edge of the seat and looks out at the woods.

She thinks of Toby on that rock in Italy, perched uncomfortably. The only time they'd been able to get away from Mother and Rosie. His prick stuck up big and round. You sit on my lap, he said. You sit on it. She did. It was comforting really. Doing it wasn't new, but Mother was a restriction on holiday.

She looks in the direction the walker has disappeared. Before Toby . . . before Toby, she . . . but Toby said it was too risky, on your own like that. Too many quiet and brambly patches, much too easy for someone . . . and how would she manage if. . . .

Through the narrow path between fern and bramble and rose bay willow herb, the walker comes on a slope of grasses. The city falls away in an instant, a draught of air in the lungs, chest widening, a draught of pleasure. She lies in the scarlet-stemmed grasses, watches them and dozes, sun hot. The clouds race and change, heavy grey, white marble, blue and white. The sun is a horizon on her eyelashes, she is falling asleep. Hand clasping the stone, oval like an egg.

Marion giggles from the champagne. Her sister slips in a remark about wedding nights, which the smooth faced bride laughs at. There is nothing new to discover about Toby. She feels at least this, is safe. She glances out of the window.

The walker wakes quickly, her sleep making her vulnerable. Her body turning sideways as if to throw off an attacker. Crunching of pebbles, someone climbing the slope of stones.

It is only two older women walking arm in arm.

The catering staff are bringing out bowls of fruit salad in the kitchens, pink and yellow and topped with white; a tray of bowls, topped with another tray of bowls and then another. They are ready to serve.

Marion smiles brightly at her mother. Toby has just picked his nose surreptitiously. Marion takes another sip of champagne and sees a kitchen, white and grey surfaces. Toby persuaded her grey and white, and it seemed so important to him. She sighs. Toby is standing up. From the side his jaw is pink and raw. Is his collar too tight? *Why, he looks like Daddy!*

She made him promise not to have another haircut before the day. But he did, anyway.

Marion, the bride, giggles. Toby has dropped his wine. Someone in black and white is mopping at the table cloth with a serviette. Everything is stiff and white, except the stupid little bowls of yellow and pink and white.

Marion looks crookedly at the waitress in her neat black skirt and white apron, standing by the door to the kitchen. The waitress reminds her of Italy. The dark haired women and the way they smiled at her, familiar and easy.

The waitress unexpectedly winks at her. Marion stares. The waitress has turned away.

Marion glances to the window. Is that rain spattering the glass? It would ruin the silk dress.

The walker will have rain in her hair.

The walker breathes in the deep brown air at the bottom of the woods away from the restaurant, away from the lookout point that tells you how far to Crystal Palace, the Telecom Tower. She climbs and sits on the bole of a tree, watches a squirrel leap from branch to branch. She throws the grey stone in the air and catches it again, firm and warm in her hand.

She remembers the great limousine at the beginning of her walk. The smooth bride poised in the back with her clasp of pretty flowers. The smooth bride waiting for release from the deep grey car. What were they waiting for?

She walks on.

Clattering and splattering noise to her left. A gang of youths, crashing through. She pauses, watching which way they are going. Watching their movements, their intentions.

They're only talking amongst themselves, not going her way.

She comes to the wide slope of stones under the beech tree, its narrow roots breaking the surface, the bright moss. She climbs. Slowly. Step by step. She walks past the heather at the top, and under the branches of beech and conifer. Almost time to turn for home.

Marion giggles again. It isn't raining. The waitress brings plates, placing them carefully, and brushing Marion's shoulder as she passes. The man in the black suit carries in the wedding cake. A man and a woman stand on the top of the three tiers. The woman is smaller than the man. He wears black. She wears white. The figures stood on top of her parents' wedding cake.

Marion is waiting for something to happen. She thinks she glimpses a figure in among the trees. Maybe it's the woman walker.

There's no time, the time is going too fast, the light disappearing from the sky. She doesn't know what it is she waits for. Has she had too much champagne?

She remembers holding her posy of flowers, sitting in the grey limousine, and waiting.

She remembers seeing the woman start out on her walk.

Daddy rustles his papers and stands up.

As she passes the restaurant, the walker sees the cascading dress, the bride's dress, and a man standing. The stone slips from her fingers. The stone bounces on the ground and she bends to pick it up.

Something hits the window with an echoing smack. Toby's chair falls backwards. His head hits the wall with a solid sound. The window is cracked in three directions, but not broken. Marion stoops to pick up a small stone from the carpet. It is tan-coloured and jagged.

THE LIZARD BARKS AT ONE

Valerie Potter

Agnes O'Reardon looked at the sky. There was a bird cage around each cloud and a nylon fishing net was draped casually over the sun. "Hm. It must be later than I thought," she mused. "Time flies where no lizard weeps."

Gardenia Watts walked by with her poetry loving cougar. "Do you understand," she fumed, "That this could ruin both of us? You'll have to go! Now! With your protractor!"

Agnes O'Reardon looked at the sky. The bird cages were empty and the sun was drowning in mid air. "Pshaw!" she muttered. "A right angle isn't such a disaster. Why there's more inches in a hymn. The lizard is always white despite it all."

Gardenia Watts lit her tongue and puffed enigmatically for a moment or two. "Well!" she screamed "Are you going or will I have to call in the nicotine soldiers? The lizard will exact its revenge you know. No freedom walks beneath concrete fruit."

Agnes O'Reardon lay down her arms and legs. A frog screamed in her throat. The air was a pastel shroud. Taking a pair of scissors she carefully cut around Gardenia Watts. It was a difficult job for her feet were multifoliate but she managed it with medium thread.

Agnes O'Reardon pasted Gardenia Watts to the oven shelf and closed the door. Fifty minutes later she was done to a turn. As the lizard flowed down from the mountains she scattered Gardenia Watts to the five winds. "No lizard cries where the body swells," she said gratefully and blew away.

DOPE SMOKING LESBIANS CAN NEVER BE GOOD TEACHERS

Berta R. Freistadt

When she took off the black leather jacket I had to look away. Literally. I turned my head and looked at something else. It was too dangerous to go on looking at her; I might be careless and let something escape from my eyes that would give me away. Then the whole staff room would rock with laughter and I would blush and they would see. Though it wouldn't be laughter would it? No, if I were stupid enough to rub their noses in what they demanded should remain a secret, if I dared to stand in the middle of the staff room fancying another woman there'd be no laughter; only a long silence punctuated by sharp intakes of breath and the creaking of eyebrows. They'd move away a little and all conversation would be stifled by steam clouds of fascination and disgust.

So I didn't look at her for that second or two. All the P.E. staff were a colourful lot, the men as well as the women; all track suits, shorts and bony knees. But full of fun, always cracking knuckles and jokes; and in the middle of them was this woman. I could never keep my eyes off her. When I did look at her again — and I really had to because she was being funny and was the center of everyone's attention, so in order to appear unconcerned it was necessary that I did look at her — when I did look the jacket was off and underneath she was wearing a shirt, a woman's shirt of pale, pale blue. And a leather tie of nearly the same shade. I almost laughed. It was so corny, so obvious. How dare she. How dare she wear a black leather jacket, black velvet cords and a blue shirt with a pale blue leather tie. Leather! I ask you! What did she think she was doing? She was supposed to be in the closet, for goodness sake.

The first time I walked into that staff room, months before the black leather jacket, I couldn't believe my eyes. I'd just been given the royal greeting by the Head, the one new Supplies are always given before you're forgotten and left to pick your own way through the punishing maze of rooms with no numbers, timetables with no times and long corridors with dead ends. These are full of children of varying ages who watch with unfocused eyes your passage to the end and back, sometimes sniggering, sometimes barring your way and always staring with just concealed contempt. And how lonely it is going from school to school like a gipsy, like a refugee. So when I walked into this staff room and saw her I thought my luck had changed. Someone I recognized. Not that I knew her, just knew what she was. It had been eighteen months among people I could never be honest with, and now suddenly there she was.

On that first day she stood there making a joke and I did one of those laughs that are more like a snigger than anything else, that seem to come out of your nose when you are more impressed with the person than with the joke. And she saw me for the first time, noticed me I mean, as a real person, and looked at me for a second. For a whole long second our eyes were joined, then I chickened out and sat down. After that first impact, of course I became unsure. I wondered if it might be my imagination grown desperate with loneliness. Ever since Annie Lennox it's been easy to make mistakes. When I go to a new school now the first thing I do is look for a woman like me. I'm always hopeful that among the rampant heterosexuality that festers in most staff rooms there will be just one other. For support. Against all the words like "queer", "poofter", "lezzie". Against the time when such a nice child will sit on your desk and declare, "I could never bear to sit next to one." Or when another will refuse to go to the library on account of "that poofter who gives out the books." And you, I mean I, sit there tongue-torn between anger, grief and caution.

Jackie; that was her name. I wonder if I can describe her. Sensibly. I doubt it. I remember that she was about my height, and stocky. But this is no criticism. It was her very solidity, her very womanly body that I craved. My dreams of her, my fantasies on the drifting twilight before sleep were always of being gathered by her strong arms to rest my head on her breast. She seemed to me, the lovely Jackie, to be expansive, generous; a romantic figure of sheer opulence. But then, as my mother would have crudely put it, if I'd ever allowed her to comment on the situation; I thought the sun shone from out the bottom of her trousers. I would watch her, I remember, across the room, secretly, with a lot of pleasure. Just to see her talk or eat or deal with the children. My eyes could never get enough of her. And if we were close enough I would observe her in minute detail, each dark curl, an eye lash, the red in her cheek, her beautiful hands with their smooth fingers and neat, blunt cut nails; details I stored that I can remember, but whose significance eludes me now. I usually tried not to get too close to her. Once I met her suddenly face to face in a doorway, me trying to go one way and she the other. In that second as we smiled at each other doing the little dance you do on such occasions, in that second, desire flooded me there in the staff room as though I'd been given some kind of kiss of life. I felt alive, hopeless, but alive. And that's how it was for those few months, from the first day when she shot me that fast look of recognition, to how she looked with her neat arse in its smooth corduroy, to her jokes and imitations; I became obsessed. Here I was, as old as my tongue, and a little older than my teeth, feeling like a school girl. I woke thinking of her, I watched for her all day at school, I talked about her to all my tired friends and at night I took her to bed with me. Some hope. I should have changed schools.

And what about the children, I hear you ask. Do you actually do any teaching or is it all sitting around in postures of lust and desire? Ah yes, I reply. Them, the children, the little darlings. And teaching, indeed. Well the one depends upon the other really. We'd all like to justify our pay slips. But it isn't that easy. It's not like it was in your day. Or even in mine. The kids are alright really. You can get quite fond of them if you're not careful. But like loving a Piranha, one must exercise a modicum of caution before exposing any open wound you might have. And in the context of school being a lesbian is like having an open wound. Keep it carefully covered or you'll get chalk dust in it or worse, a nasty little boy will poke it and make you cry. Actually, when the shit hit the fan, the fan was off as it were, and I made the catch of the season with gloves on. You may know that the children of today don't respect teachers. For that matter neither does anybody else. When I remember my old Headmistress, third in line only from the Holy Trinity and the Queen, and the awe in which she was held, I grow nostalgic. But though they have no respect for us they are nevertheless fascinated by our private lives. It's understandable I suppose, the interest that is aroused by the idea that those in authority have the same needs, bodily functions, pains and pleasures as those who are commanded. It doesn't matter who it is, parent, teacher, politician, star; that they get drunk, get parking tickets, go bald, have sex, break wind. Oh wonderful stuff! But of course, sadly, kids never know when to stop. And if you're a lesbian, yesterday was time to stop.

I was late that day. It was three flights up and they were all waiting. In a huddle, a gaggle. Leaning, groaning, a heaving Monday morning group. Suzi, it would be Suzi, said, "We know where you live, Miss." She was very accusing and somehow smug and loving at the same time. Suzi was the sort of girl who punched you to show you she liked you. I was sometimes very bruised at the end of a lesson with her. "Do you?" I said non-committally. I was holding all the books, the register, and a sheaf of mark sheets while unlocking the door and turning the handle at the same time. "Yes," she said letting me have it, "you live in that house with all the blinds and the plants." "Oh," said Lucy, her friend, and whether this was a put-up job or totally unplanned I shall never know, "I thought that was the lezzie house." It was a lovely day and the sky was blue, so consequently I merely laughed when Lucy dropped her bomb shell. And I said something even more non-committal like, "Well, the things you hear, who's going to give out the books?" And that was it. There was no confrontation, no silly questions. I suppose because I never denied anything. They knew straightaway that Lucy was right. You do don't you when something unusual is explained with the right explanation. You recognise a piece of the cosmic jigsaw as fitting. In fact, I know for certain they knew, because on the last day of term when they got drunk, a week before Christmas, a crowd of them were behind the pavilion as I passed, and somebody's boyfriend, I didn't know his name, yelled out "Lezzie, lezzie". That word is so awful. It's something to do with the precise combination of vowel and consonant that is so dismissive and yet so aggressive. "Lesbian, lesbian" isn't half so bad. In fact if anyone yelled that out at me I think I might even laugh or just say "Thank you very much." As it was, I just smiled and gave him in particular two fingers. Later, Suzi told me what I'd done and that teachers ought not to give two fingers to kids. She didn't mention why I'd done it at all.

Goodness, it was hard sometimes to be a good teacher. Take that time Suzi got caught smoking dope. Behind the pavilion again. Everything of importance happened there. I don't know why we didn't move the staff meetings there. We might have got something done then, inspired by the ghosts of real life that might be lingering along with the smell of old sock and stale sweat. Suzi was not a pretty child, nor clever. But she had a desperate boldness born from a longing to be loved despite her unloveliness. I loved her though she was often spiteful and unkind to me. She sensed my affection, I'm sure, and made me pay for it. I often wanted to take her in my arms to soothe her troubled spirit, kiss her spotty cheek and say to her, "there, there". Like you do a crying baby. But I didn't. Can you imagine the uproar? The indignation, the derision, the disgust. And I would be truly labelled, one of them. A Queer. A Perve. A Lezzie. No, school was school and my tacky sentimental feelings were quite out of place.

As it was, the time she got done for dope nearly had me in trouble too. That day I was taking French. When I say taking I mean sitting with them hoping to avoid their attention while they were sitting hoping to avoid work. That was the sum total of our responsibilities, the sitting there. Then Suzi came in late, giggling. She was obviously stoned. She was at the helpless stage when the tears of uncontrolled hysteria begin to bewilder. It is after all very bewildering not to be able to stop laughing at nothing. Later that term when I'd forgotten all about the French class, she appeared one morning very smug again and full of herself. Demanded what I thought about it all. She was most put out when I appeared not to know what she was talking about and informed me that all the staff were talking about it. I didn't want to disillusion her and reveal that the top staff topic this week was the loss of 4BLs reports and who was chief candidate for blame, so I said that I'd not been in school the day before, and, mollified, she told me herself. It appeared that somehow the authorities had got to hear of her being stoned and all hell had been let loose. Head of Year, Pastoral Head, School Head, parents and police had all been called in and there was a threat of poor Suzi being transferred. Now I know drugs are a bad thing and school is most certainly not the place for them, but I'm afraid I said something very indiscreet. I was thinking about those impotent giggles and how different alcohol would have made her — maybe violent and vomiting. I said to her "Better dope than drink." I should have held my tongue. Bad enough being a suspect perve, suggesting that dope was O.K. was definitely scandal material. And indeed for the rest of that term while I taught her she insisted that I wasn't a decent teacher to have around children because I smoked dope. And what could I say? I did. Not often, not much. And I was a lesbian. Celibate for what seemed like years, but what would such distinctions mean? To qualify my dope smoking by saying that I hadn't done it in six months would be as good as a lie in the circumstances. And trying to explain that my lesbianism involved more than going to bed with a woman would arouse jeers of derision. And rightly so. In certain cases in for a penny, in for a pound. Thus, I am revealed a bad teacher. Dope smoking lesbians can never be good teachers. Teaching is a conservative art.

For a while everything was fine. The work, the children, Jackie. But then suddenly, like a shift in the weather I lost control of it all. Like knitting wool, the threads of all my concerns started to tangle. It started one late afternoon when everyone should have been safely shut in their class rooms sneaking glances at watches and waiting for the bell. I had just left the staff room and was casually walking past the room where Jackie was taking a Maths lesson. There was a spot in the corridor outside that room where it was possible to see in unobserved. I usually couldn't resist doing it once I'd discovered it, and every week I would creep there and stand and watch her for a few minutes and pretend I was twelve again, young enough to sit at one of the desks and have a legitimate crush. All of a sudden the ominous sound of giggles came round the corner followed promptly by two fourth years. It was of course Suzi and a mate. Swiftly I translated the body language of languish and yearning into a more suitably teacherly pose. What they were doing out of class at that time of day was anyone's guess, but as I strode off down the corridor trying to look purposeful and preoccupied I caught the nudge Suzi gave her mate and knew I hadn't fooled anybody. The next day in class there was a whispered scuffle as I entered and a voice said "Are you good at Maths, Miss?"

Then I began to feel that she was ignoring me. Of course I loved her and thought about her all day long. She was my rose coloured spectacles that made even this dreadful job bearable. But why didn't she notice me, do something? Didn't she realise how I was suffering? I wanted her to see inside my head. And so my pleasure in the situation spoiled. And I began to have the dreams. In her blue Porsche she drove me to school, so fast that it felt as though we were not moving. And outside the staff room under the brown beech hedge she leant across me to open the door and kissed me. Then there was the hockey match in the desert, and I was playing with her in a pair of shorts so tiny that I pulled them down to cover my thighs as rows of girls stood in twos hand in hand around the palm fringed pitch. Sometimes I woke from these happy dreams so startled by their revelations, and made so lonely by their contrast to my real life, that I would lie crying for half an hour and be late for school.

Sometimes it seemed that I spent all my waking hours thinking of her. It was like being on a fairground swing-boat, swinging to and fro between capturing the fantasy with my bare hands and squeezing out its lies to make it truth, and believing that the truth was there as flat as an ordinary pancake with only my fear to make her inaccessible. She was so real, and yet she filled my waking dreams too. I wanted her to take control of me. I thought of her looking at me with a straight face, right in the eye. Of her facing me square on with her shoulders and breasts looking at mine. Of her making love to me and then giving me her shoulder to sleep on, her armpit to dream in. It was all so dangerous, so forbidden. I was a thief of course, to steal her like that without her knowledge. I had to stop; I was making myself sick, I was sick of myself.

I could have left the school I suppose, but that wouldn't have solved the problem completely. Finally I knew what I had to do. It was very obvious of course. I would write her a letter. I would pull myself out of the wraps of fantasy and make the situation a real one. She will either say yes or no. And that will be the end of it. I was very pleased with myself, so much so that I did nothing for at least another two weeks. The timing was important anyway. The letter had to arrive on the last day of school before half term so neither of us would be embarrassed in the staff room. So I wrote the letter. It didn't say "Dear Jackie I love you, please go to bed with me." No, I was witty, charming and said how I admired her and would she please have a date with me. That half term holiday was the longest I've ever known, as I sat there waiting beside the phone. Every time it rang I felt sick, but I let it ring five times before I allowed myself to pick it up. She never phoned. But, a day before the holiday ended a letter arrived. I knew it was from her before I even picked it off the mat. And it shivered in my hand as though a breeze had been let in with the letter. I sat down, she was probably very angry at my cheek, or shocked at my unprofessionalism. Slowly I opened it trying not to tear the envelope, and read my darling's words. And what a letter it was. So civilised, so good humoured, so generous. No, she wasn't cross; but she did have a girlfriend, and she was surprised, and very flattered and we should go for a drink one day. It was short, so I read it fifty times. Oh, how I loved her now. I didn't mind that she was already involved. That didn't matter. We would be the best of friends. It would be a strange and wonderful friendship, a mystery to the researchers in years to come as they scoured our letters for a clue to the source of our affection. We would join the ranks of other couples: Gertrude and Alice, Sylvia and Valentine, Virginia and Vita. I was off again. No longer down, I went out full of smiles, full of joy, full of myself.

Back at school I steeled myself to look her in the eye, even to sit next to her in order to give her the chance to make the date. We talked about all sorts of things: school, ski-ing, her car, the maths curriculum, my bike. And when she smiled at me with those blue eyes and I felt her bare arm against mine on the shared arm rest I felt that anything was possible. All I had to do was to wait. For the moment to come. Meanwhile, I hadn't noticed it, but summer had arrived. Windows were open and dresses were being worn. Football gave way to athletics for the boys and for the girls it was tennis. One day Jackie was in the staff room waving a piece of blue serge about. It was a tiny scrap and turned out to be a tennis skirt and I laughed to myself to remember the long divided skirts that I played games in as a girl. Next day the door flew open and Jackie strode in wearing that same tiny blue serge skirt. It was hers for goodness sake, not a child's. That had never occurred to me. The tiny pleats swung and switched about as she moved; to me she appeared scarcely decent. But no-one else seemed to turn a hair. No-one else seemed affected in the slightest by her smooth, strong, golden legs and thighs. Such poetry in motion. Oh dear, what was I to do. And I'm sure that on several occasions the pleats flipped just a shade too pertly in my direction making my heart jump, so I didn't quite know where to look. . . .

As the days ran on it became hotter, stickier and the staff room seemed to contract on an ever growing number of sweaty bodies. My duties grew less as the end of term neared but in contrast Jackie seemed never to stop. I remember her then as a whirlwind: maths, tennis, exams, matches, reports. She was never still, never even cracked a joke. And soon I discovered the reason; she was leaving. So of course I understood that she was far too busy to think about what she'd promised me, and I determined to be sensible about it. The nearer we rushed to the end of term the brighter became my smile; I even began to iron my clothes every day and wear a little make up. No gloomy face from me. Only Suzi noticed of course. She plonked herself in front of me one morning, hands on her hips, and said accusingly "You've got make up on." She sounded very cross about it so I asked "Don't you like it?" But she only tutted, sighed and raised her eyes to heaven. On the last day of term I was a smiling senseless automaton. This passed quite unnoticed in the staff room but my last class was full of mutterings, "What's the matter with her?" I don't think I even saw Jackie on that last day. After lunch the children went home, the staff got pissed and I bunked off early out the side entrance. Cycling home I allowed my smile to fold itself up and fall into my pocket exhausted.

"Cheer up," I told it, "no more teaching for six weeks." But my poor little smile made a rude noise and could not be persuaded out. I was just making myself a cup of tea when the phone went. I put the kettle down and went to the phone.

As my hand reached out I remember it didn't tremble as it had when I'd opened the letter. I had no premonition this time that it was her. I didn't count five rings nor put on a husky voice. I just said "hallo," and a voice said "Can I speak to Berta, please."

"Yes," I said. "You are."

"Oh," said the voice, "You rushed off quickly, didn't you?"

"Who is this?" I said.

"It's Jackie," said the voice.

"Jackie?"

"From school, you haven't forgotten me already have you?"

"Jackie!" It was her at last. I sat down, I could hardly breathe with delight. I was blushing, smiling again, laughing even. She sounded a little nervous, I wondered why, maybe it was just a trick of electricity. Somewhere, someone said "be careful, be a little cool." But I wasn't listening, I was talking to the woman of my dreams who wanted a date with me.

It wasn't for a fortnight, our date with Jackie. I must have filled the days with something, I just can't remember what. Then it was here: the day, the Friday I was to see her. I'd wanted to time it so that I wasn't there first. After all I'd written the letter, I didn't want to seem too keen. But that was a mistake. Instead of just arriving second, I was half an hour late. She smiled me a welcome and I nearly told her how I'd changed three times before making it out. That was a mistake too. I was in a dress with sheer black tights, she was casual. And the vodka and lime was wrong too, she didn't drink. But never mind, these were mere details to laugh at later. For the moment there was nothing but the achievement of getting us both here. I was high on a rosy glow of what I'd done. Here I was with the most beautiful woman in the world. I'd slain a bogey. I was no longer in love with a wraith. She too was to have some praise in all this, after all she'd taken me seriously. I'd wanted so much to be out of the grips of that fantasy, without her help it was like trying to stop a waterfall, or the rollercoaster at the top of the Mighty Mouse at Southend. And here we both were safe and dry at the bottom on a cosy little date.

But, I am a woman of infinite style. I can see which way is out. Gradually as I unwound, after the "Where were you born?"'s and the "When did you come out?"'s conversation flagged, smiles became strained. Her eyes wandered. It was a serious moment for me, for it appeared that, after all, after everything, we didn't have a lot to say to each other. We made up for it by finding a place that sold cake and coffee and filled our mouths with those instead of words.

All of a sudden I realised that my plan had backfired. Fantasy had indeed been replaced by an uncomfortable reality and I was no longer in love. Just like that, it was all over. There would never be her soft arms to sleep in. Nothing was real. I had lied to myself. I hadn't wanted reality, I'd wanted a better fantasy. Where I was more in control. I suppose that was a step forward. We parted that evening, her I suppose with a feeling of relief, of a duty done, and me with a little sadness, a reluctance to let go my dream. She drove me home in the big blue Porsche and as I stepped out of it I wondered if any of my friends would see me. She drove away and I stood there, the brave little woman that I was, waving goodbye to her lover as the credits came up. I slunk into my flat, tore off the stupid dress and crawled into bed. I felt as if I'd been punched. But I had no desire to cry, I was as dry as the desert.

Three months later I saw her once again. The occasion was the end of term Staff Drinks and Xmas Dinner party. I was sitting in the staff room openly reading someone else's *Guardian*, drinking hot chocolate from the machine. No need to look now as if I was busy in case the Deputy Head found me something to do. I was leaving anyway. Something made me look up. I was sitting with my back to the door but for some reason I turned my head. The door opened and she was there. In the black and blue outfit as if she had never been away, as if it had never happened. As if in that last, long, bitter winter term I hadn't suffered a bereavement with her rejection and her disappearance. Lost a lover and a dream that had brightened my life for a while and made it feel valuable. She'd been away, was back. To see old friends. At her entrance there was a general cry of welcome as she sped towards them. And though it was a matter of only a few feet it was as if she had been shot from a bow. She seemed even to have the trails of speed flowing from her that cartoonists use to denote flight. I can see her now like Superwoman, with her feet off the ground and one hand pointing before her to part the air.

Though I was on the other side of the room deep in an armchair that all but hid me, as she passed she saw my look and raised a hand to me. "Hallo," she said. That's all, just "Hallo" and a scant wave from those pink fingers that had been so kind in my dreams, that was more a dismissal than greeting. I noticed that my fingers were too dirty from the newspaper print to put to my eyes so, though my instinct was to sink deeper into the chair, I folded the paper along its proper edges and, with considerable effort since the chair was so low, rose with as seasonable a look on my face as I could muster and walked slowly from the room to the female teachers' rest room. Not until I was safely locked inside the four little walls of the lavatory compartment did I allow the tears their freedom. I thought I had held no grudge. I thought I had been mature about it. But the tears were bitter and angry, straight from the throat. Hot and bitter like chinese sauce.

Lunch was no better, I shouldn't have gone. We started with drinks in the sixth form common room that someone had decorated with tufts of coloured paper and balloons. Staff formality was abandoned and even the dourest were finding a frisky streak. Among the Supplies was an attitude of exhausted relief that should have brought us closer together as the end neared. But I could feel with horror that I was about to be seized by the strangling frigidity and coldness that often attacks me at such moments. It's as if I pull around me so much protection that not only am I made speechless by the lack of air but as others get merrier, my blanket of reserve renders me invisible. I long for someone to rescue me, but of course no-one can see me. Would they notice me now, I wonder, if I even took my clothes off. Probably not.

Soon the official goodbyes are over. Those who have served their school so faithfully and are now getting the hell out have their thanks, their applause and their book tokens. No-one thanks me for anything. Anyway it's time to go to the dining hall now so I try to be less invisible. But that's hard and everyone is in groups, patterns have been made by now. I'm like an inky blob looking for a clean piece of paper to roost on. In the dining room it's clear I shall have to be careful or I shall be condemned to spend the whole meal with people I don't like. Of course that's the wrong way round to approach the matter but my organ of self destruction is in full throttle so that's exactly what happens. I can see by all the head swivelling and the air of abandonment that others are pretending it's just a pause, that I'm not the only one in this predicament, but still I walk firmly and resolutely to the wrong table. My need to appear in control had me confused for those few vital moments when everyone was sniffing each other out. Animals at a water hole. Wart hogs with wart hogs, lions with lions, giraffes with giraffes. And I was the sick mouse. If you know that joke.

For some reason I can't remember who sat either to my left or my right. I was too preoccupied with the aura of private jubilation that still surrounded Jackie, boiling and effervescing like the pink and golden clouds at the feet of rosy cherubs that hung on the ceilings of stately houses. And still I could see, hanging about her shoulders, the ghost of my desire, blurring her edges like a carbon copy laughing at me, making me shiver. While I was concentrating on all this, looking as if I were doing nothing, two people sat down opposite me. It was the Head of Third Year and her husband. I'd never met him before; she was a strong, capable, chain-smoking woman for whom noisy classes were quiet and rude children polite. Her effect on adolescent group hysteria was like that of the hand of Jesus quieting a storm. She was a woman like a razor. He, I recognised straightaway. Sprung from nowhere, unexpected, saved up, no doubt, for the occasion by my smirking fates; Nemesis. All the other tables were full now, I was trapped. And like another guest at another feast he fixed me with a bird-like eye. A very brown suggestive eye, and a slight tilt to his head. My instincts about him were soon proved correct. He was lemon juice in milk. When the meal came he showed us all how to carve the meat. I had nut roast so I didn't have to wait. And when someone popped a party popper into the parsnips he gave us a list of all the possible chemicals that might have been responsible for the tiny propelling explosion. He seemed to think that the Deputy Head of Science also at our table needed that information most. Also a computer expert it appeared, so I dared the gods and asked a question, more in the spirit of the occasion than with any real desire for knowledge. I was trying not to be rude by ignoring him completely. They won, the gods, and I was forced to stare into his white face and brown eyes a full ten minutes while he told me which model to buy, which one was suitable to my needs as a woman and how to approach the salesman in the shop. People yawned and avoided each other's eyes. He was a little boy of course. Made no older by the kisses he gave his wife's ear.

It appeared to me to be against the interest of the school to have the Head of Third Year kissed like that. No wonder the school was going to the dogs. I tried to protect myself, tried blocking him from my thoughts. Think of your dinner I said to myself. But the poor parsnips and buttered carrots were no match for him. Once or twice catching my reluctant eye, he smiled knowingly at me as if someone had told him something about me. As if we had a secret. I longed to lean across the table now scattered with the debris of our meal and say "Listen, arse-hole, I'm a lesbian."

But I just ate the dinner and the pudding, pulled the crackers and wore the paper hat. And endured. But at the cheese and biscuits I could stand it no longer. Bear no longer sitting with these strangers, with this man who wanted something from me. As always at breaking point, the gods, bored and I hope a little guilty, took pity on me and sent a diversion in which I saw my chance of escape.

As well as the tufts of coloured pubic hair which passed as decoration, the tables had been set with candles, all part of a sophisticated ambience unheard of in the basement dining hall. One of these was set innocently beneath streamers which hung negligently down, graceful as a trailing hand from a boat. The water imagery is quite inappropriate since some fool lit the candle and it all went up. Not, I'm sorry to say, a huge conflagration, but smoldering, browning and finally catching with a small pop of flame. Then the scrape of chairs, laughter, cheers and even a small womanly scream. We all looked round. Jackie was laughing the loudest and had risen from her seat, jacket off, tie crooked. She wasn't wearing a hat. She was no clown, and as I looked at her I felt the sensation of brown eyes on me and without moving my head in the slightest I shifted my eyes to the fire. The devil could find his way to the flames, I wasn't going to help him to her. All this took a second, only a second for the world to shift in its course and for the planets to change their direction. I pushed back my chair, tore off my hat and saying the briefest of farewells I vanished for good this time. As I passed her I didn't say goodbye. I didn't say "Goodbye, dear, we may never meet again, will you kiss me one last and real kiss to send me on my way?" No, I walked out fast seeing visions of party poppers catching alight one after another after another, and screams, loud terrified screams. But before I could rescue her I was out in the corridor that stretched before me quite empty. And I was in tears again, the blue yellow tears of self pity. No-one loved me.

As I passed the front door there was a group of semi-drunk girls. They were illegally gathered, having been shoo-ed off the premises hours ago. But with admirable contrariness, they were back. It was Suzi and her mates. With Crazy Colour in their hair and Crazy Foam solidified on their uniform like streaks of luminous custard they swayed just a little. The blue in Suzi's hair looked good and the flush on her normally dull cheek made her look for the moment quite pretty. I told her, and she took my hand and shook it with both of hers. "Good-bye, Miss, have a happy Christmas," she said her eyes not quite in the same direction. And then they all wanted my hand. Their hands were dirty and sticky and getting my own back was an exercise in diplomacy that took a full five minutes. I hadn't expected to see them again. But I should have known they were still there, like the monster at the end of "Alien"; always a lurking possibility.

There were merely two short steps now to my escape. My coat and my bike. My coat was still in the staff room which was emptier than I'd ever seen it before. It seemed a different country; its whole terrain had altered. Now that I no longer had to try and make it home, now that I no longer had to learn its language, speak its words, conform to and uphold its rules it appeared to me in a completely new light. It was vast. It was stretching away from me as if I were on a height and the room were sloping down from my feet. And quickly, before the whole room tumbled away and there was nothing left for them to return to, I gathered my coat and let myself be borne out to the real world. My bike was locked in a tiny yard out of sight of the kids. You could look from this yard into the steamy kitchens and see beyond the serving hatch into the dining room. They were all still there. It appeared to be coffee and liqueurs time. He was no longer to be seen. I dare say he never existed. I dare say the Head of Third Year never had a husband. But Jackie I could see. She had risen once more and the men and women round her were for a moment frozen looking up at her. Her face was lifted and on it was a look of tenderest ecstasy. Her arm was raised with its glass and just for a second through the steamy kitchen window she seemed to be facing me, toasting me. And then the cold glass misted over and like a sorcerer's trick she was gone.

I was unlocking my bike and preparing for the road, heavy hearted and cold, when above me I heard the ominous sound of a window being flung open violently against a wall. I hurried, I didn't relish the idea of any final prank. The sort of airborne missiles that the sound of that open window suggested on a cold end of term day were not the sort of last minute memories that I wanted. But I needn't have worried. While the masters revelled in the bowels of the building the activities from the top floor only made me smile. As I and my bike were negotiating a difficult corner between the outhouse and the washing line I heard faintly and fondly from on high a last, "lezzie, lezzie".

Affectionate thanks are due to Christina Dunhill for her help with an earlier draft of this story.

YOU CAN'T SAY THAT

Rebecca O'Rourke

'Will you please collect the snails and take them to the park because they're eating the flowers off the runner beans.'

'The window panes are cracking with the weight of the night.'

'My cat trills like a bird.'

It won't do. It's the wrong kind of impression all together. But what kind of an impression am I trying to make anyway? I don't know, that's the problem. I just don't know. Smiling clearly isn't enough and besides I don't want to go through life smiling at her. I can smile as much as I like at who I like. No, I want to talk to her. I want to get to know her, perhaps I want to fall in love and live happily ever after with her. Who's to say. Perhaps I have already. Love at first sight. But I don't believe in that.

I'm beginning to find it embarrassing, in the lift and the hallway. I can't really afford the time to lurk around waiting for her to come in and out, lying in wait to catch her as she takes out the rubbish and brings in the milk, but it does mean I see her. And we talk then. About the weather. Yes, it's fascinating, I know, but we do. 'A bit warmer today,' I might say, 'Well, it is July,' she'll reply and I'll nod sagely, I like it when it rains, such emotion about rain; such endless possibility for speculation. 'I see you're not chancing it,' I said to her last Wednesday, sort of nodding and pointing at her umbrella, trying not to feel too stupid for interrupting her reveries.

I think I want to talk to her because she thinks serious thoughts. You can tell. I think so, anyway. I've thought about it a lot, well, since I first met her really. Because I don't believe in treating women as objects; I mean, how can you and why should you judge someone by appearances. Just appearances. It's disgusting. It's what men do. It really doesn't matter what she wears, how big and how little she is; the length and colour of her hair, her eyes. It's not because I like to look at her that I want to get to know her. That would be terrible. I wonder what she thinks of me?

I have to talk to her. The weather is reliable, there's a lot of it about and it's there every day, but it's not getting us anywhere. The trouble is, I don't know what else to talk about. There are good reasons why people talk about the weather. It's safe. You see, if I say 'The window panes are cracking with the weight of the night' how do I know that she will recognise my profoundly sensitive and poetic nature? She might just think I'm crazy. I want her to think I'm interesting, of course, a little bit special, a little bit out of the ordinary. I don't want her to think I'm off my head. It's a fine line. She'll know, she'll be wary: anyone who lives in London is.

Perhaps if I withdraw, go all sultry and silent, she'll say something to me. Why shouldn't she, why should I be the one to make all the running. I'll try that. Will I? No, no patience. I have to talk to her. I'll have a party. Invite her. Flat warming. She's not to know I've lived here 5 years, anyway who cares. A party's a party. She doesn't look the type to go to parties. Oh, I'm getting bored with this. What sort of a type is she anyway? What sort of a type are any of us? What a thing to think. She'd really be impressed if she knew I was thinking about her like this. Suppose she said something different to me, what would I think? I'd think she was cracked if she said any of this. 'Please collect the snails and take them to the park?' We're miles away from a park and I haven't got any runner beans. They're tomatoes and personally I think any snail making it up to a fifth floor balcony is entitled to as much as they can eat. 'I'm having trouble with my snails?' I shall have to practice my enunciation for that one. My s-nails. Not a lot of mileage in a conversation about manicures. 'I'm having a party for snails, do come.'

She might think I mean to eat them. She might get the wrong idea. Snails, ugh! On the other hand, she might think I'm French. French women are always interesting. Perhaps she'd like to go to Paris with me. I learnt French at school: I wanted to go and live there. Be a philosopher or a revolutionary. All I can remember with any confidence is how to say, 'Tu as La Grippe, mon petit.' That'll be useful, won't it.

This is ridiculous. Cats. Everyone's soft about animals, you can always talk about a cat when everything else is too difficult. My cat, my little stripey tiger will save me. It doesn't matter whether she likes them or is allergic to them: plenty to talk about either way. Witty exchanges. I can invite her in, establish contact, then we can wave and chat across our balconies, leave our doors on the latch. Become intimate friends, arms casually thrown across shoulders, chaste good-night kisses. The cat can sit between us on the settee, we'll take it in turns to stroke him. He'll stretch out and purr and offer a velvet paw, blinking his green eyes at her. She'll comment on them, so unusual. People always do.

A knock at the door. Urgent and insistent. It is her and this is Saturday afternoon. She has been thinking the same thoughts as me. 'Your cat,' she says. 'My cat,' I say, 'my cat trills like a bird,' and take her hand, pulling her into my flat. 'And so he should,' she says, 'he's just eaten my canary.'

IN AND OUT OF TIME

Shameem Kabir

PART ONE: IN TIME

The room was alive with moving women. Even those seated at tables started to tap and turn in time to the music. Ginnie felt the rhythm of the room taking hold, she swayed to the sounds coming through the speakers, her head tilting to the beat. She was watching Smita on stage, as she started to sing "Blind Date".

> *I'm never sure*
> *what's in store*
> *when I open the door*
> *on a blind date.*
>
> *Will she be nice*
> *will she like rice*
> *I sit and wait*
> *on a blind date.*
>
> *Could be great*
> *on a blind date.*

It was important for the band to be good tonight, because Joan of Disc Hits was here. Ginnie had arranged it after frequently sending demos and letters to the Company. Finally she had gone round to their offices and had persuaded Joan to come and see them on stage.

> *When she gets here*
> *the stage is clear*
> *and it's like fate*
> *on a blind date.*

Ginnie was obsessed by the ambition to get a megastar career off the ground. She wanted recognition, at any cost, and she knew the only way to get it was through a major record company deal. That's why she'd been so insistent with Joan, who had at last consented to come and see the Daughters perform.

> *Could be great*
> *on a blind date.*

Ginnie had met Smita on a blind date and had been immediately attracted to her. Perhaps it was her exotic personality that first drew Ginnie to her. She liked her being an anglicised Asian, with bits of both cultures caught in what she thought was an unusual synthesis. She had been charmed by it.

> *Should I charm her*
> *let go my armour*
> *I'm in a state*
> *on a blind date.*

More than anything else, Ginnie was immediately responsive because they had both had unhappy relationships with other partners and were determined not to fall into the same patterns. So although they realised the danger of their date, they were confident they could resist any repetition, and decided, what the hell, to give it a go.

> *The stories we share*
> *take me by surprise*
> *the stories we share*
> *make me realise*

> *the danger of our date.*
>
> *Can be great
> on a blind date.*

Smita had made Ginnie laugh in a way she hadn't for a long time. Now, as Smita sang the closing chorus of her song, Ginnie got up to do the next number. She wasn't nervous, she'd stopped counting the hours spent singing. It was a passion with her. She walked through the side aisle up the corner steps and was at her microphone in perfect time. The audience applauded as Smita turned to Ginnie, moving her arms in a sweep of welcome. The lights on her dimmed and went gold on Ginnie, who took hold of the microphone and announced "Dream of Gold".

> Met you in a dream of gold
> that's why I seem so bold
> dream of gold, dream of gold.

As Smita sat down at the band's reserved table, she saw how receptive the audience was. There were a lot of fans there that night, regulars who followed the band through the women's circuit. She was aware that many of them felt attracted to Ginnie. She always had that effect, her every gesture was enticing without design. Smita looked up to watch her, desiring her as much as she had three years ago when they met through an ad. She remembered that night. They had made love that same evening. There had been no hesitation on her part, no caution on Ginnie's. They had talked over dinner and wine, their minds meeting on many areas. Above all they wanted to avoid the awfulness of their previous encounters, where they'd either been suffocated or suffocating. Smita had thought long and hard about her first lesbian relationship. It had ended in such pain and bitterness. It had been Isabel's first lesbian relationship as well. To begin with they had been deliriously happy, but then her lover started saying how different Smita was, and how it was difficult to be with her. She said Smita was emotionally too demanding, and Isabel didn't want to make such a commitment. She then started a relationship with another woman, with whom she eventually bought a flat.

Later on Smita agreed with her friend Naseem that Isabel had been acting out a common pattern. Naseem knew quite a few women whose first lesbian relationships had been a disaster. It was difficult to know how to respond when everything was so new and intense, and when issues of autonomy had still to be worked out. Often the woman who had the control in the relationship would walk out on her lover, saying she didn't want monogamy. She would then go on and form a monogamous relationship with a second partner. The two would then make the commitment to each other which they'd previously sworn was impossible. But at the time, when this happened with Isabel, Smita only saw the rejection as proof of not being lovable. She was devastated at being excluded so totally. Eventually she decided she would build a relationship on another basis, where there would be commitment without claustrophobia, passion without pain. So when she met Ginnie, and they exchanged their respective stories, there had been the shared resolve to avoid repeating the same mistakes. They were too aware of the danger of their date.

> You're the danger in my dreams
> you're no stranger to my dreams
> you're the dancer in my dreams
> you're the answer to my dreams.
>
> So give it a chance
> to work out right
> we can share a dance
> we can share a night.
>
> Met you in a dream of gold
> that's why I seem so bold
> dream of gold, dream of gold.

Smita remembered when Ginnie had written the song for her. It had been a breakthrough for Ginnie, who had never written a lyric before. Whereas Smita had been writing them for years. She had devised many concept albums because she was sure this was the future for pop/rock. Smita had agreed to go along with Ginnie's suggestion to form a band. She wanted to put her ideas into practice. The song was ending now. She found her way back to the stage, and was at her microphone just in time for "High on You".

> *I'm high on you*
> *high as a kite*
> *I'm flying too*
> *deep in the night*
> *you start to smile*
> *your eyes so bright*
> *and for a while*
> *we feel delight.*

As Ginnie returned to their table she was conscious of a quickening of her pulse. Must have been all that real coffee she'd drunk. She could do with a cigarette, now, but resisted. It was such an awful habit, she hated being addicted to tobacco. She sat down facing the stage, as Smita sang one of her favourite songs.

> *I'm high on you*
> *high as a lark*
> *your kiss so true*
> *is like a spark*
> *we share a walk*
> *down at the park*
> *and then we talk*
> *deep in the dark.*

They'd been collaborating for nearly three years now, practically all the time they'd known each other. When they first met, Ginnie thought Smita was a jewel among stones. Ginnie liked her way with words, Smita spoke so fluently, so eloquently. Ginnie had been surprised when Smita told her she had a degree in

English, but then it made perfect sense. And she spoke so formally. She found that charming too. Smita had once objected to this. She said her speech patterns were part of her cultural heritage, and that it had nothing to do with being quaint. But Ginnie still thought she was funny. And she loved how polite Smita was. Her manners were so perfect, she said "please" and "thank you" on every occasion, she even said "sorry" when she meant pardon. Ginnie saw her customs as coming from another culture. She found that appealing too.

> *I'm high on you*
> *with eyes of love*
> *I'm high on you*
> *like skies above.*

Their collaboration had begun as a joke, with each taking it in turn to make up alternative lines to well-known songs. Ginnie had really loved the way they laughed together. And she loved working with Smita, who had taught her many a trick on how to write lyrics. They would spend hours together, writing, practising, composing and performing, and their partnership was a productive one. It had been easy to form the Daughters. The quality of their material made the band popular with lesbian audiences. They were a good working unit. Joan of Disc Hits would just have to see that for herself.

> *I'm high on you*
> *high as a cloud*
> *we know it's true*
> *to feel this proud*
> *both you and I*
> *don't want to crowd*
> *but we're so high*
> *we say it loud.*

Smita's number was ending as Ginnie went back on stage. She took the microphone and the band started on the opening bars of "Sunshine Dream".

> I was lost when you found me
> I was in waves which drowned me
> but I felt love surround me
> when you put your arms around me.
>
> You bring me sunshine like I've never seen
> you're my sunshine dream.

It had been electric for them, Smita thought, returning to their table. She let her neck relax, and the music carried her to the memory of those first days. The attraction had been immediate, signalled by their agreement to sleep together. They'd undressed slowly. When they first kissed, Smita felt a thrill of joy.

> I could feel your body swaying
> I could tell I'd be staying
> I could hear your voice saying
> you wanted us to see the day in.

Their lips were generous and gentle, demanding with passion and not pressure. They had started making love slowly. Smita felt in a state of suspension, her hands moving over the curves and contours of Ginnie's body, conscious all the time of the softness of her skin, the scent of her breath on her eyes, her ears, her mouth. She followed the line of her spine downwards, down to where it led to her buttocks, fitting round and warm in each hand. Ginnie pressed her breasts, and her legs crossed into Smita's, interlocking. Their hands were delicate in touch, alighting, stroking, then moving on to some undiscovered part of their anatomy. Ginnie kissed Smita on the nape of her neck, her breath warm.

> I never thought a kiss
> could do this much
> I never felt the flame
> quite the same
> as with your touch.

Their hands went across their thighs, and then, as they

uncrossed their legs, they unfolded themselves to each
other, silky hair brushing under their palms. They
began to move their bodies in a sway of desire, as they
radiated around each other's centre of pleasure. Their
fingers travelled up between the lips, exploring the
warm liquid joy of passion, finding the core of clitoris,
circular, firm, as they moved to the magic of each
other's pleasure. They sensed each other's needs as
they fell into the rightness of a rhythm. Smita could
feel Ginnie turning under her hand with a response
similar to her own, impassioned, urgent, but without
frenzy.

> When I felt your lips on mine
> and we moved together in time
> it was like I'd seen a sign
> I'd never felt so fine.

Now their arousal took another turn, deeper, in tune.
As Ginnie kissed Smita with the edge of a desire
neither could control, she made a humming sound at
the back of her mouth. The sound moved into her
throat, resonated, it became longer and louder as her
excitement became extremity. They started on a faster
cycle of breathing, their hearts pounding in their
breasts with beats of a frantic drum. Ginnie responded
to each kiss, each caress, by holding Smita tight, then
tighter, pulling her, reaching and responding. They
wanted each other: Smita felt a rush. And then, with
their fingers in mutual motion, they touched with a
passion of fire and flame, meeting, retreating, then
meeting together in perfect time. Smita felt release,
release in the power of giving and getting pleasure, as
they both came, explosively, both in trust and both
with surrender. Warmth glowed through them.

> You bring me sunshine like I've never seen
> you're my sunshine dream.

Then, as they lay together, spent in their exhaustion,
their eyes rested on each other, taking in each detail,
their heartbeats slowing into another, quieter rhythm.

As Smita returned on stage, Ginnie touched her shoulder, and there was still a thrill in her caress. Smita reached the microphone and began singing "Don't Do Me Wrong".

> *Don't do me wrong*
> *like I've been done*
> *don't do me wrong.*

When Ginnie returned to the table she wasn't really listening to Smita's song, she was still feeling high on her own voice. When she sang she sang with power and passion. After all, it was a performance, she believed in giving her best. Now as she glanced around the tables, she knew a lot of women were looking at her. She loved that, she loved the sense of power that this adulation gave her. She was ambitious for fame, she could be a major star. Why not, she was attractive, her voice was brilliant, she was charming. She loved being in the public eye, and enjoyed knowing that a lot of these women were fantasising about her. She was looking good tonight and was glad she'd chosen her special black outfit. She looked around again and saw Sarah at the bar. Strange how it still happened, that same shock of recognition, ever since their first encounter, meant to be casual, yet growing to more than either had anticipated. She liked her laughter, her wit, her detachment. Ginnie wondered if Smita would be upset that Sarah was there that night, but it was a public place after all.

> *You've got me reeling for you*
> *where will it lead*
> *I've got a feeling for you*
> *more than need.*

When Smita expressed her intense love for Ginnie it felt good to be the subject of such passion. But it worried her too. There was no doubt about it, Smita was intense. Her emotional attachment felt similar to what Ginnie had previously gone through with Mia.

The familiarity between them had led to Mia's dependence on her. The more Ginnie had resisted, the more Mia's clinging became something of a complex. Smita, however, claimed she really did enjoy getting on with her life separately from Ginnie, as long as when they were together it was good between them.

> *Together we're good*
> *we can shine*
> *fire and wood*
> *water and wine*
> *don't leave me stranded*
> *on the line*
> *I couldn't stand it*
> *another time.*

Smita was perfectly cool about Ginnie's wish to be non-monogamous, and didn't try to change it. If anything it was Ginnie who had felt bad in the beginning, when she first slept with Sarah. Though Smita said she could take it, Ginnie still felt a terrible responsibility.

> *Don't do me wrong*
> *like I've been done*
> *don't do me wrong.*

Ginnie couldn't understand herself sometimes, she was trapped by her own guilt rather than by any possessiveness on Smita's part. It aggravated her that she had the freedom to do as she wanted, and yet felt in the wrong. And this was without being able to blame Smita back for making accusations. She almost wished Smita *would* accuse her of betrayal, of inconsistency, anything, just so she had something more definite to go on than this vague weight of guilt she carried. As she went up on stage to do her last number for the first half, she decided she would spend the interval with Sarah. Smita would just have to put up with it. Ginnie certainly wasn't going to go through the guilt she'd felt when she first wrote the song she was going to sing next, "My Mistake".

> You said you'd go
> but you didn't show
> that night at the bar
> I was feeling lost
> and I paid the cost
> by going too far.
>
> I'm sorry, love, my mistake.

Now as Smita went back to the table, some friends came over to join her. The interval was coming up and she could have a drink. She was looking forward to talking to Ginnie, they had so much to say and so little time spent alone together.

> I saw a friend
> at the corner end
> and decided there
> I'd have a fling
> I'd really swing
> coz I didn't care.
>
> I'm sorry, love, my mistake.

When Ginnie first slept with Sarah, Smita tried to be understanding, she knew from experience not to be a guilt-tripper. It was alright as long as Ginnie still loved her. Of course it was hurtful when Ginnie started to sleep with Sarah more than just casually, but Smita still refused to let it become an issue. Without knowing it, Ginnie seemed to be pushing Smita to become possessive, so she could then confirm her suspicions that Smita was just as demanding as Mia had been. But Smita really did try. Sure, she wanted the same things as before, monogamy, sharing a flat, things like that, but there was no way this was an issue with them. Smita had learned her lesson too well to insist on such points.

> Know it's my fault
> not calling a halt
> I didn't think

> went right ahead
> went over and said
> let's have a drink.
>
> Now you mistrust me
> now you distrust me.

It was true Smita felt a sense of failure because Ginnie was obviously in need of more than she could bring to her, but she didn't resent Sarah the way Ginnie suspected. But then Ginnie's state of suspicion began to affect the quality of their time together. She kept looking for signs that Smita was being demanding. Of course Smita couldn't deny her dependence on Ginnie. Sometimes she'd get scared by it, but it was a part of her life she accepted without question, it was there and she had to live with it. What she tried to do was express her dependence with a minimum of demands. The trouble was Ginnie insisted on making an equation between being dependent and being demanding, she couldn't separate the two. Her own sense of guilt made her feel Smita was being manipulative.

> We left soon after
> I liked her laughter
> and that was that
> it was so crazy
> was feeling hazy
> back at her flat.
>
> I'm sorry, love, my mistake.

Now Ginnie came off stage for the interval, and Smita was disappointed to see her go over to the bar. Suddenly Sarah stood out. They kissed hello. Sarah said something to her and Ginnie laughed, locking into her arm. Smita looked away. She was relieved when the interval ended, and she went on stage with the energy of a fighter who can't or won't accept being beaten. She sang "Afraid" as if she was short on time.

> *When I first met you*
> *some time ago*

> *I had to get you*
> *to also know*
> *I wouldn't let you*
> *just walk away*
> *and I bet you*
> *wanted to stay.*
>
> But I'm afraid what we've made will be betrayed.

As Smita began the second half of their set, Ginnie was glad there'd been no scene about Sarah. Of course Smita wouldn't have made one. But if she had insisted on talking to Ginnie in the interval then things might have got heavy. Ginnie felt ready for a bit of drama. Anyway, they would have plenty to say when they met Joan at 11 o'clock. Meanwhile she was excited. There was no doubt about it, her feelings for Sarah were as potent, as powerful as they had always been. Sarah was looking as striking as ever tonight, in the height of fashion as usual. She desired her with none of the complexities of her relationship with Smita. It was safer because they were similar in ways Smita and she were not. Sometimes Smita's difference made Ginnie long for the stability of sameness she got with Sarah. And even though she denied it, Smita could be difficult. Her love was too intense, it frightened Ginnie.

> *Coz I need more*
> *than you give at times*
> *and I ignore*
> *the danger signs*
> *I cling and claw*
> *you meet my need*
> *but I feel at war*
> *nothing's guaranteed.*
>
> And I'm afraid what we've made will be betrayed.

Ginnie felt a great guilt at letting Smita down, which she could not confront because Smita was being so understanding. Though Ginnie blamed herself, she felt compelled to sleep with Sarah, it was a way out from what she felt was a rut in her relationship with Smita. They just didn't laugh together as much as before. It was all very well saying things were okay, but they weren't. Ginnie did not consider race as a factor in their relationship, so that wasn't the reason for the tension between them. Also, they were both middle class, so that didn't explain it either. But she agreed that there was an inequality in their relationship. It was the inequality of an emotional dependence, a devotion, that had become less pleasing. Smita said she knew Ginnie was the loved and she was the lover, but that she didn't want this to create a power imbalance between them. The possibility of this seemed to frighten Smita more than anything else.

> *Our affair*
> *has me scared*
> *and though we've dared*
> *to share and care*
> *I'm still scared.*

Ginnie was fed up with this tension she carried. She felt she had to force things to a conclusion. Smita had once had the nerve to suggest to her that Ginnie really did want monogamy. That was why she felt guilty at sleeping with both her and Sarah. Ginnie thought this was nonsense, she didn't need Smita to tell her her own mind. Ginnie was sure that setting up home was the last thing she wanted. She believed in change, and monogamy seemed mediocre to her. Ginnie liked to think she was more radical. And to prove it she was going home with Sarah tonight. She knew Smita wanted to talk to her, but she would just have to wait.

> *And how we feel*
> *and who we are*
> *has made us heal*
> *we've got this far*
> *so let's not steal*
> *what we can't take*

> *let's just seal
> what we can make.*

As Smita ended her song and came back off stage, she really was scared. She could see the danger signs but she preferred not to analyse them. They were less painful as unformed thoughts. But tonight, she saw pieces fitting in ways she'd avoided before. Now she knew Ginnie was looking for a confrontation. As Ginnie started singing "Heading for a Fall", Smita could feel her blood beating furiously.

> The moment has come
> for us to confront
> we may feel numb
> from what we want
> but we can't stall
> when we're heading
> heading for a fall.

Smita desperately wanted Ginnie to know how much she still wanted her. If only they could talk things through. But Ginnie was never there. The little time they had together would be spent in extremes of either fighting or making love, with no middle ground. Smita had been prepared to go along with the situation Ginnie had set up for them. But when her attempts to be reasonable only alienated Ginnie, she really didn't know what to do. She was trying to keep them together, but maybe Ginnie didn't want her anymore. At the thought of this, Smita's heart missed a beat.

> The anger you feel
> is really pain
> and so the wheel
> turns round again
> please don't be rash
> when we're heading
> heading for a crash.

Smita could take Sarah's importance to Ginnie. In fact, though it hurt, she accepted this importance as eclipsing her own. But she was so frightened at losing Ginnie that the pain of it made her accept Ginnie's terms. They were together in a team, and it didn't matter it was mostly around work, as long as they still shared some intimacy. Smita enjoyed the fixed routine of their arrangements to meet, they gave her a stability, and she believed in what they'd created together. She wanted it to last.

> What we've built
> shouldn't get destroyed
> I'll hurt with guilt
> you'll feel in a void
> but we'll survive
> when we're heading
> heading for a dive.

Ginnie had also enjoyed the regularity of their meetings but in a more prescriptive way. She liked making rules about how often to meet as lovers, and, more importantly, she loved the ritual that their work together involved. Performances, even rehearsals, were a delight to her. But she had become emotionally harder, inured, less giving to Smita. She had stayed largely out of habit, she was accustomed to her, and besides, they had invested a lot in their relationship. But now she was less accepting of Smita's love. Sometimes she'd be very dismissive of Smita, and had deliberately said things she knew would hurt her. Lately, Smita had not been able to do anything right. Now that Smita was out of her favour, Ginnie had a tendency to explode angrily with her at the slightest reason.

In the beginning it had worked: they had wanted each other, and met each other's want, with what was close to instinct. But now their needs and demands had altered.

PART TWO: OUT OF TIME

Ginnie knew as she put out the cigarette it was a mistake to have smoked it in the first place. It might affect her voice. She looked blankly at the stage, annoyed with herself. Then a thought came to her, out of the blue, making her want to laugh with relief at its simplicity: she would stop sleeping with Smita. Suddenly she felt light and free. The realisation that she could end the relationship had literally not occurred to her, Smita had become such a habit. Now, with a clarity she had not seen before, she knew how to put an end to her feelings of betrayal. She would stop sleeping with Smita and any feelings of guilt at letting her down would be real. What's more they would be temporary. Smita would get over it. Maybe she'd find someone who could take her emotional intensity. It might be good for her as well to start from scratch. Ginnie watched Smita as she sang "Going up the Wall for You".

> *Want you so bad*
> *need you like mad*
> *I'm going up the wall for you*
> *getting hazy*
> *going crazy*
> *I'm going up the wall for you.*
>
> *Broken pain*
> *going insane*
> *I'm going up the wall for you*
> *I'll never mend*
> *round the bend*
> *I'm going up the wall for you.*

Of course Ginnie still wanted them to be friends, and to collaborate together. But she couldn't go on being lovers with her. The relief at the thought of ending their relationship was too liberating. Things had to change. For one thing she was going to give up smoking that night. She needed a cigarette, now, but she would resist the temptation. It was an unusual sensation, but bearable. It would help if she felt under less pressure. Though Smita claimed she made few demands, the ferocious intensity of her love made things difficult for Ginnie. Smita was just too different.

> *The door shuts*
> *going nuts*
> *I'm going up the wall for you*
> *I'm in a bind*
> *out of my mind*
> *I'm going up the wall for you.*

Yes, things had to change. Smita's passion for Ginnie was now unwelcome. It was too much having a relationship as well as working on the same sets. Besides, she had her own life to get on with, she really couldn't spare the time, not even the two days a week they'd agreed on. No matter how high Smita would always rate, Ginnie just didn't have the same respect for her anymore. Now, as Smita finished her song, Ginnie went up on stage and announced "Cruel to be Kind".

> You're going to lose me
> I'm drawing away
> you have no dignity
> in some of what you say.
>
> Once you were dear to me
> now you're acting the clown
> don't want you near to me
> because you bring me down.
>
> Don't you see
> I have to be
> cruel to be kind.

Smita was sinking in pain. All she wanted to do was collapse somewhere, crash out, crush the torn nerves with sleep so she wouldn't hurt at each thought of her grief. She felt oppressed with the weight of her pain, she wanted to block it, to stop it thudding and pounding at her brain. All her thoughts returned to one central subject, drawn like seas to one ocean, all saying one thing over and over, that she'd lost her, lost her love.

> Your head's full of plans

> and contradictions
> but you don't understand
> fact is not fiction.
>
> Call me cruel
> I don't mind
> I know I'm cruel
> but I'm also kind.

Recently, Ginnie had not returned any of the attention and affection which rushed out of Smita for her. Even a kiss seemed like coercion. Ginnie wanted to maintain a friendship, but there would be a mockery in any contact they had. Smita couldn't make her understand her excessive desire. At the most Ginnie saw it as lust, to be contained and controlled. She saw none of its positive intensity, she only saw its obsessive persistence, speaking even in silence.

> Maybe soon one day
> it'll work out right
> but now there's no way
> we can share a night.

Now even though Smita knew Ginnie wanted to end their relationship, the only thing that seemed to hold her together was the desire pulsating through her, every vein aflame from need. Her hands trembled and she put them on the table, her body cut with a craving she knew Ginnie would not meet. She could take the loss and pain better if Ginnie would only return some of her desire. She knew there was no hope, but there was still the fantasy feeding her that Ginnie would relent a little, give her some token of the passion they'd once shared. All she wanted was one more night together, just one more night, on any terms Ginnie cared to name. Even as she made this admission, Smita saw the same old pattern refitting into place: this loss of power was exactly what she had avoided so carefully. But now, because Ginnie didn't want to sleep with her anymore, Smita was forced into a position where her desire was an unreasonable demand. She certainly couldn't turn it off, the way Ginnie had done. Because she had a need which Ginnie couldn't respond to, neither logic nor reason could save her. This was exactly what Ginnie had wanted. At last she could accuse Smita of the emotional suffocation she'd always suspected about her love.

Meanwhile, the audience had been applauding the set, demanding an encore. Smita and Ginnie went back on stage, together this time, to sing the song they'd co-written, "Time Will Tell".

> Only time will tell
> if we'll make good
> *and it's understood*
> *time will tell.*

Having decided to reject Smita, Ginnie felt freed of the demands Smita was now making obvious. She just wasn't prepared to be responsible for her, and she certainly wasn't going to account for her time. She resented being the object of such an obsessive sexual desire. She associated it with the worst kind of possessiveness possible. Why couldn't they just start all over again, alter the terms or something. Ginnie wanted to stay friends with Smita, they worked well together, and besides, she really did like her, she always had. Who knows, maybe Smita would accept losing her, and they'd all be good friends. Ginnie had decided to move in with Sarah. Smita might even be relaxed enough to go out with them. As far as she was concerned, she didn't want power, and was giving it back to Smita, not holding it against her.

> Time will tell, time will tell.

Smita felt Ginnie had turned her desire into a crime. Part of the fixation had to do with pure sex. Smita had never been with a woman who was as sexually responsive to her as Ginnie was. No other woman made her feel the same urgent level of intensity and excitement. Differences were subsumed in that central act of making love. But by the time sex

with Smita was no longer important to Ginnie, it had
become the most important part of the relationship for
Smita. Recently, Ginnie had been very critical of
Smita, excluding and ignoring her. But when they
slept together and made love there was equality again,
no matter how briefly, in that one act of sharing sex.
Now that Ginnie wanted to cut Smita off, her longing
had lodged into one thought alone: that just one
acknowledgement of her desire would create a parity
between them. She was desperate for this symbolic
gesture. It would give her an equality in her eyes. She
was trusting Ginnie to be generous, to grant her a need
she felt strongly about. The night together would be a
kind of acclimatization to the shock of being severed
from Ginnie. Smita was sure she could accept the pain
and start again, but she needed this one act of sharing
a night to remedy the rift between them. It would
give her the space to heal her grief.

Time will tell, time will tell.

PART THREE: TIME

As they came off stage, Ginnie said to Smita, catching
hold of her hand, that she had a surprise for her. Smita
was still in shock from the pain of thinking they'd
never ever sleep together again. When Ginnie took her
hand she felt an explosive charge run through her, a
charge of desire that touched her, touched her where
she couldn't control the pulse of passion. She was
confused, hoping for a moment that Ginnie had
understood her need, that she would give her the
token gift of sleeping with her. Smita would treasure
those moments, they would give her memories to
smooth the jagged edges of her desire, soothe also the
pain of being left hanging. Call it symbol, call it ritual,
this gift would gracefully close the chapter of her
desire. Without it she was suspended, left dangling in
desperation. She yearned for a release to her longing,
and dared to hope, but any such possibility was
destroyed as Ginnie told her about Joan of Disc Hits.

So that was the surprise. As Ginnie led them to Joan's table, Smita had no space to insist on her own needs, or even to register her disapproval at only being informed of this now.

Joan was appreciative of their songs, she liked their words and music. But Smita could see there was something she was holding back. Ginnie didn't seem to notice, and excitedly outlined to Joan their idea for a concept album, called "Stage-Rage". Ginnie told her how they wanted to do a narrative-type album, with different tracks recording the steps of a relationship. She said this had never been done before, when Joan interrupted and said it had, in opera and musicals. Ginnie was annoyed at this. She was dying for a smoke and felt doubly irritable. She felt Joan didn't have the imagination to see how novel they were being. She tried to explain their idea in another way, saying that it would be like a cabaret act, but that the main market would be the commercial music buying public. Here, Smita saw Joan stiffen in her movements, but again Ginnie didn't notice. She told Joan that they wanted to get the tension of theatre in their set, maybe with a taped voiceover, or even a third person, telling a story-line between songs. They still had to work it out, she said, but it was so obvious to write concept albums around a relationship. Ginnie said she was sure it would catch on. Their records would sell by the million. She repeated her conviction that their idea was commercially viable.

Again, Smita saw Joan stiffen with what seemed displeasure at being told her job. When she spoke, it was with tones of authority and assertion. To start with, Joan agreed that their idea of a concept album was a good one, but that Ginnie and Smita wouldn't be the ones to sell it. When Ginnie asked why, she answered, bluntly, because they were lesbians. They were too different, it made things much more difficult. It would be too risky to give them a deal. Ginnie was furious. She said that things would only change in time if people were more daring. She insisted that quality would win out, but Joan said from all her years in the music business, she knew it was hype that sold records, and the stigma of their being lesbians would make publicity a difficult matter. Disc Hits didn't want bad press. They were arguing angrily now.

Smita was distressed by this scene, by this same old story of patterns slotting into place. She was worried that they would never make it commercially, they were in their thirties, and running out of time. She had always been more pessimistic about the possibilities of Top Ten success. It was Ginnie who had insisted they try to break through on the charts. Her optimism was more unrealistic in that way. She wanted to set the precedent as the first lesbian act, to be known as such, to get number ones. She said things like if gay men could do it, so could lesbians. But Joan's response had been entirely predictable. Ginnie had seriously believed they had a chance of getting a major record deal, with network release of singles, an album, video promos, touring, television, international exposure, the works. By some irony Smita understood Ginnie's ambitions, because she knew their material was potentially very accessible. But there was no question of changing their lesbian identity or covering it up in order to sell records. Smita was unsurprised to hear that being lesbian was commercially unacceptable, and that merit was not enough.

Now Joan stood up abruptly, and said she'd enjoyed the set. She addressed them both when she apologised for disappointing them. She left them at the table. The other Daughters came over immediately, wanting to know the details. They'd guessed the outcome of the meeting from Ginnie's angry gestures. She lit up a cigarette. As Ginnie explained the main content of the conversation, Smita was again in a state of keeping the pain suspended. It had been a long evening, with even longer nights stretching emptily into the future, stretching like a sentence.

And as she sat there, Smita started connecting the threads of her life. First there was pain. But now the rage took over. Violent images flooded in as she relived the way Ginnie had hurt and humiliated her. She was enraged at herself for feeling so desperate. The rage started turning, towards another: Ginnie. It was Ginnie who had trivialised her love by reducing it to a complication which she, Ginnie, couldn't handle. She remembered how Ginnie would kiss her, with a passion that was close to violence, an aggression masking as affection. Now she felt a resurgence of desire at the memory. She wanted to be intimate with Ginnie again, so they could kiss in the urgent way they used to. As the thought mingled with memory, becoming fantasy, Smita's head took another turn: she wanted to hurt Ginnie, to humiliate her in revenge. She wanted to hold her in a vice, kiss her until she was breathless, press her body down heavy and hard upon her. She wanted Ginnie to hate her even while she couldn't resist her. Or to hate her because she couldn't resist her. As Smita's fantasy gripped her in a rage for revenge, she constructed a scenario of anger and hatred. Then she was horrified at herself. The fantasy of oppressing Ginnie held a brief perverse pleasure, but Smita knew it had to be rejected without reserve.

And then she thought about that evening, and how Joan had rejected them. Suddenly she realised that the same vein of mediocrity was at work in Ginnie. Her reluctance to work things through with Smita indicated a similar lack of courage, a moral laziness almost, in not wanting to risk engagement. Both Ginnie and Joan wanted to stay safe, not take on the difficulties of difference. As Smita realised this she knew Ginnie had betrayed her on many levels.

Now Smita knew she had to cut Ginnie out of her life, eradicate her. She was going to stop their collaboration. Tonight was going to be their last performance together. Smita knew that, even though Ginnie didn't yet. She knew there would be pain and emptiness, much longing and loneliness without Ginnie. But she could not stay in her presence, it evoked too much grief in her. Their relationship was to end, as collaborators, lovers, even as friends. A complete break of contact was the only way Smita could cope, could control the pain. She would tell Ginnie that tonight.

She knew she would never try to win Ginnie back.

this dreadful job bearable. But why didn't she notice me, do something? Didn't she realise how I was suffering? I wanted her to see inside my head. And so my pleasure in the situation spoiled. And I began to have the dreams. In her blue Porsche she drove me to school, so fast that it felt as though we were not moving. And outside the staff room under the brown beech hedge she leant across me to open the door and kissed me. Then there was the hockey match in the desert, and I was playing with her in a pair of shorts so tiny that I pulled them down to cover my thighs as rows of girls stood in twos hand in hand around the palm fringed pitch. Sometimes I woke from these happy dreams so startled by their revelations, and made so lonely by their contrast to my real life, that I would lie crying for half an hour and be late for school.

Sometimes it seemed that I spent all my waking

She had wanted to sleep with her on any terms, but now even if Ginnie were ever to want that, which was unlikely, Smita knew it would be a mistake. There was too much pain and bitterness between them. And Ginnie had understood nothing. Whereas Smita now knew she had to take control of her life. She knew she had to fight. There was no real decision about it, she had to do it. She was a survivor.

With love and thanks to Lucy Whitman for her editing, advice and encouragement, and a special thanks to Pratibha Parmar and Da Choong for their comments.

ANOTHER GARDEN

Aspen

"No, it's my hips. It's nothing you've done. I just can't lean up like that any more. They ache and ache."

This was followed by a silence. Jane knew it was the sort of silence that would be followed by Tessa starting to cry quietly. She didn't think she could stand it any longer if she had to hold her and comfort her through the hours it sometimes took her to recover. She'd been really good at it at first, being able to give blankets of energy to comfort Tess, who'd respond quickly and gratefully. But as the weeks went by, and then turned into months, and the same sort of problem came up again and again, Jane was drained of everything she had and now greeted Tess's renewed crying with tension.

Tess had always been such a strong lover. When they first got together Jane had always been overwhelmed with her strength and confidence. Of course Tess had had a few more lovers than Jane, but it was something more fundamental than that. Sometimes Jane thought perhaps it had something to do with Tess never having had sexual relations with men, but maybe it was just something to do with her personality? Perhaps some people were more contained in themselves, never stopping to think about things, just involved in their feelings and desires without any conscious elements coming into it? It couldn't be lack of trauma, because one of Tess's relationships had gone horribly wrong sexually. Tess had told her about it. Her lover couldn't bear to be touched. She'd cringe and lie like a board on the other side of the bed. Tess said she'd tried and tried not to touch her, but she loved and needed her. She'd find herself aching in her chest, her fingers touching her recoiling lover tentatively, meeting a guilty, unwelcoming body. Maybe the present mess they were in had something to do with that past pain?

But Jane wanted Tess and wanted her badly. It was ironic that it hadn't been this way with her last lover. Chris had been the woman downstairs when Jane was splitting up with her boyfriend. When she'd been with Chris she must have been kind of numb sexually. She still felt very bad about that. She didn't know whether it had been because she had been so recently abused by her boyfriend, or whether it was because she'd really wanted a mother and a sister, a warm loving relationship that wouldn't make too strenuous demands on her. Also Jane didn't have much idea of herself as a lesbian then. Not until she met Tess.

When they met, she had to admit, she was drunk. She was at a party with Chris and she felt very uncomfortable. It was supposed to be a gay party, but there was just a handful of gay men, and a lot of the women seemed to be more into them than they were into each other. Chris didn't believe in behaving like a couple, so she was making a point of not spending any time at all with Jane. In fact Jane thought she looked very affected, wafting about in a sequined T-shirt with fringes on the bottom and sleeves, waving a roll-up. But she had to admit she felt small and nervous. She didn't know where to look, she didn't know what to do. She was slowly cruising her way down a bottle of Bailey's, and trying to pretend she wasn't miserable when suddenly a large group of loud lesbians walked in. Some of the previous occupants looked peeved as the newcomers took the dance floor for themselves, shouting and swirling their way into the centre of the action, and into Jane's mind too.

Nothing much happened that night, but in a way, everything happened. Jane found herself by the drinks table, and suddenly became involved in some sexual banter with one of the newcomers. She was shocked to find she actually liked it, and even more shocked to discover she could do it back. That was revelation enough, but much worse (or better) happened on the way to the toilet, when, staggering around some bags on the floor, she suddenly found a supporting arm around her hips and that twinkly-eyed woman saying something to her. She got out of that one. In the bathroom she looked at herself in the mirror and felt more thrilled and excited than she had ever done in her life. She daren't even go out. When she did, the woman was on the dance floor and she looked over at Jane with a smile.

But Chris wasn't having fun any more. She'd got her coat and was ready to go, and it was her car. So Jane had to go. Suddenly at a set of traffic lights, Jane realised she'd left her bag behind. Chris was irritated, but they hadn't gone far, so she turned back.

"Hurry up! I'm on double yellows," she said as Jane got out of the car. Jane flew up the steps and was soon tussling through the pile of shoulder bags and carrier bags at the foot of the stairs. She took a quick glance into the living room, but she couldn't see who she was looking for. She was half-way down the outside stairs when someone called "hey", and she looked up to see the twinkly-eyed woman looking down. Her heart missed a beat.

"I was looking for you everywhere," she said. Jane didn't know what to say, so she smiled awkwardly. "I left my bag," she managed.

"Do you have to go? I had you down for the next dance."

Snakes and ladders crept up and down Jane's ribs, and she smiled again. Then Chris came into her mind.

"I have to go – my friend's parked on double yellow lines."

"Just a kiss then," Tess had said, and brought her face really close to Jane's. It had started really tentatively, just soft and kind, but something happened. Jane felt the muscles in her legs melting, she fell against the wall, and felt her hand stroking this stranger's hair. Her tummy turned over and suddenly they were in a strong kiss, tightly squeezed together.

Tess breathed into Jane's ear, "Tell your friend she can go home."

"Oh I can't," Jane said, confused, "I've got to go."

"What? After that?" said Tess. But Jane had never felt anything like that before, and it had unnerved her. She felt totally out of control, and confused about Chris, knocked back by the strength of her need and feeling it for a stranger.

"I'll have to go," she said again.

"Give me your 'phone number," Tess said. She was wet with sweat, and she looked so serious and intense. Jane muttered the number and pulled away to go. Then she turned.

"Can you remember the number?" she said, so intensely she felt ridiculous. Tess smiled. "I've got it burned into my brain."

That was the start. And the end for Jane and Chris. There were scenes, there were tears and there were screaming matches. Chris accused Jane of using her. Jane was sorry, and that hurt Chris even more. But there was the truth, and the truth was that she wanted to be with Tess.

The day she moved into the bedsit with Tess was a day of superb exhilaration. She smiled and laughed all day long, unloading chairs and boxes from the van. She sang all the way to the van hire depot. She laughed in the bath, splashing water everywhere. She was home. And it was bloody marvellous.

That's why it was so awful now. Sexually, it had been an incredible opening to Jane. She had never felt anything like the way she felt when she and Tess made love. She stopped wanting to be in control – because of her feelings, it was impossible anyway.

Things were wonderful for a long time, and then Tess started to get tired. She came home from her part-time job tired out, or exhausted. She got dreadfully tired doing the shopping. She got tired going up the stairs from the street. She got tired talking to people, and started to slur her words and get them muddled up. She went to the doctor who did tests and could find nothing wrong. The year went on and it got worse. She was too tired to bathe herself, and was irritable and snappy. She couldn't manage any of the housework without wearing herself out. She decided she wasn't fit so she borrowed an exercise bike and cut down on sugar and alcohol. But there was no improvement. She got very depressed. She was hanging onto her job by the skin of her teeth and going to bed every night terrified she was going to feel a sexual need in Jane that she wouldn't have the energy to fulfil. It preyed constantly on her mind. Sometimes she made love to Jane because she felt Jane needed it, but she got overtaken by pain and total fatigue which no amount of mental determination would allow her to push through. She went to the limits of her strength and still it wasn't enough. Her arm would ache and ache and ache. And it wasn't just that – she had lost her own sexual desire. She wanted, needed to hold and be held, but anything else was much too scary, much too risky, and anyway it had just gone. She felt incredibly guilty, and shamed. Then Jane found her crying in the middle of the night, and it was time to talk.

It had been easier in the early days of the illness to ease and soothe and nurse it in their love as a problem shared. Consciously, Jane felt her love for Tess was the most important thing, and that she could use her conscious mind to turn away the need her own body felt. But sometimes there was nothing she could do with it, and then their bed was filled with tension, and often tears. It was best if she could wait until Tess was asleep, and then masturbate, but there were so many needs that she couldn't fulfil, and she couldn't get over the feeling that really Tess had just lost her desire for her, didn't want her any more.

Then one night Jane woke to hear Tess whimpering. She was lying flat on her back with her eyes open, whispering, "Oh God, Oh God, Oh God...."

"What's the matter? What's the matter, Tess?" Jane called and rose up to gather her lover in her arms. But

Tess's body did not fall into her arms as it usually did, it was stiff, and she made sickening noises of pain as Jane tried to put her hands under her shoulders. Jane tried to lower her again, and the pain caused tears to flow down Tess's cheeks. Jane panicked. She jumped out of bed causing it to bounce which brought more little whimpers of pain from Tess. Jane rushed to the sink and got water. Tess couldn't raise her head, so Jane tried to tip some into her mouth. Too much water came out and went over Tess's chin and chest, making her splutter. Jane tried to pat her skin dry, but the touch seemed to make Tess shrink and she shrieked quietly, "Don't touch me!" Jane shrank onto the floor, her eyes bright with anguish, and wailed, "I don't know what to do, Tess! Tell me what to do!" Then she broke down weeping, crying, "Tell me what to do...."

Inside Tess's pain-ridden mind her love for Jane was overwhelming her terror. She had woken with a dark red pain at the base of her skull, pulsating rhythmically as if she were being struck with a huge bell gong. As she became more awake her mind became aware that the whole of her skull felt raw as if it had no covering, and the blood red tissues were being scratched and scraped with metal. She felt agonies of pain in her shoulders, arms, wrists and hands. Her spine was a column of fire that led to two furnaces in her hips. Her heels were tight with pain, and her knees ached agonisingly. She tried to move herself but that brought on an increase in the speed and depth of the banging that wracked her whole body. That was when Jane woke up.

Now Tess knew that she had to somehow comfort Jane. She tried to compose herself enough to reach out to Jane. She raised her arm and sharp shooting pains went through her shoulder, but she could stand it, and her hand gently touched Jane's wet hands.

"I'm going to turn on the light," said Jane and suddenly a new blinding pain shot through both Tess's eyes and hit the mass at the back of her head.

"Turn it off!" Tess shouted and Jane turned it off and sank down her head in her hands, crying, blurting out, "I'm sorry! I'm sorry," over and over again.

"It's alright! It's alright!" Tess murmured, and stroked Jane's face gently, ignoring the shooting knives going through her shoulders. Jane suddenly realised with a cold shiver that Tess was giving her comfort and support, when she wasn't the one who was ill. She felt riveting guilt and remorse, and an overwhelming anger against herself. Their eyes met and held, and somehow she calmed and held onto herself, and she saw in Tess's eyes love and tenderness behind the pain and fear.

"I don't know what's happening to you!"

"Nor me."

"Tell me if you want to, love," Jane said. She felt her own fears slide aching into the background, and a warmth flowed out of her and around Tess, which made her feel stronger. Tess told her about the knives and the aching. Jane controlled her instincts to touch her, and gradually as the pain began to subside, they talked about times past. Jane read some stories to Tess and at last, six hours later, Tess fell asleep.

Jane made herself a cup of tea and some toast. She felt weak. It had been so long keeping up a warm smile, before Tess fell asleep. She didn't know if she was strong enough to carry Tess any more. She felt sorry for herself. She felt unbearably small and alone. All sorts of morbid fears went through her mind. Suddenly she felt an overwhelming need to telephone her mother. She went to the phone. She started dialling, but in the back of her mind she could hear her mother telling her that it was too strong a burden to be carried by a friend. Only a friend. Jane had told her several times that it was deeper than that. She would say, "Hasn't she got any relatives?" No. She could ask for no support from that direction that wouldn't seek to undermine her lover-relationship with Tess. She did need support, she knew that. But not from her mother.

The following days were taken up with struggles to get to the toilet and back, struggles to wash and eat, a visit from the doctor and problems with social security. Tess found that if she could bear the initial stiffness and pain, she could bring some movement back to her body through exercise, though she quickly became exhausted. Jane massaged her time and time again until she was exhausted, but it helped. They also found in time that her problems came and went to a certain extent, and that there were periods of relative well-being when she could walk about, and think more clearly. If she stayed still for too long she began to shake inside, feel sick, lose her mental coherence and ache intolerably.

Gradually the months brought some improvement in Tess. Partly it was adaptation to the new condition, and partly it was by noticing which foods brought on a bad attack. Eventually she went out, but she was scared to death and clung onto Jane. Friends who saw her only during good periods consoled themselves that she wasn't as bad as they thought. There was only Jane who knew how it was for Tess, and she didn't know everything. But they had some lovely times of laughter and closeness, and every time a period of misery, dependency and depression was conquered it brought them more deeply together. They'd even begun to make love again. Sometimes it even seemed to Jane that things were back to normal, but for Tess they never were. Never a second went by when she wasn't consciously aware of the energy level of her body or the discomfort of her position, which made spontaneous loving almost impossible for her. She was forced to look ahead to try and gauge what she might be capable of. Her fears of being unable to carry through what she had started meant that frequently she didn't start.

"But it didn't used to be like this," protested Tess one time when she had been forced to rest despite her growing passion.

"You can't keep kicking against what used to be, love," said Jane. "Look, I'm alright!"

"It can't be much fun for you though. You'll never be able to relax, because you don't know how far it will go."

"But my love for you is much more important than that. Come on, let's cuddle."

"You'll be feeling like you want someone proper to love you soon. . . ."

"Don't talk daft, you're still you."

Reassurance was something that had to be dished out endlessly. It wasn't always easy. Things changed all the time, so that no sooner had they adjusted to one thing than another development occurred. The feelings they both went through were very complex. But things muddled along until Christmas. It was very, very hard at Christmas. Friends and relatives alike just couldn't seem to cope with Tess being ill, so she found it easier to say she was "O.K." or "not too bad", and then found herself in the confusing position of being treated as if she were well, and not someone restricted by a physical challenge every minute of her life. Tess didn't want to go out, but she went to a small party at a close friend's house so that Jane could get out.

She shouldn't have started drinking. She watched the dancers and felt a terrible rage welling up. It was unreasonable, unfair, but it just wouldn't go away. She watched Jane dancing with her friend Joanne and imagined them making love, supple, untiring, free of fears. She couldn't stand it, she couldn't control it, and she couldn't get up and walk out. She shouted Jane over.

"I want to go," she said through gritted teeth.

"Oh Tess, I haven't had a dance for ages. What's the matter?"

"I want to get you away from her before you get into bed with her."

"What are you talking about?"

"I can see you want to."

"Tess, you're being ridiculous. . . ."

"Just take me home, will you?"

Jane sighed. She got their coats, but inside she was furious. They'd been through this before. Tess was telling herself things which weren't true. They would have to spend all night with her repeating that she didn't want anyone else, that she loved Tess, that she was happy. She couldn't bear it. She felt hurt and humiliated that Tess couldn't trust her. She felt dirtied by the implication that she was lying. When they got home she turned round and walked out again. She was going back to the party. Yes, she might stay the night. Tess would just have to believe whatever she believed, she had told her there was nothing going on, and there wasn't, she couldn't force her to believe it.

Tess was stunned. Throughout all the time of her illness Jane had been upset at the nature of Tess's insecurities, she'd been reduced to tears many times, but she had never walked out. Desperation crept voluminously around Tess. She banged her head against the door and noiselessly began gasping, beyond tears. Rage and self-pity welled up, jealousy clawed at her soul as she imagined Jane carefree and happy, flirting with Joanne. It wasn't fair. She hated Jane. She hated everyone. Now the tears were coming and she got herself to her chair, aching with anguish and fear. She sat there for hours, and when eventually she began to look around the room, things began to recede. The room opened out like a vast cavern. She got up and her body seemed very long and thin. It seemed like miles to the floor. She staggered over to the mirror. She looked but she couldn't make her image fit, she was grey round the edges, distorted, unreal. She saw herself crumple into wailing and whimpering, but suddenly checked herself. She knew she could go from bad to worse. There were several edges she could go over. Briefly she saw them, looming at all sides. Then, with a shock she realised that she was talking. She forced herself to tune in to what her voice was saying: "Make yourself a cup of tea . . . careful now . . . steady yourself. . . ." She forced her attention onto the electric kettle, the one Jane had bought because it had no lid for her to manage. Jane, Jane. . . . "No, don't let go. You're such a fool," she heard herself say. There were enough tragedies that happened to people's hearts without creating them for yourself. This might be the end of everything, all the love they had given each other. Quietly she put the kettle down and gave in to quiet weeping. Grimly she realised that this aching was worse, far worse, than anything she had suffered in her body.

The next day came with a rosy dawn. Tess had been awake many times in the night, facing the empty loneliness in her bed. She looked outside – why did everything look so incredibly beautiful when her life had been rent in half? Imperceptibly she heard a small sound at the door. A dry flush bathed her and Jane walked in. Miracles were happening, Jane was smiling, but so tentatively. She was shy again, as she had been when they first met, confused.

"You don't mind me coming back?" Jane was saying.

"Jane. . . ."

"There are some things I want to say to you. . . ."

Terror, panic and awful apprehension blocked Tess's speech. But she had grown emotionally tough as well as frail with physical pain, so she smiled and nodded, and patted the bed by her side. "I'll hear them," she said.

Relief flew visibly over Jane, and she came quickly to the bed and sat down, taking Tess in her arms. "Oh Tess, I've missed you!"

"You've missed me! I've been through death and back. I'll do it again if only you'll come back to me. I'm sorry. I was so selfish. I should have known you would need another life, another love. Is that what you've come to say? Do you want Joanne as your lover? I'll cope, I'll cope. I love you, I love you, you don't know how much!"

"I do. Because I love you that much. And it's not that, you big silly. I told you that last night. I don't want anyone else as a lover. I want you as my lover. But there's got to be some changes. . . ."

"I know, I know, I'll change. . . ."

"Oh listen, I've got to change as much as you. We've both got to accept and put up with certain things, and try to move towards something else, risk things, but most of all you've got to try to trust me."

"It isn't easy. It's not because of you, it's because of me. I'm always comparing myself with what I used to be, with what I imagine other women can be. I want you, Jane. I love you, I need to love you, but sometimes I can't."

"O.K. So we'll have to accept that. But that needn't spoil what love we can share if you can trust me. I think I've been through just about every doubt there is, and I still keep coming back to wanting us to be together. I want that more than anything else in the world. I never wanted other lovers before you were ill and I don't want that now. I feel dirty when you accuse me of things I don't feel, I feel ashamed that you trust me so little."

"But I'm scared, scared I'll lose you."

Tess buried her head in Jane's hair. Jane gently kissed her, and slowly she lowered her onto the pillows. Lightly she licked the line of her hair. Her smell was sweet and pungent. Jane felt her love rising up. Her breath was hot on her lover's neck. Tess shuddered slightly as Jane opened her mouth and gently sucked on the flesh of her neck. Jane realised she'd often been afraid that leaning over on Tess would hurt her, but at that moment she was caught by a powerful need. Her mouth covered her cheeks and her body lay on Tess, as she pulled the bedclothes down. Tess gave a little cry and Jane hesitated, again afraid she was hurting Tess, but Tess moved her hips, open like a flower, a move that could be understood by any woman. Jane felt Tess trying to move with her and then heard her familiar sigh of hopelessness and frustration as she couldn't bring her body in motion with her desires.

"You don't have to do anything, you know. You can just rest still and let me love you," Jane said, and Tess laughed, and Jane laughed with her, covering her face with kisses and stroking the soft skin on the inside of her waist. Then their lips were touching. At once Jane felt a storm of love; she bore down on Tess with a power that was completely new to her and she felt Tess give way. Tess was receiving this force of energy with an incredible mind-opening delight. Her body was giving her pain, as Jane moved on her, but her mind was blowing out beyond it. She had never known Jane like this. Perhaps she had never let her? Perhaps she had never been able to give herself up completely? She'd always been comfortable when she was the one making love, but vaguely she remembered tides of longing having to be replaced with well-worn sexual fantasies before she got her climax. But now she was out of herself and she couldn't believe the sensations she was having as Jane licked and tickled her skin and plunged back ravenously into her mouth.

Suddenly Jane's hands pulled Tess's thighs apart, and her hand was in her cunt, moving, opening, pushing into her. She couldn't believe it, Jane was rougher and more urgent than she'd ever been before, but as she plunged into her and shook her inside Tess felt a terrible feeling of calm come over her, a new feeling, and she heard the strange sound of her own laughter before she was pulled further out with new shocks splashing like a raging sea on her body. She let go completely and clung to Jane.

Jane herself was angry, bloody angry, with Tess. She'd nearly spoilt their relationship with her mistrust, and Jane valued that relationship unfathomably. But now her desire was taking her to a place of storm within herself. She felt the lack of protection which surrounded them, and the magnitude of the trust which could hold them together. Her nervousness was gone, she gathered up her lover Tess, who was moaning beneath her, looking at her with eyes that reflected all she herself felt. Her own cunt felt warm, and ached slightly with a rich, orgasmic feeling. Suddenly she understood why Tess had been the way she had. She saw her enormous courage in having to readjust her view of herself, having to put up with limitations and pain, her life ripped out from beneath her feet. Her spirit filled with tenderness, and her tenderness washed over Tess. Gently she stroked her belly and her lips, gently she stroked her until she came with a quiet sigh, and lay resting in her arms.

Jane's energy had made Tess feel powerful, beyond herself, fully a part of it. She said it carried her up through the clouds to where she didn't have an ill body, but a powerful, feeling one. They found out they both liked slow loving, with softness and rests, as well as energy. They found there were a million ways of expressing their love which weren't necessarily energetic. Their sexual relationship became truly an affirmation of their love and commitment, and incidentally more erotic.

The old insecurities didn't just vanish; they had both been locked into them, even before Tess's illness had destroyed their old ways of being. And sometimes Jane felt it was the most loving thing to do to leave Tess alone, but their eyes held it all just the same.

THE SECRET OF CHANTAL GREY

Margaret Melvin

My name is Chantal Grey. I'm called after a holy nun but there is more to that than meets the eye. I'm 45 and still young looking, I'm neither fat nor slim, I like the way I look. I've always had something in the way of looks since I was 18. Before that I was the usual adolescent mess. I am accustomed to the odd glance of approval from others. It's a question of pride I suppose. The glances were all from men when I was young and so were the love affairs. Nowadays I am a lesbian. I have gone through many changes of heart and mind since I was a muddled and yearning teenager battered by my vicious father. He worked in the shipyard, and he hammered his children into the church the way he hammered rivets into the vast steel hulls at his work. I cried inside for my mother, so silent and scared, and myself. I took consolation in religion then; later on, I abandoned early Mass and took consolation in sex. Now, I dress neatly, I am an illustrator by profession, I value myself. I am in a long-term deeply committed relationship full of intertwining obligations and mutual needs. We have non-religious Christmas rituals together. I do my partner's child's homework. And I am bored. My first proper lesbian love affair has become a marriage.

At 45 there are the first whispers of the menopause,

and beyond that I can dimly discern an old woman with a lined face, a stoop, a stick, a head full of memories and no teeth. I'm old enough now not to panic. I put my hands in my pockets, I stroll in the park, I look the old woman of my future in the eye. I notice my teeth getting worse, the visits to the dentist more frequent. I notice my breasts, still round and young, and wonder what changes they will suffer. I walk in beautiful places as often as I can, in the Botanical Gardens, by the Water of Leith, and the only sadness is that I no longer break into a run like a child and rush at the wind, hurling myself at it like a bird or a diver, there are limitations. I stay within limits. I stay cool. I cope.

Last year my mother got very ill and had a hysterectomy and depression at 75. The ground shifted under my feet. I added another name to my list of obligations and visits to be made. I suffered panic and had physical symptoms myself, breast lumps, upheavals in my period, a grotesque and belated longing for a child. My father, the old tyrant, now arthritic and dependent on my mother, stuck it out till she got better then went down with stomach ulcers and shingles. My brothers and sisters and I managed, but the emotional tensions were exhausting. I was forced to see how far I had drifted from my family. Their religion does not allow lesbians.

Nowadays I bear it all with an ironic smile. The hopes I might have had once, of real intimacy with my mother and my sisters, have gone. This is what it seems to me to be, middle age – more obligations, fewer hopes, more detachment.

My work keeps me alive. The running child, the downtrodden but hopeful girl, express themselves in line and colour, in paintings for children's books. My wicked stepmothers are a sight to be seen, my sweet babies cradled in loving arms, my heroines setting out on adventures, my ambivalent, handsome princes. I work in bursts, finish a job, go lazy again, potter, value any time I can snatch from obligations. My lover, a teacher who is not "out" at her work, gets busier as the Government piles on extra tests in the schools, and more worried as the climate hardens against lesbians. We listen less to each other, do more things automatically, cook a meal, sleep together. I am grateful for her warm arms round me on a cold Edinburgh night, with the gale stalking the rooftops and rattling the windows of her flat. But we have stopped making love. I can't do it any more, even as an obligation.

I go to women's socials now and then, not to discos with the music I can't bear, too old to put up with the booming and roaring in my head which is a forerunner of deafness. I go to socials and cabarets, meetings and so on, I am often eagerly welcomed as a new face or an old friend, I sense currents of desire and eroticism, I do nothing. I feel sometimes that women are interested in me; I get occasional phone calls ostensibly about joining some activity or campaign, a women's writing group, a lesbian rights campaign. I hear something in the voice, I acknowledge the response I feel, the running child who wants out for an adventure, I do nothing. I tell myself that I do not two time my lover, there is no space in my life for an affair. I am afraid of it all anyway; the intensity, the out-of-control mess of it all.

I used to let men walk into my life, wave their magic wands — their fast cars, their good jobs, their need for a devoted listener, their admiration and their lust — and turn me into a passive princess for a while. I let myself become as shapeless as a half-melted ice cream. I gave up ambition. I had something to fill my life, take away the agony of choice. I let myself be turned on by a handsome face, a deep voice, authority. I let go. I went to bed. I had orgasms. In between men I would make another effort at independence, till the next one came along. It took me twenty years of adult life to get out of it. Never again.

Perhaps my expectations of life with a woman lover were understandably too high: that it would somehow heal all the hurts, be unimaginable bliss, perfection. It hurts to think that this might not be so, it hurts to criticise. The dream of perfection, of the wounded girl made whole again in perfect joy, of running in the wind and flying towards each other, is too magical to give up. What else has kept me going all these years?

Lately on my walks I have taken to imagining another woman walking by herself, not far away from me. In my mind I study her, wandering circuitously round the rock garden to emerge, as it were, across her path, aware of her even if she is on the other side of the gardens. I have never done this before. I know I am playing a game. I want to make a move. I feel a crack in the wall of boredom.

She is taller than me, she walks confidently, she has presence. So many women seem sad or eclipsed, harassed and bent. Of if they are young and vigorous, they are dressed for men, they clip along in high heels and seem less than themselves, less than they could be, prettified up with hair bleach and lipstick, like myself twenty-five years ago. I scan women all the time but rarely see what I am looking for, a woman who belongs to herself.

This woman has short grey hair, a lined face, brown and clever, bright eyes. I imagine walking right past her to look. She wears a grey coat and black trousers and walks like an athlete. She looks like someone who has escaped from the reservation we are all supposed to live in.

My parents called me, their first-born, Chantal, after a mediaeval saint who became a famous nun in her middle age, Saint Jane Frances de Chantal. I am glad I was not called Frances, such a respectable name: Frances Grey, someone who writes flowery verses for the Sunday Post. Or Jane: after all Jane Grey was loved by a king and executed. My saint was clearly a survivor, took to the convent after a no doubt turbulent marriage. Perhaps my parents wanted me to be a nun. Perhaps they wanted to preserve me from the evils of sex. Little did they know. Saint Jane Frances de Chantal, on the run from a brutal mediaeval baron of a husband and endless childbirth, running to the convent, to peace, women and probably lesbian love. Chantal, my name: a good name, a singing bird.

In my fantasy I return to the gardens. I walk. I stay

cool. I walk on till I reach the Water of Leith by the path with the trees. It is very quiet, most folk are at work, I am queen of my own universe, I walk and dream, I smile to myself. I find a place by the water and lean on a railing surrounded by trees. I look at the water. The season has changed and burgeoned, there are long green tresses of weed streaming on the water and beautiful delicate white flowers which make me think of Ophelia's hair. The tree beside me is a cherry and it bursts into white blossom, I stand and look at the rushing water, a blackbird sings. She comes down the path, unhurried, graceful, strong, she saunters to a stop, leans on the railing beside me, we look at the water in silence. I feel a sense of destiny, I turn to look at her, she is in the act of turning to look at me, I see a smile starting in her clear brown eyes, my heart sings, inside me a child is running, running in the wind. I wait for her to speak.

I have not told my lover about my secret, that I am considering being unfaithful to her in my thoughts. I am afraid of the hurt. Seven years ago we fell in love, and came together in a blaze of passion, so extreme that commitment seemed inevitable. We have shared our lives since. I cannot risk it all with a few careless words. We talk as usual about my work, her work, my mother, gossip about friends, her child's school work, our holidays, the latest local lesbian gossip, everything under the sun. Except love and sex. Except my secret.

In my imagination she sees me in the gardens and she knows I am a lesbian.

We lean on the fence by the river. We look at each other. Her eyes smile at me. I cannot breathe. She says something. It is hard to imagine an ordinary conversation, nice weather, lovely spring day, what is the name of those beautiful flowers on the river, none of these will do when my heart is shaking, when this moment is so significant. She must say something incredible, the atmosphere must heighten, she must be ordinary yet at the same moment be about to lift us both out of the ordinary, into adventure, into another world.

She smiles at me. Her eyes shine and dance with life and energy. I feel myself wanting to preen or bask in her gaze. She lets her gaze become sexual. Wordlessly she lets me know she has been watching me for days and has followed me here. I begin to feel very real, taller, beautiful, my real self, a lesbian with no need to hide. I play at being shy. I look away and blush. She asks me to have coffee at the outdoor restaurant. I agree. On the way there she walks almost touching me, giving me a message of desire, a continuous compliment, nothing excessive or frightening, just infinitely pleasing. We drink tea and coffee, we exchange conventional details about each other in this public place, she holds my gaze, her hands rest an inch from mine on the table, electricity flows between us. She asks me to meet her again a few days later. I agree. I go home intoxicated, drinking air, full of wild energy.

She is an astronomer, a botanist, a doctor, a famous writer, a woman of independent means, a woman of power, the woman of my dreams. She is a lesbian and she is lonely and she wants me.

I go home. I work well. I think of her from time to time and smile. I buy myself flowers for my room. I hum love songs from old movies. I attend to my life, wash my clothes, write to my mother. At night I fall into a fever of desire. I do not tell my lover. I wash and brush my hair, I clean my jacket, polish my boots, wear scented oil. I go back to the gardens several times. I stare at the spring flowers with delight and gratitude, I wait for my new lover. She comes, we walk for hours, we talk quietly. People pass us and look twice at us, because they see there is something between us. We do not care. We feel invulnerable.

One day she asks me to come to her house. We walk to a quiet street of expensive houses with beautiful gardens. A black cat meets us at her door. She lifts and strokes it, it purrs with pleasure, a tingle runs all the way down my spine, I shudder with desire.

She gives me wine, she looks at me. We look and look at each other. She comes over to me and sits beside me. She kisses me and tells me she loves me. I fall and fall towards her as if I have been waiting for this all my life, I swoon with desire, I fall and fall into this other world, and all the time I can feel her lips on my face, my neck, my breasts, she is revealing me and kissing me and opening me all at once. Her lips touch me with infinite kindness and infinite power, she holds me so I will not be lost, I cry out, I rejoice, I am loved.

I carry on with my life. I keep my secret. Occasionally I go to a women's meeting and we discuss oppression, male sexuality objectifying women, the horrors of porn, our lesbian ideals for sex, our rejection of butch and femme and domination and submission, we construct an ideal lesbian feminist world of harmony and equality where no woman dominates another and there is no poverty. I do not mention my rich, powerful fantasy lover. I feel more alive, my work is going well. My real lover of seven years and I lie in bed and listen to the Edinburgh gales and rub each other's sore backs and give each other affection. We talk about our old age together.

I know I am fortunate. I know I have more than I perhaps deserve. I try to hold it all together like a fragile bowl, with our lives inside it. I dare not mention my secret. I keep it as a silent picture in my mind. In some strange way it gives me life.

BELOW ZERO

Alison Ward

Hell froze over long ago.

When they asked me to make a documentary about a dinosaur in the Arctic, I agreed without even pretending I needed time to think it over. An unforgiving wasteland was exactly where I wanted to be.

I needed a break. I needed a break from making preachy little films for schools, about Man's Abuse of the Environment. I worried about poisoning the kids' minds with all that guilt and ugliness. I needed a break from lovers. I fell in love all the time and regretted it all the time. Let them touch your body, and they think it gives them the right to stick their fingers in your soul as well. As for the kind friends who pointed out that I shouldn't take life so seriously, I needed a break from them too.

I did the research: sat through the Polar Survival classes, and read the books of prehistoric fairy-tales about Laurasia and Gondwana, when all the world was a swampland mottled by spindly trees which bent, dripping, under a blazing white sky. The dinosaur came from those times. Its skeleton had been drifting northwards for millions of years, until the ice closed over it.

I took the same route as the dinosaur, only measured in hours of flying time rather than millions of years. It makes the imagination feverish, flying for droning hours with nothing to look at but sea and ice. I wondered about the dinosaur, vast indifferent creature without any other name. How would I feel standing inside a ribcage the size of a cathedral? And then I wondered about the leader of the excavation, Dr. Thea Christiansen, who had devoted her last three summers to this skeleton in a wasteland. She was probably mad. I pictured her emerging from the Arctic mists, bundled up in caribou skins and flourishing an ice-axe. Moving or ridiculous? I didn't care. Either way, I was going to enjoy myself filming the story of a monster being hacked out of the ice by a crazy old paleontologist.

I was wrong. Thea wasn't old.

She shattered all my fantasies, right from the first time I saw her. She was dressed in sunglasses, bunny boots and a grubby parka lined with nylon fur. And she was sitting on a bright yellow skidoo, eating – this was what shocked me the most – eating an ice-cream. I was too stunned to say anything. Where were the caribou skins? the axe? the mania?

She smiled back at me, but when she took her sunglasses off her eyes were cool and hard, as though she guessed what I was thinking.

The next day, we quarrelled. I didn't want to waste my time doing here-we-are-in-the-Arctic scenes. I wanted to get straight to the dinosaur.

Thea refused to let me go near it.

I took a deep breath, put down my camera, and asked her why.

"You don't have enough experience."

That was a ridiculous reason. I pointed out that I'd made three full-scale documentaries already. I wasn't exactly a novice. Hadn't she seen any of my work? The one about the woman with the hippopotamuses had won a prize, and –

She interrupted me. "I know. I didn't mean that.

Your work's very brilliant, very sharp. But it's too neat to be truthful."

I let that one pass. It stung then and it still stings. I can't help how I am. I was born neat, one of those sweet, neat little girls who are supposed to grow up into sweet, neat little women. At any rate I grew up neat, with a knack for sidestepping all the messy things like having babies or asking questions without answers. What was wrong with that?

"Thea, if you're not going to let me film the dinosaur, why did you ask me to this death-by-freezing nowhere in the first place?"

She shrugged. "I didn't ask. The Institute just told me you were coming, whether I wanted you or not."

"Oh, really? The Institute was very grateful I accepted the job. No-one else would have. Who else would agree to spend all summer on ice, tell me that, for the sake of filming you and that skeleton out there —"

"I suppose you had your reasons."

"Is there something wrong with the dinosaur, or what? Is it still alive? Is it dangerous?"

Her eyes widened, and then she laughed. I liked her when she laughed, even though I was angry with her.

"No," she said, "it's not alive." She stood up and looked at me for a moment from the doorway. "I'm sorry to disappoint you."

This is all the film I managed to bring back: these reels here. It's surprising how much has survived, when you think about it, but I'm not sure how to make sense of what's left. They're not in any order except this: this was the last reel I took, and it's the last one I'll show you. Shall we look through the others now? Let's try this set: "Research Station".

Exteriors: very grand, sledgehammer photography. See this, all you tired viewers of other people's lives, lounging in front of your centrally-heated TV sets. A plateau of ice as wide as the sky and an ocean rolled out like sheet steel, splintered by icebergs two hundred feet tall. The research station, by the way, is the little string of blocks along the shoreline, underneath the cliff. I stood on the roof of the station powerhouse to get this next shot: the camera pointing up, sheer, to that great blister of sheeting and wooden props bursting out of the cliff face. Inside the blister, the dinosaur is still asleep. The excavation team won't start work until the weather's right, in about a month.

Interiors: Thea in her study, pondering over a huge claw. The camera moves close and stays a fraction too long over her hands: beautiful hands, broad and long-fingered, honey-coloured except for a few scars left by the frost. She's explaining how the bones are hewn out of the ice and numbered, one by one. It's her job to work out how they should all fit together, but – catch her smile, it's gone in a moment – that's not easy when nobody's seen a fossil skeleton quite like this before, and some of the pieces seem to be missing.

Me, at midnight. Alone. Wide awake. Hard to sleep when it's the sun that shines all night, not the moon. So I lie in my bunk for hours, counting sounds instead of sheep. Clatters, rustles, bangs and drips, all the machinery that keeps us alive.

I've stood in Thea's doorway, and watched her sleeping.

I go to the indicator and check the wind-speed. I hate that wind. It looks harmless enough, stirring the loose snow into grainy patterns along the ground; but step into it, and it hits you like a lash of broken glass.

There's no wind tonight. Tonight, I'm going to climb the forbidden cliff, and see the dinosaur for myself.

When you look down, the space between you and the ground seems to stretch. I'd often stood at the foot of the cliff, staring up fifty feet to the dinosaur and yes, it was high enough to make an exciting camera-angle but that was all. I'd never realised how terrifying fifty feet can be, when you're hanging on the highest rungs of a ladder.

I reached up and dragged myself onto the platform,

trying to calm my mind by concentrating on the state of my body. My armpits were running like melted wax, and I couldn't stop my legs trembling.

Wise of me not to bring the camera, this first time. But I hadn't brought any lights either. I looked across at the bleary sun, praying for it to break out of the mist and not let me walk blind into the dinosaur's cavern.

Heavily, I turned back to the wall of sheeting over the entrance and snapped open the clasps, mumbling to myself.

"It's only a heap of old bones. Why be afraid?
There's enough light to see. . . .
See what? Is this what you came for?
Don't wait too long. Go in now. Go in."

Colossal grey forms growing out of blue shadows. The ribs, arching up to the roof, further and higher than the light could reach, massive pillars of bone held in place by beams like flying buttresses. I stepped underneath them, holding my breath as though I were trespassing on their silence by being alive.

After a while, I began to see the outlines of bones breaking out of the ground, a blurred jumble of curves and dislocated slabs flung down at random. And then, as I reached out to feel them, the sunlight flared up. It streamed through the entrance, stabbing at the chips of ice on the rock face, and turning the whole vault of the cavern into a dark sky flickering with stars.

If I'd let myself, I might have stood gazing at these until the cold lulled me to sleep. I tore my eyes away and walked around to keep warm, exploring the rest of the skeleton. Snaking away behind the ribcage was a row of flanges, crushed into the rock and ending, a few feet up, in a skull.

I almost felt pity for it. Had its neck been broken by something in life, or only by the passing of the ages? Oh, this place was bad for me. I was getting lightheaded and sentimental. I turned back towards the entrance.

And I saw the crack for the first time.

It began in the middle of the ribcage and ran outwards as far as the platform, a slit only a few inches wide but too deep for the light to penetrate. I crouched down, reached inside it and then snatched my hand away. Had it been there when I came in? The skeleton had been opened up by a landslide. What if the cliff face had started to split away again, and the whole thing was going to collapse underneath me?

"You've seen it, then."

Thea's voice cut across my panic like a slap. Sharp and cold. I got to my feet.

"I told you not to come here." In the half-light, her eyes glittered like the ice-chips. "It's dangerous, if you don't know what you're doing. Don't try to step over it. Go round."

"Thea —"

"I said, go round. This way. Don't look like that." She reached across the crack. "Take my hand, if you're afraid of slipping."

By the time we were back at the station, she seemed more thoughtful than angry. I told her I was sorry.

She shook her head. "No, I should have warned you."

"About the crack? Why didn't you?"

"I thought you might tell the Institute."

She'd noticed the crack a few weeks before. It was growing wider. Sooner or later the face of the cliff would break up, and the remains of the dinosaur with it. If the Institute found out, they would close down the station. I sat stiffly, rubbing my head and listening to Thea slate the Institute as a bunch of termites who didn't understand anything.

"I don't think I understand either. What if somebody gets killed?"

"If I'm the only one up there, whether I get killed or not is up to me."

"And the rest of the excavation team?"

"They're not due in for another month. Oh, then I'll have to say something about it. You're right. But not till then."

I wasn't sure I believed her. But for the moment, I

thought, why should I say anything about the crack either? I had a film to make. And Thea was part of that film, the part I cared most about. She went to sit with the dinosaur every day; she wanted its silent presence so much that she would rather risk her life than leave it. I asked her how long she thought the crack would hold.

"As long as it needs to."

She sounded very sure, almost serene.

When I couldn't sleep, I tossed over other things now apart from the noises. The dinosaur, Thea, Thea, the dinosaur. I didn't understand either of them. Perhaps they were both mad. I fell asleep over an old photograph, this one here. Thea aged four, pushing a toy pram just like all the other litle girls in the high street. But those aren't dolls nestling under the hood, they're dinosaurs. Mummy Stegosaurus and Baby Stegosaurus and old uncle Tyrannosaurus Rex.

"Didn't you have any dolls to play with, Thea?"

"A couple. I chopped them up and threw them to the dinosaurs for lunch."

"Yes, I see . . . why do you think they fascinated you so much?"

"Is this one of your in-depth interviews? All right, let's have an in-depth interview. You've beat about the bush long enough. What do you really want to know?"

Point blank. "What made you come here?"

"Boredom."

I waited. If you wait long enough, most people will blurt out something else. Anything to fill up the gap. The battle of the silences. I lost.

"Try again, Thea. I want to hear about dark, irresistible forces. Tell me about your passion for dinosaurs."

"Boredom is a dark, irresistible force." She jerked her head forward and stared into my face. "Do you believe in dinosaurs?"

"Doesn't everybody?"

"Two hundred years ago, nobody even dreamed of their existence. I was born believing in them. I wanted to see, I wanted to know, everything about them. How were they made? Why were they here? Where did they go when they died? I made up all kinds of answers, when I was small. And they were much better answers than the ones I read in books when I grew up."

"What answers? You don't get those sort of answers out of books. Even I know that."

"True, but where do you get them from? You'll laugh, I even tried sitting at the feet of all the great dinosaur experts. Anything to avoid thinking myself."

"Did you get bored with all the answers, then?"

"No." Thea stretched out her legs, and yawned. "I got bored with the questions. This blanket's a bit scratchy. I'll give you one of mine, you'll sleep better. Only the living can perceive the living, and all the dinosaurs are dead. It doesn't much matter what they were made of, and they didn't need any grand purpose for being here. Don't turn up the lighting like that. You'll make me look sick, like you did the last time."

I nearly dropped the camera, trying to keep the focus as she rocked herself in and out of the light.

"Thea, there's a film in here. And it's running."

Am I boring it? Switch it off then. Let's go for a walk instead."

The sun has shone all week. I meet Thea on her way back from an evening rendezvous with the dinosaur. She looks distracted. Has the crack widened again? Surely it has, with the heat. . . .

"I pegged it over with extra sheeting." She dismisses the problem. "Do you want to see something beautiful? Bring your camera, if you like. It's not far."

We walk along the shore, not too quickly, the sound of our boots in the shingle muffled by the vast curving silence all round.

"Can't you get used to living here? Is it too sad for you?"

Sad, that was a curious word for her to use. I'd never thought of the Arctic as sad, only dead. Bare and cold and white, world without end.

"Too many Arctic travellers are haunted by the phantom of their own death: if you don't worry about it, it won't haunt you."

Thea raised her eyebrows. "Who told you that?"

"I'm not sure . . . I think I read it somewhere in my Polar Survival classes."

I wondered if the thought of her own death haunted Thea too, but that's not the sort of question you can ask when you're out for an evening stroll.

"Thea, do you know where your dinosaurs went when they died?"

She laughed. "No. I don't think they went anywhere. They just existed for their own sake. Like these. That's why they're beautiful." She took my arm and drew me to the top of the slope. "This is what I wanted to show you."

Flowers.

Thousands on thousands of tiny flowers. All along the tundra the ice has thawed into glittering blue and turquoise strips of melt-water, ribbons round the clusters of pink, yellow, white. I must tread carefully, so as not to crush a single one. Even these sunflowers only reach as high as my ankles.

I might have spent hours filming them. Wide-angles, close-ups, more light, less light, faster and faster film as the sun sank. The last one I took was this little blue flower, standing apart from the rest. I knelt down beside it, in the snow.

In a few weeks they'll be gone. And me?

"You don't belong here," Thea said.

"No, I don't belong here." I stopped, feeling her eyes on me. I wanted to tell her that I didn't stay just because it was a job, to make a film. I didn't care about that anymore. I stayed now because this was where she was.

She pulled off her gloves and bent down to touch the flower. Its petals were closing up. Then she held my face in both her hands, and kissed my forehead.

Twilight, the spell of ambiguity. "We should go back now."

The sun was so low that our shadows reached almost to the far end of the shore.

She takes my lips, slowly, and her teeth are sharp.

Even her sweat is cold, it smells of the snow. She drags her fingers down my back and I shiver. I want to cry out: Thea, you're freezing me! How many times have I felt warm, close to her? I'm afraid of her now. I touch her and all I can feel is the skeleton under the skin.

They didn't go anywhere when they died. They existed for their own sake, and that's what makes them beautiful.

I know now, this place is too sad and I don't belong here. Tomorrow, or the day after, or the day after that, I'll leave. I twist myself out of her arms.

"Come here."

"Thea, I'm cold."

"Come here."

That's not blood I can feel shimmering through my veins, it's melt-water. It seeps out of me with despair, not longing. If I reach out and touch her again, I won't be able to tear my hands away. She knows that. I grip her shoulders and bite back, hating her, listening to her breath hissing in my ear. Is it my rage or hers, filling my whole body? I could weep with it. Thea, Thea, Thea, I don't want this, but it's too late. She's enjoying my rage, riding it as it moves and thickens and swells in waves, tensing, flexing her muscles to dance with mine. Oh, I want to slow the dancing. I want this wave to rise and rise upwards, and never break. But it roars away, finite, to the point where it hangs motionless, and then shudders, and bursts apart.

We lie silent for a time, listening to the whispers behind each other's eyes.

Then she's gone.

Everyone was very kind, very understanding when I came home and said I didn't want to go through with this film. The editing would have been too painful, I couldn't have been objective enough – well, you know all that, that's why you're here. It's up to you now to piece all these bits together into fifty minutes of prime time, with a break for the ice-cream ads. It's all right. I know your picture will be different from the one I would have made.

This is some footage of the gravestone. In Memoriam Thea Christiansen, who gave her life for science, time and place. You might want it. I didn't shoot it and I wouldn't have used it anyway. I like my truth neat, remember. Here's what I could have chosen: these few minutes I shot the day she showed me the flowers.

"Thea? Thea, look at me."

She turns round slowly, smiling not quite into the camera, but somewhere beyond it. Then she tosses up a handful of ice-crystals, up into the sun, and the air between us sparkles as though it's caught fire.

Freeze it there, credits over, the end.

This last reel? Yes, I'll show it to you, but I won't let you use it. I'd sooner destroy it. I made it the night ... that night she left me to shiver myself to sleep. I knew where she was going. Up to rest in peace with her dinosaur.

I followed her. I don't know why I took my camera, I still don't know. Perhaps I had some idea of taking her for the last time, because I was going to leave her.

She was sitting inside the vault of the ribcage, hugging her knees and staring out at the sky. She couldn't have known I was there behind her, at the back of the cavern, standing in the shadows underneath the skull. Then I heard the sound, once, twice, very softly. A sighing rumble that vibrated through the dinosaur's bones. But Thea only nodded and touched the bones as though to soothe them, and kept looking at the sky. I shifted the camera onto my shoulder and turned it towards her.

I can't sit still and watch what happened then. The thing that haunts me and terrifies me most about this piece of film is that it's soundless. No, let it run. Watch the sheeting alongside Thea's leg, the sheeting over the crack. It's stretching, tearing away from the pegs either side. Then the bones shift, leaning inwards over that great dark wound opening up the ground.

Thea's running towards me, through the cracked arches of the ribs, scrambling for the bones still sunk into the rock at the back, like the skull I'm clinging to. Even if the edge of the cliff collapses, these bones might hold. And if I let go with one hand, I could reach down to her.

Only I don't let go. I leave her out of reach.

The platform heaves and vomits out slabs of rock, wood, steel, down onto the station below. The whole ribcage is tilting, dragging Thea over with it and crushing her legs. Her eyes are still open. Is she looking at me, that albatross of a camera still hanging round my neck, watching her slide away? I can't be sure. I don't think it hurts her anymore. She doesn't even seem to be afraid.

THE RUNNERS

Char March

We are travelling by night. I'm tired and I take my specs off. Narrowing my eyes the white oncomers and red tails split and flash across the ink black. They converge and separate. Retract to wobbly orbs of heat and stretch – streaking out in hair-thin scores of energy. I enjoy the spectacle and practice other methods of distortion with my myopia. The contorted images dance in the dark.

The swooping up and down, the jockeying for position of the red and white lights that stream out in front and behind – they have no reference points save themselves and so equate well with space traffic. The conurbations we pass by on our black airlane are flickering orange fields of light. Alien settlements hanging in space.

2001 – only three more years and it still doesn't sound like a real year – I suppose it will have some strange sort of a ring to it even when we've passed it – like 1984.

I am lulled by the swooping lanes of lights. Everything's becoming a little disjointed. Fairy lights and star ships; roundabouts and flyovers. Spaced out fairgrounds. I yawn and stretch. Tilt the seat back and

work on making the distortions dance. The seatbelt is
uncomfortable. I shift forwards to try and adjust it and
am thrown off balance. The guy standing behind our
car has just started us whirling.

My head is pushed back and I feel the hard
wooden top of the seat pushing in on my neck. I
hunch down further on the vinyl bench to stop my
head being torn off by the spinning and lurching.

I find I'm enjoying the speed and sit, seemingly
nonchalantly, not using my hands to grip the well-
polished steel handrail in front of me. My feet are
jammed hard against the front rim of the whirling car.
My legs feel strong, tautly braced to take the pressure
of intense centrifugal force.

Ella looks really green. Her hands are black vices,
screwed tight round the steel bar, but her face seems
to be loose – joggling and shuddering with each
reverberation of the mad machine.

The Waltzer slows, you don't get as long for your
money these days.

"You awake again love? I'm aching tired, could you
take over soon? The car's thirsty so I'll pull in at the
next station."

Gaudy neon of the petrol arena strains my eyes and
the penetrating interrogation lights in the toilet are
even more disturbing. A grey face stares back at me
from the polished steel disc. Eyes rimmed with crust,
hair alternately flattened and spiked. I emerge from
the stale smells and the night air knifes through my
jumpers. Ella motions me from the pump to go and
pay. I change course under the neon, my shadow
rotates and lengthens.

Nothing is said. The digital display tells me the
amount and automatic relay lights up the yellow
numerical eyes of the till behind the cashier's grill.

Cold, my fingers fumble with the change and I glance up to see "Diane" pulling a sneer across her lipstick. The request for chocolate freezes on my paler lips and I thrust my hands deep into my pockets and stride back across the oiled tarmac and again the warm stuffiness of the car and its smells surrounds me.

I open the air vents and pull out onto the silent road, glad to take the controls of our star ship and slip back into my space fantasy. The scarlet sneer nearly grounded me.

Ella checks the scanner, it glows calm and green, and then she settles back, her hand warmly cupping the nape of my neck. The dark miles brush past my window as her breathing softly evens out.

Out of a bank of mist comes a convoy of bright cargo lorries steaming up the long hill in the opposite lane. Decked out with dancing coloured lights and chrome on all their angles, multi-coloured streamers flying from mirrors, they wheeze and gasp loudly with gear-changes. The billow and flap of their red tarpaulins makes them appear to undulate, romp almost, up the long haul. They seem like Chinese dragons – a festive spectacle from the mist.

To my right and far below now, the shape of a city's hills are picked out by strings of wildly discarded necklaces of light. It looks sumptuous – the greedy opulence of winking colours – like huge shimmering mounds of lazy treasure.

We've turned off onto quieter roads and now onto familiar lanes. These last sixteen miles of high banks, hedges, sharp bends and crazily angled humpbacks over "our" stream. They stretch out and out, ours the only lights.

The wind has picked up steadily and snatches at the car through gaps in the trees that now crowd close and thick. It's still three hours 'til dawn so we'll have at least a couple of hours rest before we have to move again. It'll be bloody hard to pull ourselves away so quickly.

A scattered cloud of moths wobbles towards us. Dancing white motes like the first large flakes of a snow flurry. Some splat into the windscreen, the others, veering into the slipstream, are swallowed by the dark.

I drive fast, but smoothly along the known way, feeling at last part of the night. Ella's hunched form beside me is picked out dimly by the glow from the dash. The hump of her shoulder. A light triangle of turned up collar against the dark of her face.

A red line of blips appears on the scanner as we start the long descent towards the river. I have to force myself not to throw the brakes full on. Instead I slow gradually, indicating to pull in beside a low banking.

Tick Fl-ick Tick Fl-ick. The rhythms of indicator and wipers. Ella pulls her hand slowly down from my neck and massages some life back into her arm. The removal of this patch of her warmth makes me shudder and I pull my scarf round. We look at each other. Ella shudders slightly too, rubs her face briskly and reaches for both pairs of binoculars. I douse the lights, but keep the engine purring.

We wait. The rain drumming on the roof – feels so like a can.

Almost together we see them – matt black and powerful, a different species altogether from the dragons we passed earlier. Even with their engines they are only crawling up the long hill of the main road that cuts across our route.

We watch them through the powerful binoculars. There is movement in the cab of the seventh lorry. I zoom in; the window opens and there is a swill of orange sparks on the road – the silent explosion of a cigarette butt. I turn my binos on the cab and watch the driver's mate pull his next cigarette alight. He shifts the heavy rifle and turns to stare at me and puff bored smoke into my eyes. It clouds almost my entire field of vision. I feel the urge to cough. I lower the binoculars and the matchbox-sized lorries drone on up the hill.

Ella is craning forward with binos, searching the moon for features. I wrap my arms round her.

The red blips die slowly from the screen. A dogleg across this intrusive dual carriageway and then only three miles to home. I dash to the central island and tear on up the empty lanes, eager, willing us home.

For sheer joy I slip the car in and out of the cat's eyes before slowing down for the turn-off. The shots ring out as I see the dark figures run onto the road and I try to haul us away. The wheels squeal and lock, then bite into the gravel and I career the car backwards, swinging it wildly to shake their aim. Slam into first, fear tearing at our throats, and away again, back down the main road. I cut our lights and jab the switch to send our distress call. The car bucks sideways, wrenching the steering from me. We head for the banking.

It has stopped raining. The wipers squeak up the windscreen and judder back. Behind this noise I can hear a delighted chortling – the petrol tank, it's emptying itself. Squeak, chortle, judder, chortle. Gods, I can see the heavens clearly from this angle. Cassiopeia, Pleiades, Taurus, Andromeda. Squeak, chortle.

"Do you think if I can reach the bino's we could see the moon's smile, love?" I ask Ella, but as I turn to look over and see why she's not answering, there is another noise – it seems to be me, screaming.

They are crowded round the car – some flail whips across the bonnet and roof. I pull the keys from the ignition and stab the security lock. My right arm is very numb . . . all of me is very numb. I try not to look to my left – at Ella.

They are shaking the car – swaying it back and forth between them and chanting. Some deform their faces against my window, licking at the glass and rolling their eyes. In other words – they are enjoying themselves.

I sit inside with my dead lover and wonder what they are waiting for. For me to crack up?

It amazes me how deadly calm I am now that it has at last happened. All the warnings about each Runner's operating life I know have never sunk in, but I find I am counting up for the first time how many over the average we have done together. All I feel now is a kind of release.

I am slipping into the automaton response expected of a reaction trained Runner except I'm beginning to feel a little sick with the rolling motion of the car and the crushing reality of everything. I hate death.

About six of the chanting bodies on my side of the car are blown to bits by the first explosion. Confusion breaks out and some panic – canned girl it seems is okay, but only if she plays along with what you have in mind. I'm not about to wait for them to collect themselves – as it is a sharp volley of shots smacks through Ella's window just after I've released her hand and dropped low through my door, rolling under the car and hefting another grenade into the nearest clump of legs I see.

I've made the gap I need. I drop two slight delay incendiaries and head for the mass of smoke caused by the last explosion.

My back is seared by the huge puffball of fire that takes Ella's body well beyond the reaches of the screaming men as I stumble over the top of the bank and throw myself forward to avoid skylining an easy target.

I hug the box to my chest and roll fast down the tussocky hill. My specs slip from my face and I feel them crunch under me. On my feet as the slope levels out – running hard, trying to guess at boulders and grass. I grab a squelching handful of peat bog and smear it all over my face, hands and neck and into the white V-shape of T-shirt on my front. Run. Peat-juice trickles with sweat between my breasts. Run.

I don't think of the "real" reason, in terms of my indoctrination training, for destroying the car and its contents. The pain of my back and singed head has brought hot tears through the frozen core of my mind.

Behind me I hear the heavy revving of engines and then the sky overhead is lit by strong, slanting beams of light. I risk a quick, useless look round and run even harder, my feet pounding across the surface of the bog. They are trying to get the vehicles to the crest of the banking to light up their target.

Several hundred metres ahead of me small hillocks loom out of the flat bog and behind them what I think may be thin woodland. I can only just hear their shouts now above the engine noise, but the beams of light in the sky aren't levelling out – they can't get up the banking.

I run into the water without seeing its dark surface. Floundering in the cold, trying to tell the relative firmness of bog from pool.

The engines stop. I am instantly aware of the loud, sloshing noises that I'm making. I stop, still, and slowly, carefully, sit down into the water. It closes darkly up round my chest. I lean my head down to its surface, my breath makes quick fluttering marks across it.

They start shooting. Strafing the bog. Bullets hiss

and splat into the water and wet peat around me. I sit still. My back feels huge, rising from the water, aching with waiting for the heavy thump of a hit. I stay still. They stop firing and the engines start up again.

It's so hard to run with everything so wet, but Ella is running beside me now, helping me with the awkward box chained to my wrist. Flashing me a wide grin in all that blackness – "Never be afraid of the dark again huh white girl?" she says – same as she did after we'd been making love the first time.

I've done the three-quarter circle route as drilled and my breath is coming up in rasps – like continuous retching. The pain is bad, but the savage fight inside myself is worse. Willing myself to scream her name again and again and the training forcing my gagging silence. It keeps my legs going, my footfalls light, my breathing – though rough with tight-held anguish – as quiet as possible. But the training had always stressed that we would be able to think of nothing but the required survival and flight reactions. I am choking on Ella, on leaving her, on incinerating my lover. . . .

I am back on the dual-carriageway running on the soft verge back from where we'd come.

I know they won't have lights. I know I must quiet the drumming in my ears if I'm to hear the engine. I can't believe I haven't been shot . . . maybe I have.

I must concentrate – can I hear anything? Is there any pursuit? I keep on running. I consist of nothing but pain. Total physical and mental pain. Ella dropped away what seems like several miles ago . . . I can't have gone that far. Do I know where I am? In the blackness, afraid of the dark without her.

I push my tongue out at full stretch from my mouth and loll my head back as another misty flurry of rain comes over. My throat and mouth are very sore and dry, but trying to catch moisture like this just makes breathing even more difficult and the root of my tongue aches like it has been twisted on its moorings.

My feet sink into the grass and my legs bends all ways under me. Ahead of me, maybe 500 metres, the road cuts through a hill. Diffuse moonlight catches on what looks like the wetness of stones in drainage channels.

The stones are rough and sharp as I scrabble at them. They yield nothing but an acrid-tasting and gritty sheen of wet to my sore tongue. No water lies under them in the ditches – only damp sand. I clutch up a handful and squeeze, hoping for a drop or two of water, but the stuff just oozes through my fist in a damp sausage, breaks off and splats back into the ditch like a soft turd. If I had enough breath I would swear at it – or maybe even laugh – why not?

I want to stay here, sunk on my knees half in the ditch, gulping in cool, dark air to heal my lungs. I look at the metal box. My arm takes up the weight of it as I get up.

Walk thirty, run thirty, concentrating on counting, on keeping my legs moving. I mouth the numbers through cracked lips – they are right after all – I can think of nothing now, nothing but these numbers.

But I must listen too, I remember this – it floats up at me from somewhere buried. "You must listen"; "They won't have lights"; "You will only get one chance".

Every fifth set of running I stop. Quite still. I allow myself ten long gulps of air and then – quite still. Listening. No use to trust my eyes. My ears feel like they are reaching out, straining to sample the air's vibrations. It is so silent at first that I know I must be deaf and then faint, faint sounds edge in – of wind in the grass, of very distant birds. A sludge-grey dawn is starting behind me.

17, 18, 19 — I am looking forward to 30 when I get my ten gulps of air again. They step out together and grab my arms. I flail with the box. Try to shout. Knocked down onto hard road. Air forced from me. My mouth is stuffed with woollen scarf. Struggling. Pinned to the tarmac. I feel the chain on my wrist tighten and then go slack; they have taken the box. Then my head is lifted by a strange apparition; a young woman with starched hair. Her face, macabre in the muted light, is heavy with blusher, eye-shadow and lipstick. She stares at me hard and signs, "Other one — where?" My head shakes mechanically while my mind tries to unravel what has just happened. There is a long pause. Both of them stare hard at me and then the other — another perfectly painted doll — pulls the scarf from my mouth and pours sweet, cold liquid into my parched throat. It vomits — weakly, and I am sucked into oblivion.

My knees are up under my chin. My left arm and shoulder feel very dead. My head thunders with pain and it takes some time before any other signals get through. It is totally dark. I would try and touch my eyeballs to see if they're still there, it's so dark I can't believe they are, but I can't move anything. I am in a short coffin. My feet — freezing blocks of pins and needles hanging from trapped legs — wobble a bit now and then, I don't seem to be telling them to, they just do it. This is my first clue.

My whole body feeling dragged into one end of the coffin and then into the other gives me my second. My head hurts so much I don't hear the quiet purr of the engine for quite a while. By then however I am certain I am travelling. Where? What in? Who with? I have no clues on these.

Ella cradles my head gently in her lap. The curtains are drawn on the sunshine, but it still finds its way into our room. Colours from the curtains' patterns sidelight Ella's face as she leans forward to put a fresh, cold flannel on my forehead. My head heaves with thick pulses of pain. "A real live Black Florence Nightingale – turn out that bloody lantern will you?" I manage to slur. Concern and held-in laughter creases up her eyes and I love her. "My name's Mary Seacole actually – why use a blacked-up white reference when you've got the genuine article?"

Much later, when evening blues and deep greys are calm behind the curtains, we sip hot camomile tea and sit close under the blankets. My head feels cleansed, light-weight. The clamour of roosting birds has settled and no longer beats like pain against me. I reach over to refill Ella's cherry-red cup with the pale yellow heat of the tea. Instead she shakes her head and takes the small teapot from me and places it, with her cup, on the windowsill by her shoulder. "I need to pee," I say, but we slide together under the covers, her hands lifting my shirt and my lips brushing along her neck.

I feel us stop which makes me realise I haven't been conscious for a while. How many migraines did Ella come through with me? There are voices. I must concentrate. Male voices – sounding amused. I hear the vehicle doors open and the sounds move away. They return a while later – I have no sense of time left. The vehicle rocks as bodies get back in. Doors slam, there's a couple of slaps on the vehicle and we move off slowly.

My head collapses into pain again after concentrating so hard to pick up this meagre information. We are travelling fast now and it slops from side to side, spilling pain in all directions as the burns on my back and head are ground into the coffin.

Again we stop and this time there is quiet. Then doors open and there are low, female voices. Very close. Sliding noises as if heavy things are being moved. The lid of the coffin is lifted, the light is too much – I can't see anything but the torch beam, "Turn it away from her!" I see the two women's faces again, their scarlet cupids' bows still look completely out of place.

I lie on my side on the big bed, while Alex cleans up my burns and Cathy wipes the last of the peat and the lipstick imprints off my face. I look up at her own dishevelled face. "I don't know how you got through that road-block – those blokes should have spotted you a mile off – dykes never can get false eyelashes on straight," I say, and then make enough room to start crying.

THE GREAT TROPICAL HARDWOOD WALKOUT

Frances Gapper

I woke up with a terrible jolt, to find my bed moving at top speed down the corridor. Wheels creaking, springs groaning. Before I could collect my wits or do anything – scream, leap out, faint – suddenly it stopped. On the very edge of the staircase.

In the dark hallway below, I could see faint outlines of furniture. But something was wrong: it all seemed strange, out of place. Surely the chair had moved – and the hatstand should be on the other side...? And the front door was opening – closing – opening again –

A police siren sounded loudly down the street. My bed jerked back and *scuttled* – that's the only word to describe it – back to the bedroom, settling itself in its usual place, by the window.

Everything was just as before, except the blankets were in a dreadful mess, and I'd lost a pillow.

But how can a bed move, by itself? That's ridiculous, surely. It just doesn't happen.

Next morning at breakfast, I mentioned the incident casually to Marjolein: but she was attempting to mend the toaster and not really listening.

"My bed moved last night," I said. "I think someone's trying to murder me."

"Mm. Hold this screwdriver a second...."

"It wasn't a dream – you can still see the wheel

marks in the carpet. Someone must have *pushed* my bed all down the top corridor...."

"Um. Sounds awful. You poor thing...," Marjolein scratched her head, peering into the toaster's depths. "This damn machine is full of crumbs, no wonder it fused."

Some mornings, Marjolein is just impossible to communicate with. Eventually I gave up and went to get dressed – stumbling over my pillow in the hallway. I glanced suspiciously at the hatstand, but it was back in its normal position.

On my way to work I bought a newspaper. Not much of interest happening. Friends of the Earth were running one of their weird campaigns, this time about tropical hardwood furniture – wastes rainforests, kills parrots, makes spiders homeless, etc.

Immediately I got into the office, the phone rang. It was Marjolein, which surprised me. "Have you heard?" she cried. "Isn't it *fantastic*?"

"What?"

"They've stopped all the trains, they've blocked the traffic – they've –"

"Who? What?"

There was a click, as the phone went dead. I shook it and tried to dial, but it was silent as the grave.

This was the beginning of the great tropical hardwood walkout, due shortly to change the face of Britain and life as we knew it; that difficult transitional period when – as you can no doubt recall – telegraph poles cast off their wires and walked in the streets, teak lavatory seats refused to be sat on, coffins resurfaced, and it was all most upsetting.

By the time I got back to the house, shaken and breathless from several potentially nasty confrontations along the way – and I witnessed one cupboard making a suicide leap from an upstairs window – Marjolein had liberated all our furniture. This really annoyed me. "They're going home," she said, defensively. "Where they belong."

"But they belong *here*. *This* is their home."

"No, Frances."

"It was *my* kitchen table."

Marjolein sighed. "I know it's hard," she said, "to recognise yourself as the oppressor. We must find ways of dealing with our guilt – I'm setting up a consciousness-raising group –"

"I want my table back. And my bed; what am I going to sleep on? And I was very fond of that hatstand...."

"Don't be so childish. You don't seem to realise, this is one of the great movements of our time. They're going back to their roots – the tropical rainforests of Amazonia, South East Asia, Central Africa and Central America – the forests we've pillaged and destroyed, for lack," Marjolein added, pointedly, "of a suitable code of conduct guaranteeing that all tropical hardwoods sold in Britain come from forests that are sustainably and renewably managed."

"Oh."

"We're establishing a refuge for them in central London: it's open to all tropical hardwood products –"

"We?"

"My Friends of the Earth sub group. They need time to repair all that psychic and emotional damage: and while we're raising the funds for their fares home –"

"But listen Marjolein," I said reasonably, trying to introduce some sanity into the conversation, "most furniture is made from particle board with only a thin surface veneer of exotic hardwood –"

"You sound like the Timber Trade Federation."

"A kitchen unit isn't a tree any more, it's a manufactured commercial article. How could it possibly acclimatise – how could it *survive* in a tropical rainforest?"

But she never answered; for at this point the room went dark and the air was filled with a strong, spicy smell of pine needles. Marjolein grabbed my hand. "Don't be frightened," she whispered. "We hoped this might happen. We needed their support; but I never thought they would come."

"Who?"

"*Them.* The Norwegian pines and spruces."

"What, Christmas trees?"

"*Don't call them that.*"

Branches pressed up against our windows, blocking out the sky, darkening the daylight to an eerie shade of green. Marjolein, in high excitement, pulled me down the corridor. I didn't resist, scared of being left alone. There was no front door: we walked straight out into the deep forest....

The police – I heard later – had cordoned off Trafalgar Square. There were new laws against spontaneous marches and demonstrations – only strictly applying to human beings, but no one argued this point. A state of emergency had been declared. The Trafalgar Square Christmas tree broke out to join its sisters and brothers: nobody tried to stop it.

People huddled in their empty houses. It was a cold and cheerless Christmas that year, what with no furniture, no trees and few remaining means of heating. The streets were a sea of mud, churned up by marching roots.

"But where are they *going*?" I said to Marjolein. We had followed the forest, now proceeding steadily at a slow walking pace. With trees on all sides and silence apart from the crunching of roots and the sighing of branches, it was difficult to believe we were still in London.

"It should be perfectly obvious," she replied, "to anyone of the least political conscience. What time of year is it?"

"Nearly Christmas."

"It's December 11th. Tomorrow is the anniversary of NATO's decision to site Cruise missiles in Europe."

"Oh yes – sorry, I forgot."

"Well, then. We're going to Greenham Common."

"We're *what*?"

"The Greenham women stand as a symbol against all kinds of political oppression and injustice. Racism, classism and sexism of course, but that's just the start. There's also torture, police violence, wife and baby battering, homophobia, food mountains, prison conditions – and most certainly the rape and destruction of tropical rainforests.... You've never been to Greenham, have you?"

There seemed no way to avoid it, so I went. By the time we arrived, late next day, the base was already surrounded. The tropical hardwood contingent was there in force, blocking all the roads for miles around. I think I saw my hatstand.

Women were lighting candles, weaving coloured wool through the fence and singing. It was lovely. Chairs, beds, cupboards and tables from all over Britain had come to show solidarity – and while I carefully refrained from sitting on them, lying on them, opening them or using them in any way at all, I did make some small tentative efforts at communication. Given time, I think they might begin to trust us.

SOMEONE IN SOME FUTURE TIME

Shelley Anderson

They say you threw yourself into the dark waters for the love of a man – a sailor named Phaon. Unhappy suicide, is your shade wandering now in the grey world bound by that other dark river? You, who loved women and poetry and music, who worshipped love itself?

I sit and ponder these things, almost as old now as you were then. Cleis was still young enough to need you. Your pupils adored you. Atthis had returned to you. It hurts even now to say this. Wherever you are now, the deities greet you and listen to your songs with pleasure. While we who remain, wonder. Remember.

The sun on the mainland is brighter – it stabbed me after leaving the cool darkness of the temple. It was a shabby temple, the priestess overjoyed by my patronage – but then, my offering had been small. My mother taught me to bargain both with men and with gods. There would be a bigger thanksgiving when the return journey was completed.

Myro had given me stern warnings to be back on board by midday. Ostensibly, of course, I am the head of this voyage – my mother Chrielyssa owns the ship, while Myro is only the first mate. But he was protective because this was my first trade visit. I was the one my mother gave the pieces of Scythian gold to dispose of quietly. Chrielyssa did not believe in paying any more taxes than necessary to the Athenian overlords.

That was when I first saw the girl. She was reading the marks on the border stone. She was just on the verge of womanhood, perhaps 13 summers old, her breasts still girl flat but her glossy black hair curled and arranged like a woman's. The air of difference about her came not only from the strange cut of her robes, but from the kohl and powders on her face, the rings on her small fingers. She looked very vulnerable standing there in the dust, reading.

I wasn't the only one to notice her. My eyes caught the glint of the sun off bronze helmets just as I heard their sandals slapping the dirt. There were four of them, a small patrol with spears and short swords, seeking relief from the dock's noise and heat near the edge of the woods. One pointed towards the girl and their barking grew louder. The gold under my robe suddenly felt very heavy. Those lists of salted fish and olives Myro wanted me to look at before sailing seemed very pressing.

Hatred can be very empowering. The girl's vulnerability dissolved, replaced by a look of palpable hostility. If looks could kill, the soldiers who surrounded her now would be in Persephone's domain. The soldier with the curly blond beard reached for her robes. Another jabbed his comrades in the ribs and made some comment that set them all to laughing. What fools, I thought. Her robes were garish, but not the colors of a prostitute. She didn't wear the short jacket whores had to wear on my island. She was obviously rich and her kinsmen would have their heads on a platter. Is it a crime now for a woman to travel alone?

She cried out a warning in a rich deep voice that resonated in my throat. I realized in shock that I'd heard this accent before. Some traders from the East, dining at my mother's table, spoke in the same silken way. At least I knew enough to recognize the name of the Goddess Cybele. Her priestesses danced with cymbals, perfumed and oiled, in richly colored robes to make themselves beautiful to Her. Something else about them tugged at my memory, but disappeared as I stepped forward to prevent blasphemy.

It was then that things got really confusing.

The soldier who had grabbed the priestess dropped to his knees. He had finally understood her warning, I thought, until I saw the red ribbon staining his tunic, a ribbon that grew wider and wider. His partner began shouting while the others gripped their swords and looked around wildly. The girl stood stock still.

There was a whirling sound, like locusts, and another soldier dropped. Then a horrible scream, a rilling, ancient sound that came in waves, splitting the air. A figure danced out from underneath the pines. Dressed in a bulky traveller's cloak and the same broad brimmed hat, he made a dash for the priestess.

"Stay or come, but decide fast!" he shouted, running with the priestess towards the woods. The two soldiers began their own scream and ran after them, brandishing their swords. It didn't seem the best of times to argue. I ran. Straight into the woods and the arms of a monster.

Fortunately, this monster was on our side – at least, it hated Athenians. It reared up on two powerful back legs and kicked out with vicious front hooves. Its nostrils were huge and it snorted and pranced sideways, avoiding the soldiers' blows and getting in its own. Long hair, like a woman's hair unbound for mourning, tossed from its neck. A centaur. Not the clever beast of my nurse maid's tales, but a sweaty, heavily-muscled killer.

There was a sickening crack, and the brains of one soldier spilled onto the forest floor. The last man turned to run. That whirling sound again, and then both of them lay crumbled on the leaves, their spirits racing towards their ancestors.

The stranger began stomping the ground in a joyous victory dance. Then he stopped and looked up at the centaur.

"I'm getting better, aren't I?" he grinned.

"Better we get away from here before the next patrol," the centaur answered. The voice, like gravel in a river bed, came from a head that was brown and leathery, with cropped hair shot through with silver. The brown eyes were small and deep set, like candles shining from a cave, and they looked at the younger stranger with amused respect. A human head attached, I realized looking closer, to an equally sun browned human body whose legs hugged the creature's sweaty flanks. The priestess was already on his back, her arms clasped around his waist and her kohl rimmed eyes fear wide.

"Right," said the man, walking towards a huge oak. From behind it he led another centaur, smaller and roped around the neck. "We can leave these two at the temple." In one swift movement he was on its back, and holding out his hand.

"Come on, I'll help you up," he said to me.

"You want me to ride a centaur?"

"You'd rather explain four dead Athenians to the next watch?"

I turned to the centaur, to ask permission, but the man gripped my arm and pulled me up. We rode.

My thighs felt like they were being pulled from my body. The up and down rhythm of the horse, as Atthis called it, was as sick making as a boat at storm. Pine boughs slapped my face and a short, quick rain left me shivering. I was too miserable to learn anything more about Atthis other than his name.

It was night when we reached the market town. One look at the horses and the guards ran, their game of knuckle bones unfinished.

We trotted through the deserted square, the road tilting upwards until we reached the hill's top. The temple gleamed faintly in the moonlight. It was dedicated to Hera. The priestess of Cybele seemed strangely reluctant to enter inside, as did Atthis' companion. They stayed in the courtyard with the horses while a priestess, her eyes bemused with sleep, led Atthis and I inside. She guided Atthis through the dark interior and into another room. I sank down on a marble bench, exhausted. The stone's coolness soothed my aching thighs but made me shake even more. After some minutes another woman brought me wine and then I was left alone in the dark and the silence.

I still shook, perhaps from nerves, perhaps from the long, unfamiliar ride. I thought of Atthis sliding off the brown horse as graceful as water falls from a mountain. The horse had a strange smell, not unpleasant but very earthy and moist. Not clean like sea air, sharp as a knife rubbed in salt. Their hooves had sent clods of earth flying in our wake. I dozed against the temple's wall, my body still rocking inside from the horse's run, still breathing in the pungent animal smell.

Slowly I became aware of another scent in the night air. The shadows seemed to gather before me, to coalesce and grow heavier. I smelled roses. An outline began to form. The very air seemed to shimmer and a woman appeared to me, a woman with blue black hair cascading over creamy brown shoulders. She flowed before me and the air was rich with the sweet tang of fresh apples and roses. I looked into her shining eyes and lost myself. My thighs ached with a sweeter pain. The Lady laughed, her teeth startling white against her red, full lips.

"Stay with these new found friends." Her voice was music and a blessing. "You have work to do for Me, Phaae of Kreta. See that you do it well." Her brightness was blinding. Then a crack opened in the night and I fell through.

I was weak the next morning. The little priestess of Cybele had spread her cloak over me and curled up beside me on the floor. She smiled at me when I stirred, and then left, to return with barley bread still warm from the temple's ovens. Then she left again, to where I did not know. My thoughts were desperate for home, but the Happy Ones had different plans for me. I would have to send a message to Myro and to my mother, and talk with these strangers.

The older man was tending the horses. I felt foolish, having first mistaken him for a centaur, but I also was still afraid of these animals he so obviously loved. I stood in a shadow, unsure of how to tell him of the visitation last night.

"Observe her closely, Phaae – you'll never see her like again," Atthis said behind me.

"Her? But he –."

"Is an Amazon. Her name is Mekka. She belongs to a tribe that was old before the first stones for the walls of Troy were ever set. One of her people's queens died in the battle that saw those same walls destroyed. I've heard it said that you once had to travel for days until you saw an end to their tents during one of their festivals. They still follow Artemis, though I'd need the Goddess's own help to pronounce Her name the way they do." Atthis stood staring at the older woman.

"Amazons are just stories! And she doesn't even have one breast."

"She's got two very nice breasts," Atthis said, grinning. "Just like me. You shouldn't believe everything you hear. Now come along – the priestesses want to talk to you and our other guest from yesterday."

I did not like Atthis' smooth assumption of authority but I followed her, trying to hide my confusion. She led me to a room where seven other women waited. The two younger priestesses kept silent, as was proper, while the older women questioned me about yesterday's events. One woman, her hair almost pure white, translated for the priestess of Cybele, whose version matched my own. There was much whispering and exchanges of glances between the women, Atthis and Mekka, as if they all shared secrets unknown to me. I was glad to tell them of last night's visitation, which produced even more whispered conferences. Atthis was upset, I was very happy to note.

The priestesses, it turned out, needed a message delivered to the main temple of Hera on Lesbos. Atthis and Mekka were to deliver it. After much arguing back and forth, it was decided that the visitation was a true one, and the horsewomen were ordered to take me with them. Atthis was vehemently against this, but was overruled. We were all to ride to Siraeus and find a ship for the island. Siraeus was ruled by a minor tyrant who had her own reasons for turning a blind eye to the temple's business.

Mekka remained as impassive as ever throughout the discussion and seemed to have no objections to my journeying with the two. It was like a mountain storm then, sudden and explosive, when she began shouting at a suggestion proposed mildly by one of the younger women, who wondered if the Goddess also meant for the Cybeline priestess to join us.

"Never! I don't ride with this half-man! It's his tribe we're fighting against," she snarled. And then I remembered, the little thought that had been nibbling softly at my mind's edge, ever since I had seen the Easterner. The male worshipers of Cybele, the *fanati*, in a divine frenzy would cut their maleness off and put on women's clothes, to become as much like the Goddess as possible. The Cybeline paled when the Amazon's words were translated for her, but made no answer. No one spoke in favor of her going to Lesbos.

I was embarrassed, remembering how my arms had curled around her waist last night, which felt as soft as any of my other girl friends'. I thanked the Goddess my mother would never know about this — I am 14 and will marry soon, to a man who would not be happy to learn I'd spent the night next to another of his kind, no matter how muted. It's said he is a nice man. He has given two ships already to mother, and that is just part of my bride price. I've even seen him once, at a feast.

We left later that day. Just as we were to ride out of the temple's courtyard, the Cybeline approached, with a temple priestess behind her. The priestess hesitantly touched the reins of Mekka's horse.

"The Easterner wishes to say something to you before you leave, Amazon," the woman spoke, embarrassed. "She says it is true that you and she do not belong to the same tribe, but that it is also true that the Athenians hate her kind as much as they hate your people. She wishes me to tell you that when the temple she served was desecrated, the Holy One's *fanati* were used like women. She hates the Athenians also, and gives you Her blessing for your work, which is sacred. She hopes sometime to meet you in friendship. That is all." Mekka stared at the Cybeline, who dropped her eyes.

We left the temple and headed for the sea. No Athenians bothered us that first day's ride. Perhaps they did not know, or did not care. Or perhaps they simply watched and waited.

I did not look forward to riding on the horse again, but I was happy to be riding behind Atthis, my arms around her. I had many questions. My mind was full of images of smashed statues, of groves cut down, priestesses violated. Once I tried to ask Atthis some questions about our journey. She looked at me hard. "Don't prod any rubble if your stomach is squeamish," she quoted, her voice going back to a school girl's sing song. I took the warning and kept silent.

My body silenced the questions also. My legs felt they were being split apart. We were climbing through pine forests and the air was becoming chill. Each step made my bones rasp. I clung to Atthis' lean body for warmth and support. The Amazon, whom Atthis sometimes raced in a gentle rivalry, surprised me by her sympathy. She brewed me tea from the plants gathered along the way so I could sleep at night. She would slip away, silent as a mountain cat, and reappear as soundlessly further up the trail. She always beat Atthis at their games.

One night I woke whimpering. The pain was nearly gone, but I missed my mother, Kreta, the sea. A hand reached out and began to stroke my hair. A husky voice whispered a children's lullaby in my ear. My body still swayed from the horse's gait, but another, more comfortable rhythm took over as the other arm circled my waist and began to rock me. My hand curled around a small breast. The lullaby trailed off.

I kissed her lips. Soft, moist. The world was dripping honey with the earthy smell of moss packed between strong tree roots. Skillful hands took the reins of pleasure. We mounted a different horse and rode to the moon. When I opened my eyes again I saw the Pleiades, the seven sisters, smiling. I fell asleep, the scent of apples and roses mingling with the whispers of the pines, muttering about the stars in Atthis's perfect ear.

The new found joy that was mine was interrupted next mid-day. We found the body of a baby girl exposed on the hill side. Mekka had seen the vultures earlier and headed towards them. They had found other babies before, Atthis explained, before the slavers had. They had been able to save one, and given her into the care of some priestesses. We were too late for this one. She would serve in neither temple nor brothel. Mekka made the small pyre. No more lewd jokes or jarring slaps on the back came from her for the rest of the day. That night I dreamed of a lost child screaming for her mother.

We were descending and the path was rocky. The pine forest became thinner, and gorse and brambles multiplied and grabbed the horses' legs to trip them. We caught glimpses of the sea. The blue, so startlingly beautiful with white waves, caused an ache in my heart. All three of us were thirsty and dusty.
Suddenly I heard Mekka swear. Atthis jerked her brown bay swiftly to avoid a collision. Shaking my arms off, she reached for her dagger.
Mekka slid off her horse and dropped onto the ground. Her stocky body took on an astonishing grace as she slid through the dust, towards a lichen spotted boulder. Slowly, she raised her body, swaying to some inner rhythm, making soft hissing sounds.
Coiled on top of the rock was a snake. Her eyes glittered with cold fire. Her thick scaled body swayed to the same rhythm as the Amazon. They rose together, eyes locked, mesmerized. They lifted each other, suspended in the hot shimmering air. There was no sound, only the two figures swaying in the heat, an ancient fulcrum for prophecy.
The snake struck in a blur of scales. She bit the Amazon in her left forearm and Mekka crumbled. We rushed forward. When I looked back, the messenger had disappeared from the rock.

She was nauseous after the message, too weak to travel anymore that day. Atthis wrapped her in a wool blanket, chaffed her hands, fed her a healing broth. We sang and gave thanks for the Mother's visitor. The priestesses of Kreta had visions this way – I had not known that other people had the same gifts.

Mekka had been told to wait, that help would come to us. The green one had not told her how long the wait would be, or in what form the help would come.

The woods were alive that night with hundreds of sounds. Every twig snap brought on images of satyrs. Atthis and I lay stretched out on each side of Mekka, the three of us talking quietly.

Glancing up, I saw the shadows move.

Mekka always had her knife on her, I knew. But Atthis' short sword was near the pack, under another tree. I stood up.

"I need some food, it's in the pack," I said loudly.

"It's all right, Phaae –," Mekka began, when a bolt of brown lightning hurled itself at me and sent me sprawling.

"– they won't hurt us," she finished, but I was shouting to Atthis and there was something growling, clawing at my arms, pinning me down.

I looked up to see Atthis laughing. And to see five shaggy bears ranged around the fire. Six, if you count the one who was sitting on my chest.

To call them bears is to exaggerate – they were cubs. Girl cubs. They stomped and leapt around the fire, shaking leaves and dirt from their skins. The air smelled musky and vibrated with their deep-throated growls. The fire tossed the lumbering shadows into the pine boughs, where they lengthened and twisted. A taller cub broke from the circle and advanced with as much attempted menace as possible towards Mekka, who was grinning weakly. The cub clawed the air in front of the Amazon's face and growled. Nestled between her small brown breasts was a streak of silver. It glinted in the firelight, dangling from the dirty leather thong around her neck, a silver crescent sliver.

I pushed the cub on my chest off. She yelped. The

dance wavered and moved towards me. My cub stood up and glared at me with all the fury an eight-year-old girl is capable of. My indignation melted like snow in spring, faced with this circle of grubby but angry faces.

"Praise Artemis!" Atthis' voice rang out. "And Her bears for their help! May we ask for a blessing before you leave? We wouldn't want to delay you any longer on your business for the Queen of the Wild Ones." The taller girl danced closer to Mekka, her crescent spinning, cutting through the black night. She bent towards the Amazon and lightly raked her claws over the older woman's cheek. Then they shambled back into the woods, to their cave temple and the Teachings. But not before one pushed me over the outstuck leg of another, sending me sprawling while Atthis and Mekka burst into laughter. Beside the Amazon lay a dripping honey comb, like an offering.

The arktoi, the girl bands that worshipped Artemis, left tokens of wool in the pines and took our horses. The tokens gained us an audience with the chief priestess in Siraeus, and passage to Lesbos was quietly arranged.

It was not a pleasant voyage for me – Mekka was sick and Atthis, my star, grew more and more distant the closer we came to the island. There was little of the usual joy in watching the sailors make magic with knots and sails. Gliding over Poseidon's domain, I felt little pride in our human cunning and muscle, but rather sadness at our insignificance.

Back home my mother would be taking stock, counting bolts of cloth from Chios, Phoenician crystal, Asian spices. Her thick black hair would be tied back in a simple purple headband, her stylus poised over the tablet. We spun the wool for that headband from our own sheep. I would help her count the new jugs of wine, then go for a walk along the beach, to see our ships. The beach, covered in gold broom, is a gift to eye and skin. I would curl my bare toes into the warm, wet sand and watch the fishers come in, the nets bulging with silver fish.

Salt water burned my eyes, breaking the reverie. Before I left the deck I saw the rocky edge of Lesbos in the distance.

A young woman was waiting for us at the dock in Mitilini. She led us past whitewashed walls that dazzled in the bright light. The island itself was radiant, glowing with a special quality of light, a light it seemed to hold inside and release at will. The day was so clear that across the bay we could see the blue hills of Asia Minor. Somewhere out there, Atthis had her home, before her mother sent her to this island, to the poet's school.

Mekka slipped her hand around my shoulder and muttered a prayer of thanksgiving. Atthis was already running after the yong woman. She led us past the poorer houses that clustered together like chicks under a hen's wings, up to where the air was cooler and into an elegant courtyard.

We were led in after a short wait. My first impression of her was – disappointment. To be bested by such a rival! She was not a pretty woman. True, she was dark, but she was small, and thin, too, with none of a bigger woman's robustness. Her hair was black, the shining black of obsidian in old ritual knives. It made the gray streaks stand out all the more. Her motions were too quick – she was like a tiny bird, hopping from grass to grass, looking for worms. A handful of dull brown feathers and hollow bones.

The sparrow sat on her oak stool and looked at Atthis.

"You never did know how to dress," she finally said, arranging her yellow Chian robe into an even more sophisticated fold.

Atthis flushed. "I didn't leave of my own free will, Sappho. And I suffered too. Anyway, we've got to work together now, despite what we may feel."

"Yes, we do have work to do together," Sappho echoed. She managed to make it sound unpleasant. "But that can wait until you've bathed and been refreshed. I wonder how much you really do remember of civilized life," she drawled, glancing at the

Amazon, who was inspecting a tapestry. "We'll find out."

We were being regally dismissed when Sappho, as if struck by an afterthought, told a servant to put new pillows in Atthis' room. Sappho looked in my direction when she said this. Atthis did not.

I saw Atthis only later, at a feast where we were the guests of honor. Atthis, in a soft blue robe, was seated on Sappho's right with the poet's little girl, Cleis, nestled in the crook of her arm. Mekka's grunt first alerted me to the fact that there were also two soldiers among the guests. Sappho rose gracefully and made the offering. She was small, but a force radiated from her thin hands and beautiful voice.

"Power is a strong aphrodisiac," Mekka grinned as I stared at the poet. Then the smell of meat roasted with herbs drove thoughts of elegiacs away.

Servants were passing trays of apples and nuts when a slender young woman, dressed in a loin cloth, walked in front of the tables. Her oil sheened skin glistened in the torchlight and her black curls fell to her muscled shoulders. She walked with the surety of a born athlete. She saluted Sappho then strode toward the center of the floor.

She slowly bent backwards, until her hands grasped her ankles. Then she began a series of somersaults, her body gaining momentum with each spin until she suddenly uncoiled and sprang straight up into the air. There she spun not once, but twice, before landing on her feet. There were loud murmurs of appreciation as she stood, chest heaving and wiping the sweat from her eyes, grinning and very pleased with herself. She was as lithe as a bull dancer from Knossos. The man next to me said she was a track star from Gyara, a pupil of Sappho, named Hero. Her praise was cut short rudely.

"I've got something for the slut to jump for!" The larger soldier, his eyes riveted on Hero, was swaying and fumbling under his tunic. "Come here, girl, I've got something you need." Anger and a catty delight at this breach of manners mingled. The Athenian's companion, a hawk-faced man who had said little but watched much the whole evening, apologized and sent the man away between two servants.

A pupil named Mnasidica recited poetry after Hero. I did not listen, being fascinated by the conversations around me. Most of it was gossip of this one's latest villa and that one's latest lover. This side of the table was far enough from Hawk-face to indulge in speculations about war between Lesbos and the Athenian colonists at Sigeum. The poetry must have been good, as Sappho complimented Mnasidica when she took her seat again, only rebuking her mildly for reciting bareheaded. "It's always better to wear a garland," she said.

The girl sat down and the mill began again, grinding the incident of the drunken soldier into a fine meal. They were still at it long after the torches burned low and I made my way to bed. A bed with no new pillows on it.

Everyone slept well after sunrise the next day. Sappho had announced at the feast that she would be singing herself at tonight's celebration. Cleis complained that she could not concentrate on her spinning with all the preparations. Atthis took one small hand and Sappho the other and the trio wandered off to find the right goat to sacrifice. The endless discussions over which sandals to match with which headband were intolerable. I went in search of the only other person I knew who found Mitilini as confining as I did.

Mekka's leather pouch was as bottomless as the sea. Out of it came goat cheese and another pouch of wine, which we drank as we walked through the outskirts of the city. We climbed up, past the sycamores, to a rocky outcrop overlooking Mitilini.

"This is named after an Amazon, this place," she said, nodding at the villas below. "My people travelled far. It's said, farther south, there's a place so hot that our skins burned forever black. The women there are very skilled builders – and powerful hunters. Up north, women ride through plains of grass, as wide as the sea." Mekka shuddered, glancing at the blue waters of the bay. "But we all belong to the horse. And tonight, for the full moon, we all dance for Her. That makes my heart happy."

She leaned back against a tree and looked at me. "With my people, if your special one finds another breast to nuzzle, there's no bad feelings. There's plenty of other mares. Sometimes, if someone cares much, there are hard words. It is settled with knives. Maybe," she said thoughtfully, "we should learn from these Lesbians, and settle with words only. There's not so many of us now, to be killing each other off."

"There's nothing to learn from these people except how to tear your ex-lover apart in a poem," I burst out. "They're all such snobs! They're petty and stupid. And that priestess," I spat out her name, "she's the worst of all! She's a witch!"

"They like beautiful things," Mekka said after a pause. "And they moan too much about losing one lover, when six others are already climbing into bed with them. Strange, that. But stupid? No. No one gets as rich as these islanders by being stupid. They play politics too well. Atthis told me Sappho was in exile when younger. Political exile."

Mekka turned to look at me. "We have a saying, little mare – 'Before you shoot, choose your mark well.' It's not the Lesbians you have your quarrel with."

We walked back to the city in silence.

The full moon spills silver over the apple grove. The wind stirs the branches. There is the sizzle of grease dripping from the thigh bone on the altar, the smell of burnt flesh mixed with the cloying fumes of myrrh. The wet grass has been beaten down by the feet of circling women. Throughout, above, between all of this is the rhythm of the tortoise shell lyre, the sound of that voice measuring out the pulse, breathing the cadences, taking possession of the bodies retracing the sacred steps, over and over again. The rhythm is a living force, no longer conscious or controlled, but controlling, superseding all thought and will. Thin dark fingers free the music from the strings and the music invades bone, blood and sinew.

A fury leaps into the circle screaming, cutting slices of moonlight with the double sided axe. The axe is tossed, caught, tossed again, weaving an intricate pattern of its own as the fury chants and stomps. The swaying circle absorbs this frenzy too. The women dance under the moon and the night smiles.

I slept where I dropped. Sun and heat woke me. My leg muscles were cramped and I was thirsty, but inside I felt more at peace than anytime since I'd left Kreta. Last night I had heard a creek singing nearby and I stumbled towards it. Was it Hero I had seen Mekka slip off with when the chanting had died down?

The pain was so swift and sudden I did not recognize the cause at first. He had crept up behind me while I knelt by the creek bank and twisted my arms behind me. It is strange, the things you think of when in danger. Perhaps fear is a mystery also, and cannot be looked at too closely, or we go mad. He pushed me down, the rocks cutting into my breasts, but all I thought of was the borrowed robe being torn and dirtied.

He wanted me to see his face. I must not have looked frightened enough, because he slapped me a few times. He wanted me to be afraid. I felt like the essential me had been curled into a ball and thrown far outside the body he was hurting, where it hovered over us both, watching, waiting. I think he was one of the soldiers from the feast, the one who had been so drunk.

Had he been waiting, spying on the ritual last night? Cold anger filled me. Before you shoot, the gravelly voice came back to me, choose your mark well. He lowered himself on top of me and I bit the only part of his body I could reach, his nose, hard and swift.

He bellowed like a speared bull and smashed my face with his heavy fist. The blood flooded his lower face, bright red like one of Sappho's beloved roses.

Another burly figure appeared, and knocked him off me. Mekka had her obsidian knife in her hand. She moved quickly, dealing with him in only one or two strokes. She picked me up and walked away from the screaming, bloody mess.

It took us four days to travel to the other end of the island. We hid in the sacred groves at night, skirting the bay of Kalloni, moving southwest to Eressos, which Sappho knew well. The town was near the Hellespont trade route, so I would be sure to find a ship to the mainland and safety. Sappho was convinced the Lesbians would be at war soon with the Athenians, and she spent the days drilling me on messages for Hera's priestesses, messages of sabotage and political alliances.

Mekka stayed near Mitilini, planting a false trail for the soldiers. She left us after the first day, after helping Sappho gather herbs to heal me.

"You should have killed him," she told Mekka. "If he lives, he can identify her."

"If he lives," Mekka had grinned, "he'll live in shame for the rest of his miserable life, losing both his balls and his nose to a woman!" She clapped me on my shoulder, as if we had ridden the plains together, horse sisters and shield sharers.

The land became rocky and barren the third day. A great fire from time's beginning had turned the trees to stone. The sighs from the stone forest still filled the night. A peasant gave us olives and cheese and hid us in a cave until night, when she returned to guide us. She also gave Sappho a homespun tunic, like boys wear. The old woman said nothing when Sappho blessed her, but her eyes were full of pride.

Sappho cut my hair and smeared my face with dirt. I went over the instructions, the names and dates, until I could recite them in my sleep. I wrestled with my own message those four days. Atthis was sure to be followed if she tried to meet us in Eressos. If I wanted to say good-bye to her, it would have to be through my rival.

Gratitude and jealousy are horrible horns to be

stretched between. Sappho was risking much to smuggle me off the island. It was clear the islanders themselves regarded her as semi-divine. Their respect rubbed off on me. But respect is not love, or even friendship. How can you be comfortable with perfection? How can you forgive someone who doesn't even know they need forgiveness? Sappho needed nothing from me. She had every blessing the Holy Ones can give – including the love of Atthis. I wondered during that time what would happen when her perfection stopped. What would she do when her steps began to falter, when her memory failed? How can you go back to being merely human when you've brushed the divine?

We stayed in one of the poorer taverns the night before the ship was to leave. Sappho wrapped me in her cloak and we were given a place nearest the fire. We woke with the others, the traders and thieves and whores that all port towns attract.

The binding cloth around my breasts itched terribly. I was ready to push the ship myself, I was so nervous to be gone. We had finished the morning porridge and Sappho had settled the account. We turned to leave.

And I stepped right into the broad chest of a soldier. "Careful, boy," he growled and pushed me away.

The thieves faded into the shadows. The traders eyed their bundles anxiously and the whores prepared to display their own wares. The Athenians basked in the uneasy silence and made the most of eyeing each customer. One soldier, his sparse beard marking him as not much older than myself, ignored the whores and eyed me.

"We are looking for a girl, one Phaae of Kreta, who maliciously assaulted the Athenian sergeant Praxos. She may be travelling with an older woman, Sappho of Mitilini. If anyone knows where they are," the soldier caressed his sword meaningfully, "you'd best tell us now and save us all a lot of trouble. There is a reward."

They were stupid to think any Lesbian would turn

in Sappho. At least in front of other islanders. Better to wait, I thought uneasily, until backs are turned and you could collect your drachmas in secret.

The sergeant nodded to the soldiers. Two soldiers dove toward a whore and began to search her. Little Beard grinned and came straight toward me.

Sappho suddenly pressed me against the wall and began moaning. "Oh, Phaon, don't! Don't! You promised you won't leave – I can't bear it." She wept, pushing me into the shadows. Her body spoke of betrayal and abandonment more than her tears. The room was filled with her suffering. The sadness touched everyone in the dingy space, weighing our own hearts down. Her face cradled mine, her tears fell down my cheeks. I smelled her own perfume, the heady scent of roses in her hair, felt the curve of her hips under the thin robe, and knew a hunger I had never known before.

Little Beard was frowning. Another soldier, watching him, laughed, and the spell was broken. The sergeant gave one more arrogant sweep of the room with his eyes. And then they left.

Sappho released me with a chuckle, and I collapsed.

I remember little else of that day. I joined the crowd of passengers waiting to board. The fear must have returned, for Sappho murmured in my ear, along with her blessing, "Have courage, people will remember what we do here, now, in some future time." Salt water stung my eyes, whether from the sea or my own tears, I do not know.

She stood on the cliff watching the ship leave, her cloak bellowing in the wind. This is how I remember her. Later, when I heard the rumors, I wondered. Did her foot slip? Did the soldiers come upon her again, alone this time? Or, and strangely I fear this the most, knowing her own inevitable loss of perfection, did she choose to embrace what others feared the most?

I am older now. I worry about my own ships and the future of my own daughters. We make what trouble we can for the warriors of that many-pillared city. They find their own blond bodies so beautiful and tell us ours are dirty and obscene. They make slaves of more and more peoples, spreading war and destruction wherever they walk. This is blasphemy.

Atthis lives in Sardis, using her own wealth and power to thwart the Athenians. I hear no stories of Amazon body guards surrounding her. I hope Mekka still rides the plains with her kinswomen, but I fear the sisters of the horse grow fewer. What will happen to the world when they disappear?

The power of the warriors grows stronger day by day. I worry for my daughters, and for their children and the children after them. Will they be able to sail and command like I have done? To create beauty like Sappho, to ride free like Mekka? Will they worship on the hilltops at night, free from fear? Can they fight the warriors' lies and power? Choose your targets before you shoot, my daughters. Aim well.

SACCHARIN CYANIDE

Anna Livia

Lauren was just reflecting that she wouldn't want a car if someone were to ring up and offer her one, when the phone rang. Last time the phone had rung, three days ago, it was someone from a timeshare company in Spain offering her a free television. There is no such thing as a free television. There is always the licence fee and, for this set, you had to sit through a two hour presentation in Leicester Square on the glories of collective tenancy. The penultimate time the phone had rung, sometime last week, it was a young woman offering a free quote on a new fitted kitchen.

"I don't have a kitchen," said Lauren.
When they rang offering free insurance quotes, free help with buying your council house and a free questionnaire, Lauren would reply,

"Oh my, how exciting. I am glad you've rung. Now just wait while I get a pen."
She would put the receiver back on its cradle a couple of days later. Often the sales negotiator would still be extolling the finer aspects of the insurance cover, plastic waste disposal, political party....

Lauren answered the phone. It was her brother. Would she like his old car. Free.

"There is no such thing as a free car," she replied. "There's the M.O.T...."

"It's got eleven months to run."

"The insurance..."

"Included in my cover."

"Licence..."

"Bought my annual last month."

"Then why're you giving it to me?"

"I just won a metallic blue Ford Grenada with air conditioning, fuel injection and six year anti-corrosion guarantee."

"What do you have to do for that?"

"Shake hands with a household name and collect the keys."

"Aren't they going to pull down your existing kitchen, reinsure you for twice your market value or make you vote Conservative?"

"Got the kitchen done in January on the last insurance deal and I've voted Conservative ever since they sold me my council house."

Despite her better judgement, Lauren shook her brother's hand, collected the keys and drove off in a five year old beige Ford Fiesta. It was the ideal car for gliding through road blocks; the cops would never be able to distinguish it from all the other beige Ford Fiestas they had already searched. Not that road blocks figured high on Lauren's horizon. She was at that moment reflecting that a car would be useful for fetching calor gas refills and she'd be able to park at the new Sainsbury's to take advantage of their economy 36 pack of Andrex which she'd never been able to carry home before.

As Lauren kicked open her flat door, arms laden with a harvest festival of toilet rolls, gas cannister waiting at the bottom of the stairs, the phone rang. Assuming it would be aluminium double glazing or timeshare parking, Lauren picked up the receiver. It was Muriel from the Women's Centre. Since Lauren now had her own transport, would she mind collecting the hi-fi system for tonight's disco?

"How...?" Lauren began.

"Delia saw you in the parking lot up at Sainsbury's. She couldn't help noticing you walked round to the driver's side."

The phone had used up a fortnight's calls in one

day. Lauren unplugged it. The next four hours she spent transcribing tapes and recording the contents of various official letters for her boss, a blind research doctor. Then she set off to collect the hi-fi equipment. The car wouldn't start.

"Battery," she thought. And, scraping together what car folklore she could remember, "Choke."

She had passed her test at the first attempt a month ago, but she'd never had to start a cold car. It came to her door warm from the last pupil.

Lauren drove neatly off and into the main road. Then she stalled. She stalled again at the zebra crossing, at the traffic lights and in a queue of traffic waiting to turn right. She stalled five times in the first mile, the last time right in front of a police car with its siren screaming. After that she turned into a side street, stopped, considered the situation and formally burst into tears. She slammed the door and strode off up the road, turning her back on the car never to return. She was half way up the street when it struck her that if she left the car in the middle of the road the police would be knocking at her door. She had closed the choke and reversed into a more orthodox parking position, when she remembered that a hundred women were depending on her to add grace and rhythm to their finger clicking, hip swaying, heel tapping, low diving, slow jiving courtships. By now the engine was purring prettily. She reached the Women's Centre only twenty minutes late. Muriel was on the front step.

"At last. Any later and you'd have been as popular around here as Edwina Bacon."

Edwina Bacon was the local word for poison.

The disco was blasting, fingers, hips and heels moving to a well-regulated beat.

"Okay Muriel," said Lauren, "So tell me about Edwina Bacon. If you old ones don't pass on the gossip, us youth of today might make a mistake and invite her back onto the collective."

"Over my dead body."

"Funny how everyone offers their corpse whenever Edwina's mentioned."

"That woman is poison. She's a power mad, puritanical racist tyrant. Took a full-blown court case to get her out of here. Even then she carted half the stuff away with her."

"What stuff?"

"Books, magazines. I don't know, nothing valuable. Don't suppose she even wanted them. Just a sour loser, had to grab something."

"What was the row about?"

"Row? That woman created so many rows you couldn't get to the bottom of one of them. But the big thing was the café. She was determined to get that café closed down, called in an outside auditor, said someone was fiddling the books. Paranoia. The others were running the café very well without her and making a handsome profit, so Edwina had to find something against it. And there were the film nights. They organised a series of lesbian movies in the café. Edwina picked on one and declared it soft porn."

"Was it?"

"That wasn't the point. Edwina had never seen it. It was for her like a successful film series was the last straw in losing control of the Centre."

"I don't get it," said Lauren.

"There's a lot about Edwina nobody gets," said Delia, popping into the office to pick up some raffle tickets. "She said the lesbian film was porn but in the court settlement she opted to take all the 'violence against women' stuff in the Centre. There was a whole section: books, films, tapes . . ."

"Oh yes, that's right," said Muriel. "I forgot. Edwina had collected most of it, so I suppose it was fair."

"And amongst that stuff was the film she'd made all the fuss about. Can you beat it?"

"Sounds like she was confiscating it," observed Lauren.

"I heard she turned her spare room into her very own porn library," said Muriel.

"That woman's sicker than saccharin cyanide," said Delia.

"There is no saccharin to Edwina," Muriel corrected.

"Let's dance. I'm sick of Edwina Bacon. All that was over with five years ago but it's still the big scandal," said Delia.

"Once you hear of Edwina, you never hear the last of her," said Muriel. "That woman is . . ."

"I know," said Lauren, "Poison."

"Paraquat," confirmed Muriel.

"Harpic," added Delia.

"Neat lye," was Lauren's suggestion.

The merry list was interrupted by Joy.

"These women just told us that some boys have been smashing car windows in the street. Any of you parked out there?"

"Couldn't be my car," said Lauren, "After all the trouble I had getting here, that would be too much bad luck."

"Better go to the cop shop," advised Muriel, shaking her head over the broken glass. "You'll need a crime number for the insurance. I don't know why they do it, unimaginative vandals. Smashed car windows wouldn't make me happy."

"Don't start. Give them imagination, they'll smash an atom," said Lauren.

The glass was everywhere: all over the seats, the floor, in the glove compartment. There were even some fragments on top of the sun shades.

"Offside front," noted the policeman, "Park it with the broken window to the road, less risk of opportunist crime. And don't leave any valuables in it."

Lauren decided to leave the car outside the station over night, safe there as anywhere. Nothing in it but cassettes she'd been transcribing and no one in their right mind would bother to filch those. In the morning she rang her brother.

"I see," he said abruptly, "Where is it now?"

"Outside Wood Green Police Station," said Lauren.

She did not want this gift car used to apprise her brother of her every move.

"Which garage are you taking it to?"

"Dunno. Nearest. Why?"

"Insurance."

"Nonsense. Muriel told me that was automatic. Wouldn't even affect the no-claims bonus."

"How'd she know? Just tell me which garage and have them send the bill to me."

Lauren shrugged into the phone, leafed through the *Yellow Pages* and read out the name of a garage up the road. As good as any, no doubt.

What happened next, and in what order, would have slipped Lauren's mind, like washing hung out to dry in other people's gardens, were she not soon to have reason to go over every fine detail. She dropped the car off at the garage as arranged. Then she walked home, about five minutes away. That evening, just as she was pouring a second cup of tea, she remembered that the tapes were still in the car and she needed to finish indexing them. This was the most skilled part of the job: without a proper index Dr Akoba would have to listen through fifteen cassettes before she could find the part of research she wanted to quote. Lauren composed the initial index, being most familiar with Dr Akoba's work; then she gave it to the RNIB braille pool who would translate the aural into the tactile form. Reconstructing these details was easy because all braille work was sent off at the end of the month and this was the 29th, so even if she hadn't remembered, Lauren could have guessed quite accurately that she would be finishing off index work that evening.

She put a saucer on top of her cooling tea, shrugged back into her coat, and walked round the corner to the garage. The yard was dark and Lauren had not thought, not being in the country, to bring a torch. She located her car and began gathering up cassettes. She could find only fourteen in the glove compartment where she'd left them. Maybe one had fallen on the floor when she was clearing up the glass. She searched under the seats, hard work in the dark.

Finally she bent right over and began to feel around with her fingers, worried she might collect an inadvertent splinter. And there was the missing cassette, or rather the missing cassettes, for her finger tips felt the hard plastic of two cases. She dropped them into her coat pocket. Did she glimpse a shadowy figure approaching the garage as she left? Or did hindsight provide the figure after the fact? Lauren hurried home.

She began to check references to 'sickling', certain she'd missed one on tape thirteen. She listened carefully right the way through, still the reference eluded her. Maybe at the beginning of tape fourteen? What a waste of time; which just showed the importance of a trustworthy index. She surveyed the stack of tapes. One of them was unmarked; she didn't remember putting any blank cassettes in the car. More likely she just hadn't written its series number on the J card. Better have a quick listen and mark it up now.

But the unmarked cassette was indeed blank. She fast forwarded a little to make sure. Nothing. Then, as she poured milk into yet another cup of tea, she heard a little click. And a woman's voice, not her own. The voice of an old woman, calling for help. Screaming. Oh my God, screaming blue murder in a shrill, breaking pitch. Then the woman spoke,

"Help me, please, help. Are you there? Can you hear me? Police! He's in the house, he broke in. He's coming up the stairs. I can hear him. Please." Then a muffled noise, a thud, but the voice went on, now an inarticulate gurgling, choking, gasps. Then nothing. As though a phone had been shoved back in its cradle.

Lauren let the tape play right through to the end, until the transcriber clicked. She was unable to move, to think, to breathe. She was terrified. Terror was the man who had broken in, who was, even now, climbing the stairs towards her flat, who would open the door and swoop down upon her, wrap his hands around her throat and choke the life from her. Her body was old, it could not move fast, she had little strength in her arms and she walked heavily with the aid of a stick. She could not get away; there was nowhere to hide. She had rung the police knowing they would be too late but unable to give up and go, abandon hope. Her screams were pleas for something to intervene, for a residual goodness in the air she had been breathing for eighty-three years, for general indignation that the world was so brutal a place for old women, to come forward now and throw her attacker down the stairs.

At last Lauren roused herself, switched the machine off and sank into an armchair. She was shaking. A bath, perhaps, a warm bath and all the mindless small actions needed to accomplish it. Surrounded by hot water and many soap suds, Lauren thought over what had happened and what she should do. Clearly she had picked up a tape which did not belong to her. How it had got into her car, and when, she had no idea. But these were rational thoughts, devised to block out others. Who was that old woman? What had happened to her? Had she been choked to death by an intruder while in the very act of calling the police for help? Or, was it part of a play, a radio play, perhaps? Lauren wondered. Had she inadvertently recorded a few frightening moments from a play? Or, from the News? There was that woman, what was her name: Syriol Lewis? She had indeed been murdered in just that way. Lauren sought desperately to remember. It had been on the News earlier that month. That must be it. She must have had a blank in the recorder and turned on the radio at the same time. Lauren began to feel a little less shaky. She played with the soap suds, heaping them up into piles and calling them sheep as she had when she bathed with her brother years ago. It was a long excerpt for radio news, though, ten minutes at least. Very long. And so frightening, surely there must have been complaints if even Lauren, who was used to listening to unpleasant recordings through her job, had been terrified. Lauren surveyed her store of bath oils, bath pearls, bath essence, bath salts and bath seeds. She threw a mixture into the water and turned the hot back on to produce a churning Hellespont of foam. She smelt like Sissinghurst on a hot day when all the sap is rising and a thick cloud of perfume hovers over the flowerbeds. Simple comfort to calm her until she was recovered enough to think again. Before she took her hot water bottle and warm milk to bed, Lauren threw the poison cassette into the dustbin. The smell of all the bath scents wafted around her as she raised the bin lid: sweet and rotten. Saccharin cyanide.

Next day passed in a leaden whirl. Lauren had to rush through the rest of the index without checking back over earlier work. Dr Akoba was as pleasant and courteous as always but clearly impatient. Lauren was a conscientious worker, and, knowing the index was not up to her usual scratch, she phoned the braillers and explained that they might have to pay closer attention than usual to make sure everything tied up. Dr Akoba had overheard the phone call and told Lauren off. It simply was not the braillers' job to check the work of the indexer. Did Lauren need more time? Why didn't she deliver the new tapes to the RNIB herself later next week; now that she had her own car it shouldn't be too much trouble. A reasonable solution, but Lauren was in no mood for polite reason. She would very much have liked to confide in the Doctor about the poison cassette but after she'd been ticked off it hardly seemed appropriate.

That evening she had a phone call from the garage. The owner didn't know how to put it; did she want the good news or the bad news first?

"The good news. I've had such bad luck with that car I could do with some good news."

"Well, we've fixed the side window for you. Won't even lose your no-claims bonus," said the owner.

"And the bad?"

"It's been in an accident and, I'm afraid, it's a write-off."

"You're joking. Look, just don't. It's too much. I'm sorry, but I can't take a joke at the moment. I really can't."

"No. It's true. Another car bashed into it. Volvo. Built like a tank, volvo, built like a tank."

"Was anyone hurt?" asked Lauren weakly.

"Fortunately not. And we've got an independent witness so it'll come out of the volvo's insurance."

"I don't believe it," said Lauren, "I don't believe it. It can't be a write-off. I've only just got it."

"Want to dispute with their insurers?" asked the garage owner. "You could do; we'd back you. We feel a little bit guilty cause one of our mechanics was driving it at the time."

They ought to feel more than a little bit guilty: it was their fault. What the hell had the car been doing out on the road anyway; weren't they just fixing the window?

"We had to take it round the block once we'd finished it," said the garage owner, as if answering Lauren's unspoken question. "Not enough room in the yard to keep them there when they're fixed."

Lauren rang her brother.

"Oh bad luck," he said with the Raj drawl he was cultivating now he owned his own council house. "Better still, I have a very good chap in south London who could fix it for you much quicker. Used to weld World War Two bombers. Very good chap. Tell your garage they're off the case and my man will tow the car tomorrow morning."

Lauren felt, if anything, relieved that the car was going back where it came from. It had brought her nothing but suffering. She would go to the RNIB by bus and forget she'd ever had a car. Right now she really must get on with checking the index.

Lauren looked forward to a calming few hours with no interruptions. When there was time to do it properly, she enjoyed the precision and system of her work. She went to the shelves which held her copies of the latest 'Sickle Cell' tapes. She had left them in number order last night, but now they were all out of sequence. It didn't make sense. Someone trying to steal Dr Akoba's sickle cell secrets? Marvellous, let them develop a cure! What was happening? Someone must have broken in, gone through the tapes and not known how to put them back in order, or even, perhaps, that there was any order. They were very clearly numbered, for anyone who read braille. A sudden suspicion occurred to Lauren and she darted into the kitchen. Under a pile of wet tea leaves lay the poison cassette she had thrown away the night before.

It ought all to fall into place: her brother's second hand car, the broken window, the accident, the poison cassette and the break-in. For the life of her, Lauren could not make sense of any of it. What had it to do with the death of Syriol Lewis? for Lauren was uncomfortably certain that it was the murdered woman who connected the sharp fragments. All day Lauren had tried to get on with her work and be sensible, and all day the old woman's dying screams had echoed in her head. She had to do something.

The phone rang.

"Hullo, my dear. I hope I'm not disturbing you," said a familiar voice.

"Oh no," said Lauren, "I'm glad you rang."

"I was a bit short with you today and you know the old saying, 'Let not the sun set on your displeasure', so I want to say I'm sorry if I was harsh."

"Dr Akoba, that's very kind of you. But it was true, it is my job to do the index, not the braillers'."

"Is everything all right at home?"

"Yes, only . . ."

"Only?"

Lauren told the Doctor about finding the cassette.

"Very nasty. Sounds like the Moors murderers recording those poor children's cries," was Dr Akoba's first comment. She did not appear to think it could be a simple practical joke.

"What would anyone do with such a recording?"

"I don't know much about it, but there's a whole market in 'snuff tapes' as they call them. I tell you who would know, the young woman at the Bacon Library. She was very helpful when I was collecting information on female genital mutilation. But I think you should take that tape straight down to the police station. You don't know what you may be dealing with."

Dr Akoba rarely recommended the police station.

Lauren pondered in silence. The police already had a copy of the tape, or it would not have been mentioned on the radio. They weren't exactly known for their efforts to stamp out violence against women. Besides, and an even nastier idea occurred to her, the car had sat outside Wood Green cop shop all night with a broken window, ideal for some bent copper to hide his latest money-spinner. Maybe she should find out more about these 'snuff tapes'. If she could stomach it. She looked up the Bacon Library in the phone book.

"The Bacon Library is closed now. Opening hours are from ten a. m. to six p.m. Tuesdays and from nine a.m. to one p.m. Saturdays. Researchers from abroad on short stays may arrange an appointment outside these hours. If you wish to lodge material, or have any other message, please leave your name . . ."

"This is Lauren de Haan and I, well, I wanted information really. Someone said, that is, Dr Akoba told me, well, I need to know more about 'snuff tapes'. Oh, and I think I'd like to lodge some material."

As she made the offer it occurred to Lauren that a library might indeed be a good place for the poison cassette.

Hardly had she put the phone down, but it rang again.

"Bacon Library. Lauren de Haan, please."

It was one of those abrasive English school mistress voices which will always make sure to pronounce the girl's name right even while delivering the soundest tongue-lashing.

"Yes? Er, speaking."

"You want to lodge some material."

"Well, yes and . . ."

"You are not a member."

"No. I'm afraid not. Is it members only?"

"You wish to apply for membership."

"I suppose I should. Do I just fill in a form?"

"You must state the nature of your research and pay a joining fee."

Sunday found Lauren in Broxby-After-Bliss knocking at the door of the Bacon Library. A tall thin woman showed her in.

"I am Edwina Bacon," the woman said.
Silence.

"I see," said Edwina at last, "You have heard of me."

Lauren shrugged. "All that was five years ago. Things change."

"They do not," said Edwina. "I was right then, and I'm right now. If I hadn't been right you would not now be seeking information in my library, Europe's largest collection on violence against women. If I had been right quicker, you would have been able to consult my material in the comfort of your local Women's Centre."

Edwina's tone went straight to Lauren's backbone, rubbed sandpaper in between her vertebrae, pinching nerves as it went.

"You want to know about snuff tapes," Edwina informed her.

Lauren nodded.

Edwina showed her rooms filled with magazines, rooms filled with videos, rooms with tapes, books, letters; a catalogue of horrors, an anatomy of the female body sliced thin, sliced into specialised sections for specialised atrocities; from the new born baby to the old, old woman, the myriad uses and abuses to which flesh of different elasticity could be put.

"So much?" said Lauren.

"The way violence against old women is going," Edwina said, "I'll have to build another alcove."

"You're cynical," said Lauren, "I didn't expect that."

Edwina looked at her. "I wouldn't have thought anything would surprise you about Edwina Bacon."

"I don't know you."

"No one does."

That old line. No one knows me. No one understands me. What was Lauren doing here? Peering into the dusty corners of Women's Liberation Movement history? More like raking through the accumulated hairs, slime and tea leaves of a partially blocked drain.

"Why don't you tell me what you're here for?" Edwina suggested. "Cut short this agony."

Agony.

"Is it that bad?"

"You can hardly expect me to be pleased to see you," said Edwina.

"I don't know you," Lauren repeated.

"No," said Edwina, "You don't. But you know what you've heard."

"I heard you were asked to leave the Women's Centre. That they had to take you to court. You were ... very ... suspicious, and the others couldn't work with you," said Lauren, "Something about having the café investigated and objecting to a film night."

"'Suspicious'," savoured Edwina, "Is that what they say these days? The movement has grown ... polite. I thought I was poison. Saccharin cyanide."

"Well, what did happen?" asked Lauren.

"You're opening old wounds."

"I seem to have opened them by walking in here. Has no-one else from the Centre ever been to the Bacon Library?"

"They haven't the wit. They want to have fun. They want to have a nice day. An endless series of endlessly nice nice days. They want to include every woman who ever lived in their all-inclusive 'we' but they don't want to think about the violence men do which binds us, binds us to each other, binds us hand and foot. Or the women who help the men and do their binding."

"I would find it hard to live in a place like this," Lauren gestured at the walls lined with card indexes in case of computer break-down, "In the midst of all this horror."

"We all live in the midst of it," retorted Edwina, but more softly now, as though the constant abrading of her sandpaper voice was wearing itself down into the finer sand of an ocean beach. "And we all find it hard. I prefer to know; in all circumstances, I prefer to know. I cannot say with those others, 'I can't bear to look', 'don't tell me, it's too upsetting'."

Edwina's body was as taut and as finely balanced as a

bicycle wheel, the spokes sprung out from the centre with the grace of the lightest of the new alloys, but the balance was so fine, each spoke tuned so high, that any dart or arrow coming horizontally, when the whole, meticulous make-up of the body was toward the road ahead in one, unwavering line, must throw her over, spokes snapping against the one pressure they could not, for their own nature, guard against.

"Do not mistake me for a spider's web," said Edwina, with a hint, almost, of amusement in her eye, "I am thin but not frail."

"I have heard what the women at the Centre say of you," said Lauren, "I would like to know your story."

"My story?" Edwina paused, then let it pass. "I was prosecuted by my friends. I lost the Centre I built. I was publicly vilified. Women spat at me, or they crossed the street to avoid me."

"Why?"

"'Political Differences'. I was, even then, the national expert on violence against women. I see you bridle at the word 'expert', a well-trained response, but we are not horses. We were all supposed to be 'equal', weren't we? But I knew what was going on, and those women did not. They could have known, but they didn't want to. The woman running the café was an agent."

Agents. Oh brother. And what a sense of bathos.

"I checked the accounts. There was too much coming in. Regular payments from an unlisted source. How do you prove that? I notice, however, that they never opened the café again. Just couldn't quite manage, somehow, to balance the books."

"I heard there was a film . . ." said Lauren.

"Pornography. Lesbian pornography," said Edwina. "Why the hell should I spend every moment of my waking life for years and years and years setting up a Centre for women, a place for lesbians to feel comfortable and have a good time together, oh yes, I wanted a nice day too, collecting massive evidence of the profits and networks of the money men make on buying and selling horrors done to our female bodies, only to have two lesbians make the same kind of film and show it at my Centre? It is not different when lesbians do it, it is merely worse. Merely worse."

It had been a long time since Lauren had heard anything approaching a political opinion, let alone a passionately held political opinion. It happened to be a different opinion from her own, but she felt a grudging respect for a woman who could maintain her passion for so many years with no-one to say "how right you are."

"You are looking at me as though I was crazy," Edwina observed drily.

"Oh no," said Lauren, "I feel a, a . . . a grudging respect for you."

"Why do you grudge me respect? You have come here to my library because you think I'm the only one who can help you. Do you grudge my help? The circumstances which have put me in a position to help you?"

Lauren sighed. It gave her time to think. She remembered this. This prickly, on your toes way of talking, where what you said mattered because the other woman was listening, acutely, to the phrasing, and the tone, every nuance. And Edwina had kept this method alive over five years, by herself?

"Why don't I make us a cup of coffee," Edwina was saying. "Then you can tell me what you're looking for, and need so much that you're prepared to venture into my lair to seek it. Rage is tiring and, probably, misdirected."

Lauren smiled, a little smile to herself it was meant to be, but then she laughed. Edwina looked down upon her, consideringly. It would have been too hard for her to smile, now, after so many years of stiff-lipped, straight-backed silence. Her mouth wouldn't do it, couldn't find the grooves. She cast around for something else.

"There's cream," she said at last. "One of the researchers brought strawberries and cream. Would you like cream in your coffee?"

Edwina listened while Lauren retold the story of the cassette and Syriol Lewis. By the end Lauren found herself shaking. It had been hard to keep going all week with that piteous voice ringing in her ears. The shaking embarrassed her. She was afraid she would cry.

"The Lewis tape," Edwina was saying, "I thought that would surface sooner or later."

"What?" said Lauren.

"As soon as I heard it on the radio," said Edwina, "I knew what it wás."

"What?" said Lauren again.

"Well, you were right. It's a snuff tape. They had it played on the air for authentication."

Lauren could not follow. She had hoped for reassurance, she was not getting it.

"To raise the value," said Edwina.

Lauren frowned, then shook her head.

"There is a lot of money in turkey porn these days. Sex with old women."

"Stop. You're making me feel sick."

"I think Syriol Lewis must have felt a lot worse."

"You mean, someone murdered her, recorded what they did, and sent that recording to the police?"

"Possibly someone on the police force. So they could be sure to get the story onto the *News*."

"And some man listens to it and jerks off?"

"Probably. But what they'll do is edit that voice and those screams into a porn movie – real terror, as seen on TV. Or, in this case, as heard on BBC Radio *News*."

Lauren stared at the tape, still in her hand. Sick. Sick. Sick.

"It isn't true," she said.

Edwina only looked at her. "Have some more coffee."

"What can we do?" asked Lauren, unaware in the fear of the moment that she had included Edwina in the solution.

"I think you should be careful," replied Edwina. "They won't like to think a copy of their tape has gone astray."

"You mean I'll get back to find my flat turned upside down, drawers on the floor, dustbin emptied on the carpet?"

"It depends whether that's the master or a copy," said Edwina. "If you're lucky, it's only a copy. Tell me again how the tape turned up, when, how you got the car, everything."

So Lauren told her everything.

"Your brother was very keen to trace your movements," said Edwina at last.

"For the insurance," said Lauren. "He needed to know because the car was still on his insurance."

"Convenient."

Lauren said nothing.

"I think," said Edwina, slowly, "You should make another copy of the tape, take this one to the police and phone your brother. Tell him all about it; it was frightening finding it and you just don't want the car back. Girls are superstitious about these things. He'll know that."

"I don't see . . ."

"Whoever put that tape in your brother's car will be very anxious to get it back. They will, by now, have gone through your flat inch by inch. It would, in a way, be better if your brother was involved in it because he can call off his watch dogs."

"My brother? My brother has nothing to do with it. You're letting your imagination run away with you. My brother is not like that. He just happened to let me have his old car," said Lauren, as evenly as she could. Edwina was trying to scare her, use fear to win her over. Well, she'd made a mistake throwing Lauren's brother into the plot. That was plain ridiculous. Not to say insulting.

"Your brother rings up out of the blue to offer you a car. A car you never even suggested you might want. He says he's won a new one in some competition. Next day you phone and tell him the car's in the garage getting a window fixed. He makes a big performance how he needs to know which garage. That night you find the snuff tape. Next day your whole tape collection has been tampered with. Then some volvo writes off your car and your brother has it towed back to south London. Lauren, that guy's in it up to his neck, and trying to use you to throw someone off the trail."

"Stop this, Edwina. Stop it at once. You're not going to intimidate me like some little student or a new acolyte. The whole story is fantastic, it's a complete perversion of what happened."

"Then where did the tape come from?"

"I don't know. Someone put it in my car by mistake."

"Like leaving an umbrella on a bus? I suppose that man's hands around Syriol Lewis' neck were a mistake too."

"What man? Edwina? Are you saying? Christ that's sick, that is perverted. You're crazy, you're . . ."

"Poison?" supplied Edwina. "That's where all our careful analyses always fall down. We never can believe, really believe, that it could be our own brothers, our little brothers, our gay brothers, our Black brothers, our Jewish brothers, our poor, oppressed, working class brothers. Well, it's your choice: believe me and follow through or back off; tell the world you met Edwina Bacon and she's as poisonous as ever. Then convince yourself it's my mind, not your world."

SCARLETT O'HARA

Mary Dorcey

I

Sometimes you wondered if you might have done less harm to women if you had stayed heterosexual. Loving women, after all, you had to consider was not perhaps the best way of loving women. You had seen the damage and attrition; the blackened eyes and mauled hearts. And had not been innocent yourself. But could there be any doubt (as you said when other women complained of this) that it was those you loved and lived with, inevitably who did the wounding? Those you chose to desire of whichever sex, you invited, did you not, to be the agents of destruction and loss? Anger, what's more, that should have been turned outwards; the grief and pain of love suppressed, was turned in on your own vulnerable fragile selves. And when you went running in the street, kicked out by a lover, eyes streaming, blood on your cheek, who would take you in? Who would comfort a woman maltreated by a woman? Women were supposed to be nice, were they not? Why else after all, bother?

The time you walked into the Royal South Hotel, round about midnight – staggered in, drenched, almost fell through the revolving doors, an April night turned treacherous, your hair dripping, your shirt clinging to your back. And oh god, you were desperate, desperate for a drink and just downright desperate. They could see it of course, you knew that, the doorman, the barman, the bellboy – the eyes red rimmed (not black this time; oh no, that much at least years ago behind you) recognised at a glance, as who doesn't; the ravages of romance and heartache, so much of it staggered through the doors round about midnight. You would have to make your way into the lounge and up to the bar without rousing too much interest. One sidelong glance in their direction would be enough to evoke hours of free drink, consolation, a brotherly shoulder to cry on, "and who knows what else might be going lads if you get her when she's down?" And you were down – low as you could go, parched for a drink and a kind word from any other human being, so godawful she had made you feel, you had made yourself feel with the rotten things said and done. So low even a barman in the Royal South was a companion unworthy of you. There were four of them ahead, an old barman, a young barman, very pink and up from the country looking, an american tourist in emerald green lambswool and a business type in a dark striped suit. You would have to steer your way through them, head down, up to the counter and order your drink, side-step their predatory sympathy. Keep the mind blank. Think nothing and they can pick up nothing.

It was not true that you regretted the first day you had laid eyes on her or was it? You were too miserable to tell. Or that you regretted every touch that had passed between you? Jesus, why did you say these things? Bad enough thinking them but what kind of fool would say them, straight out, as if in cold blood, as if fully serious? In the pub you had tried to placate her, touching her shoulder, smiling – will we go you asked? Her face turned from you, "Why don't you just go back to her if that's what you want?" "But I don't . . . I want. . . ." "Fuck off" she said, not caring who heard. And you did. "Alright," you said, "at least she'll be glad to see me." And flounced out. The moment the wet night hit you after the warmth and clamour of the pub you knew your mistake. Rain in your face and nowhere to go in the whole miserable town. You started to walk, blind with anger, not caring until you reached this place.

"Well now," the older barman leaned towards you with what's known as an avuncular smile, swishing his cloth over the mahogany counter. And you almost started off again, tears in your eyes, god where did it come from? Salt so strong it corroded your cheeks because he had said "bad old night" (meaning the filthy wet rain) "wouldn't let a dog out in it"; the thing so ordinary, so sane, it struck you with new blasts of contrition and shame. You alone freakish and cruel in a world of such easy uncritical kindness. And he asked what you wanted to drink. A double. Double what? Don't know – double anything – whiskey, gin, vodka – make it a vodka, and he did, swinging off with his polished gestures. The american at the end of the counter threw you a fine country you have here glance, making friends with the natives and the business type in the suit watched covertly, appraising mood, need, how many drinks it might take, and would it be worth getting started?

"Room number Madame?" the young one scrubbed and pink eared wanted to know. "Five o three," you answered, saying the first number that came into your head, the number of your first lover's car as it happened. The things that stuck in the brain. "Very good Madame," and off to the opposite end, the american tourist requiring attention.

Lift the glass now. Slowly. Get it to the mouth without spilling. First mouthful down things will feel better. The shivering calmed. Rest a moment. Sit up on the barstool. Nonchalant looking at least. When they'd got used to you you could make your way to an armchair in the lounge. Your body was stiff, and sore, a bruised feeling in your back and limbs, as though you'd been beaten. The words coming home to you like waves of seasickness. Why was there no better way to handle these things? Years of experience and you hadn't discovered it. Another swallow. Steady. Keep the mind empty. Warmth in the gut. Better soon. Patience. Unemotional. Imagine a summer's day, walking the beach, sun on the face, driving the motorway with the headphones on. He was watching again, the one in the suit with the red tie. At a loose end obviously, unexpected break on an empty evening stranded in a provincial town, you arriving in, looking maltreated and vulnerable. Preparing his opening line. In a moment he'd ask if he might borrow your ashtray and after that it would be "can I buy you a drink?" And why not after all? You could stay here all evening under cover of a resident. You wouldn't mind letting him talk you into amiability and oblivion. You could easily spend the night drowning your sorrows with any of them. Except that even in that the joke was on you letting a man console you for the pain caused by a woman. Knowing, they were sympathetic only because they assumed some husband or boyfriend was behind your coming in here at this hour. Well, why not? It would serve her right if you did. God . . . serve her right? Where was the right? It was all wrong, fouled up from the first moment you had opened your mouth.

She had called you a bitch and a hypocrite. She had asked were you in love and you said, "What does that mean?" "You bloody well know what it means," she had said. You should have said nothing. You should not have told her tonight. Tomorrow when you were quiet in some less public place, when you had re-established some kind of rapport. It would not have been impossible to have said nothing at all. You would probably not see S. again, or at least you were sure to see her but would probably not go to bed with her. But when Alanah had asked, some insane need to confide; as though no experience was complete, not even sexual infidelity until you had shared it with her. And oh Jesus – you had even wanted to boast! Yes, something like that. There had been an actual impulse to impress on her what a good woman S. was. You had wanted Alanah to like her; appreciate your taste. Even when you were in bed with S. the thought had flashed through your head. You had found yourself thinking, when she told that wonderful Virgin Mary joke, how much Alanah would enjoy this woman. A bitch and a hypocrite, she had called you. And *she*, you said, was a possessive, deluded, maniac. What did she expect? Fifty years of unfailing fidelity (stupid word – what had faith got to do with it? It was an excess of the quality rather than its lack that led to this mess – too much faith in yourself and all round you) like some shitty bourgeois marriage? But even while you were shouting at her you knew how you would act in her place.

"Very mild up to this." "Oh yes, can't complain up to this." "Two out of three's not bad." They were doing the weather thing now between the four of them, discreetly keeping their eyes from you while you knocked off the drink. Letting you settle in. And it was working, you were beginning to thaw. First knot in the intestines loosening. The banter and vodka doing its thing. You could lift your head now, risk a sentence or two without fearing your teeth would chatter.

"Labour might do well in the city," from over the counter.

"Labour!" the business man scoffed, "all labour and no delivery with those boys." Tossing remarks towards the young barboy that you knew were intended for yourself. "Sitting on their hands for forty years, keeping them clean." His own hands immaculately groomed; buffed nails, skin smooth as the day he met his wife, twenty years ago; no dish-washing, nappy changing blemishes or wrinkles for him. Voice smooth too, easy authority. A no problem, can do type. The suit was good, pricey; pure wool. You were swilling dregs to keep him from asking can I get you another, corner of the eye kept on your glass. And why bother? Wouldn't he keep you in from the rain?

"A bitch and a hypocrite!" she had said. "How could you do this to me now, when my whole life is coming apart? And here? Why did you come down at all if it was just to dump this on me five minutes before going on?" She was always on edge before speaking, though no one would think it, she looked so incredibly cool and together and expected your understanding support. And, of course, it *was* the wrong time but when was it ever the right time? When had you ever in your long life of such matters heard one lover say to another "thank you I'm so glad you're doing this now – this is exactly the right moment and place!" It was more than usually wrong though you knew that; the very title of the weekend "Twenty years on – what do we carry into the future?" inviting doubt and self-scrutiny. Blood, sweat and tears and very little else it seemed at such times. "You might at least have waited...." But you had waited, almost six months while her life came apart, almost half of the time you had known her, and you could not go on waiting, could you, a bottomless well of empathy, solace and comfort? "At any other time...." And you said, "It wasn't planned you know – I didn't go out there and say now this, this is exactly the right point in history to be unfaithful to Alanah. It just happened that way – that's all." "Like hell – like fucking hell," she said. "Nothing just happens!"

And she was right in that too when you thought of it. It was, of course, she who had made it happen!

"Can I get you another?" He was leaning forward, an ingratiating, self-deprecating smile. Nice smile. Nice hips too. Couldn't stand men with fat hips! Sexist it was and why not? You chose men when you had chosen, the way you would a horse, the way they would a woman. Getting your own back was it? Or merely that that was all you could find to respond to, the physical?

"Another vodka," you said, "no ice." Might as well. You had to sit somewhere. At any moment they might start to get awkward about the room number. He could provide a safe alibi. You might even have to book in at this rate. No going back now. The door locked. No chance she'd forgive you yet. Anyway could you deal with it? No, not tonight – neither recrimination nor pardon.

"Are you sure vodka's the best thing?" he asked, man of the world decides for you, knows the best course. Nicely, oh so discreetly sympathetic, letting you know that he *knew*.

"Probably not. But it's what I'll have all the same!"

"A vodka it is then – no problem," smile broadening, least line of resistance always, got you further faster in the long run.

You shouldn't have told her. Needn't have told her. The whole thing would have been redundant with a little passage of time. You wouldn't have told her if she had not seen it the very second you arrived in. "You might at least have wiped the smirk off your face," as you sat down in the coffee shop half an hour before she joined the others. And seeing her eyes you were glad there had not been time to buy the bunch of violets you had seen at the corner stall. Written all over you she said, no good denying it, as you shifted uneasily in your seat. Reeking of it. You felt like hiding your hands under the table. As though you had forgotten to wash. As though if she leaned any closer she might smell S. from your skin; the sharp almost citric tang of her flesh. "You didn't waste any time," she said, "did you? I leave on Thursday and you're fixed up by Friday." "Fixed up," you said, pride wounded, "it wasn't like that . . . not at all like that." "Oh wasn't it? And what was it like then?" She looked at you her eyes gleaming, her wide pale lips drawn back. She was wearing a black linen jacket, loose in the fashion, over a lime green tee shirt, her nipples jutting under the clinging fabric. A pang of desire shot through you. And you felt guiltier still. What was rousing you? The bright flush jealousy had brought to her cheekbones? Or the memory of S. returned to you now – almost the same flush of blood at the neck and cheeks, the eyes dark when she came – returned by these questions?

"Anyone I know?" she asked. "Well yes – who else was there? Though not very well." She had stood in the same room at a party or meeting. "Her!" she said. Whatever that meant. Envy, admiration, contempt? Too little taste or too much good fortune? Her hair was falling about her face in bright yellow tendrils, escaping a loosely tied pony tail. You looked at her hands, the lean sensual fingers, the one ring with its deep jade stone, placed palms down on the table like weapons between you. You wanted to touch them, you wanted to edge your own hands forward and touch, inch by inch across the gulf you were widening with every word. "Go on," she said. And you went on.

"A woman who knows her own mind," he said, swishing back his jacket to drop the change in his trouser pocket, revealing the slim, exercised waistline, the clean cut, debonair jaw thrust towards you. "Out of the ordinary, I thought, the moment you walked in."

The lines didn't change it seemed, no matter how long the interval. How long was it anyway? Five years or more since you'd had anything to do with one. Never missed them – never gave it a thought until now – times like this, alone and wretched, self-loathing. Glad of any distraction. Any paper thin compliment that might restore equilibrium. How long now before he would launch the main campaign? Would he tell you his problems – the broken marriage, renegade son, failed opportunities or go for the dazzling facade – invite your collusion in the game of well organised, golf, squash playing world, clean cut limbs and cleaner shirts, power and good nature, everything going his way. And you might even surprise him, call his bluff, go up to the room when he asked. Or before, taking matters into your own hands, speed the night up (he'd like that – strong minded woman). Take the easy way out. The quick road to oblivion, wallow in the well heeled compliments. Play representative types; the old stupefying ritual acts. So many women you knew did it. Went running back to men when some woman had broken their hearts. Who could blame them? Where else was there to run?

"A woman like you," he was saying, "would have a sense of proportion. Keep your head. Not run to extremes."

God it was so much easier with men. Another world. Soothing. They talked so much more slowly for one thing, calming effect. And think more slowly, one idea at a time. And so caught up in pride at their own thoughts they have no time to wonder about yours. Privacy, that was it. No privacy possible with a woman. She knew everything you were thinking before you had thought it. Men knew nothing, you didn't tell them. And you could tell them anything. Also they needed so much less. Look at this one – for all his air of sophistication – if he had regular food and regular sex and his work to go to, he'd be content. Women? Women always wanted more. More of what? More anyhow than you seemed able to find or to give.

He would be ardent. Oh yes. You imagined the gold, almost invisible hair on the lightly tanned squash playing thighs, heard the familiar gush of used flattery, felt the excitable hands; careful to hang up the jacket just the same.

"Grinning like a cheshire cat," she had said. She told you she wanted the truth. All of it. Now that you had begun you might as well go on. Go on. She was sitting opposite you still, the café emptied of all but last stragglers, you sat riveted to your seat by her eyes. You wanted to kiss her mouth, the faint blonde down at the edge of the upper lip. Instead you were explaining what had taken you to bed with another woman. Every word striking like a hammer blow, a flush like bruising raised under the skin with each one delivered. "Go on," she said. You went on, blow by blow. The meeting at Christine's. The walk home, out of your way, the drink that led to another. Asked in to see her paintings. "I don't believe this!" Yes, paintings. And then you heard yourself say, at the last, that you supposed it was the first time in months you'd felt reckless, light hearted, felt needed, for *yourself* – not just a shoulder to cry on. That did it. She rose to her feet. Her face blanched, oddly distorted. She looked like an accident victim. Like a face glimpsed at the edge of the road at the site of a car crash. "You make me sick," she said, and wheeled round, nearly overturning the table, out and into the street before you could protest or help, leaving you with the gaping crowd.

"Great excitement at the weekend with this

women's thing on," the business man was saying, "a big crowd down I believe. O'Shaughnessy addressing them. After the women's vote, smart lad."

"Whatever the women want, that's where it's at," the elderly barman remarked, having returned to your end to fetch whiskey for the american.

"Ah, but do they know what they want?" the business man said with an air of grave insight.

"That's it – the sixty thousand dollar question. We'd all be rich if we knew the answer to that one!"

Alanah had to get up, despite all that you said to her, and demand what some women wanted. Needed. Set herself against the tide. The new mood of rephrased orthodoxy, the new politicians and agency workers, the academics, the women's studies people, professional women being professional, moving on past the old divisions and labels; making sure of next year's funding. And Alanah had to rise to her feet and remind them of mess and squalor; of the women unable to move on; the women stuck at the end of the battlefield in the mire of lost causes, while the cavalry rode on into the sunset, briefcases glistening. "What do we take into the future? Some women will have nothing more than their scars and the clothes they stand up in," she said, fire in her eyes. And you were proud of her, the familiar throb of pride hearing her tell it like it was in the teeth of their pleasantries. At the end of the room, applauding, your back to a pillar struggling to catch her eyes that would not turn to you.

Alanah. You should have said nothing. You should have come down and had a good time in spite of the lousy conference: the lies and the posturings, the old tired enmities, the old faces putting out the old lines, dodging the issues and dumping them on others. None better than Joan O'Malley with her long years of practice. All of it adding up to the wrong time for you. Adding new fury to Alanah's mood. As she walked to the pub with the others in the aftermath, you caught hold of her arm to draw her aside. "Alanah I wanted . . . ." "I suppose you're in love," she hissed, "I suppose that's what you crossed the country to tell me?" "After one night?" indignant, "what do you take me for?" "Oh bravo – well done! Are you looking for brownee points for staying detached?" And you felt such a shit, such a miserable eel talking this way. Passing S. off as some casual fling, a bit of adventuring – like some bored Don Juan coming out with these lines to make Alanah feel better. Or yourself. No, you were not, whatever that meant, "in love" but neither were you in the least. . . . But you would not go down this road into more definitions and justifications. You remembered her mouth at your shoulder, the scent of her . . . you could not regret it, and yet . . . these phrases seemed to have hold of you, coming out pat before you had thought them, each one of them taking you further from truth.

"My wife now," he said, "if only she knew what she wanted. Time on her hands . . . with the children . . . ," moving his stool a little closer, his blonde shield of hair, smooth as his voice, his expression nostalgic, penitent. "Restless maybe . . . people change . . . different interests. . . . Time of life. Nothing serious mind . . . a marvellous woman . . . kept her looks, always . . . still have . . . well you know . . . nothing wrong in that area at least. . . ."

But you would not be drawn in. No, not even here, half pissed and spiteful in the small hours of the only drinking place open. You should make a move now. Shift to one of the tables in the lounge. Give it a moment or two, finish your drink, then make your exit discreetly.

"Wonderful woman and mother . . . but something . . . somehow, over the years," he was pulling at his striped silk tie, running his hand down its length, rolling the tip over his fist: "well . . . missing. . . ."

And you were grown philosophical now, detached, steady enough almost to sit on your own. Having reached a familiar pitch, a small plateau of calm and wellbeing when events slide into perspective or out of them; great happenings becoming trifles in the far distance. Something, somehow, over the years, missing. After all it came to everyone did it not? The same unravelling and disillusion whether it took twenty years or one. Whether you took the jog-along, ready-made path of security and contentment or struck out for something new, something not yet in existence. A course you had to forge along the way, hour by hour, with your own hands. Whichever. The same cul-de-sac waited at the end.

"She tried various efforts," your business man was telling you, twisting his wedding ring on his finger, reddening the pale flesh, "part time work, counselling, that kind of business. Then she went along to one of these meetings," he glanced at you doubtfully, "a local housewives' affair, you know the style – get together once a week for a good gripe about their men. Well, after a bit she got close to one woman in particular, an odd sort; over intense, a malcontent and gradually it began to infect her. She said to me . . . do you know what she said to me?" his face was flushed, his voice suddenly vehement, "she said to me that the excitement had gone out of her life! I ask you! And how many people, I said to her, how many people do you think have excitement in their lives? Well, she didn't answer that, did she? It's like that book I told her – 'Bring out the Magic in your Mind'. For most people, let's face it – there's no magic in there!" he was staring morosely at the high polish of his shoes. "What's the point I'd like to know," he asked more or less to himself, "of raising impossible expectations?"

Yes, yes who could argue? Where had they got you, half a life time of little else? Drunk and wretched at one in the morning, drowning your sorrows with stray business men? But yet, even tonight were you dismal enough to want to exchange it for the alternative? For his life or for his wife's? Sheltered and supported by an amiable stranger who left her, after 20 years, just enough leeway to pass him out without his noticing? You wondered where she was now, this wonderful wife, while he talked about her problems – while he chatted you up.

"She said she wanted to go to this conference nonsense at the weekend, the girlfriend egging her on. A lot of hot air, I said, a lot of shit stirrers, too fond of their own voices," his own voice returned to good humour now having retreated from the particular to the general. "That Joan O'Malley one, she was down, wasn't she?" He asked with a small knowing grin. "Did you read what it said in the paper? Do you think she means the half of it or is it just for the crack?"

"Oh yes, Joan was down." Up there on the platform, keeping them laughing, keeping them guessing, dodging the issues all weekend. Elegant, eloquent on every corner of women's oppression, but her own. But what could one expect? She couldn't afford to get stuck with a label, to tarnish the image now could she? She had her career to think of. Her family after all. And hadn't she a right to a private life like anyone else? Oh, you knew all the excuses. You had heard them so often they had taken on an air of inevitability. You nearly forgot all the women who had, years ago taken the risks she wouldn't chance. Ah, but she would say, sure didn't everyone know? Why make an issue? And who would listen if she got too political? If she lost her sense of humour?

Ah indeed. She would have the nation with her on that. Just what they liked – turn a blind eye, let you get on with it so long as you kept it quiet. Didn't frighten the horses. Juno Galloway, home from London, called it something else. "The conspiracy of silence," she said, rising from the floor to launch her attack: "a silence that diminishes each one of us, lessens our capacity for love, for joy, for self-criticism. A silence that makes freaks of the few who dare to break it!" Well that was telling them! It even cheered Alanah, for a moment, brought a smile to her face. But not for you. No, not for you. With you she was adamant. Vengeful and cold. Damn it! You couldn't afford to fall out with her, tonight of all nights. With so much needing to be talked about. A hypocrite, she had called you. Well, she should know. In one breath demanding the whole story, in the next castigating you for giving it.

"Tell me something now?" the business man was asking, fully restored to his early good nature. Finished with the wife story now, free to move on to the evening's main business. Ships that pass in the night. You wondered how he'd change tack? Admire your eyes or your mind? Shuffle his knee close to yours and measure how long you would let it remain there? "Tell me, all this man hating stuff, is it for real would you say, or effect? Mind you when I've seen her on the chat shows she seems fairly reasonable. Sense of humour – I'll give her that. But then she'd need it wouldn't she?"

"Man hating," you said, feeling the alcohol taking its toll, the edges of your patience fraying, "I wouldn't flatter myself with that. . . ." For a moment you toyed pleasurably with the notion of telling the truth. You would enjoy watching his face; the clumsy attempt to cover disappointment, distaste. But no, you thought, he wouldn't be shocked – on the contrary. He'd be turned on. Want to hear all about it. You had seen it before. Titillated. One hint and it would take the night to escape him. And you needed to leave, badly. Restless and bored you had grown. A relief that at least. Yes, he had done that much for you. Transformed pain and guilt into tedium with the steady wash of his platitudes.

Time to go. But where? In this town, at this hour? Go back to her? Would she let you in even if she heard you? She would have the phone off the hook, the pillow over her head. Besides you had your pride. Or must pretend to have. Maybe you should check in at reception? Go to bed? Well, you could order another drink before deciding. That was it. Take it into the lounge to a quiet corner table. You would have to make your excuses nicely. He'd be put out, that was for sure. Crestfallen. "So soon," he'd plead, "must you? Why not one for the road? Life is so short."

"A lonely bloody life all the same. . . ." he said out of the blue. But then you hadn't been listening.

"What?"

"I mean living the way she does. . . ."

"Who – your wife?"

"No, no . . . Joan O'Malley. I mean it can't be a bowl of cherries, can it?"

"What?"

"Well . . . her kind of life . . . you know?"

"Telephone call for Mister Michael Crowley . . . if you'll just step this way, sir?" The young barman was there to show him the way. And down he stood from his stool, many apologies, assurances of a speedy return. "Take up where we left off, in a moment?" And the brisk stride, the executive off to clinch the big deal. Though you knew it would be his wife, of course, calling to tuck him in. To check him out.

II

"A sense of timing . . . of the essence . . . am I right or am I right?" Oh no, not another conversationalist. You had thought you were safe. You had borrowed the barman's paper and made your escape to an armchair by the fireplace at the far end of the lounge. You had not seen her come in and she certainly was not here when you arrived. But she was here now, standing over you, leaning for support against the mantelpiece, a cigarette in one hand, a half empty glass in the other. "If one cannot trust an individual to be in a pre-arranged place at a pre-arranged time, pre-arranged a month in advance, for what can one trust them? Do you see what I mean?"

"Oh yes, I see."

"That is what I would like to know. Do you see?"

"Yes, I do. I do indeed see."

"Well, he doesn't. That is the problem." She teetered on her high heels and hiccuped softly. Mascara was smudged under the left eye, the voice slurred, pissed as a newt of course, but holding it well. Aggressive, pre-maudlin stage. Looking for someone to pigeon hole. God, why was it you always attracted this kind? Well she could just take herself off. You were not going to encourage her. You needed to be alone, long enough to think things out.

"He says what is one night? Can you not wait one night? Is the hotel not the best in the town? God help the town! But my point, you see is not the matter of waiting. No, no, I have waited before ... I can wait again. It is the simple matter of a de ... ro ... gation of trust ... do you take my point? A de ... rogation of trust. And I am, to my cost, a trusting woman!"

She lifted her cigarette to her lips, craning her head stiffly to meet it half way: "Men!" she said. Two plumes of blue smoke snorted dragon like from her nostrils: "not one of them worth a mouse's fart. Am I right?"

She looked at you consideringly. You saw the livid red of her cheeks under the frosting of rouge.

"Are you waiting for one or just left one?"

"One what?" you asked unhelpfully.

"A man of course," the drooping eyelids gave her a knowing, flirtatious look she might well have had sober.

"Neither, as it happens."

"Very sensible if I may say so ... extremely bloody sensible ... the condition to which I aspire." She sloshed the last of the alcohol round her glass, setting the ice cubes clanking and knocked it back. "May I offer you a ... another restorative?" her lips pursed oddly as though attempting some expression they could not quite remember.

"No thanks ... I'm fine as I am."

"Fine as you are! I congratulate you. I do indeed. I would not be fine if I were unrecognisable." She hiccuped again loudly: "Perhaps I am. Perhaps that is why I find myself alone, lodged in this hole of a town."

Oh lord! Were you reaching the maudlin stage already!

"Men," she said, "not worth a pig's fart ... am I right? However ... cannot live with them ... cannot live without them. Just about the size of it," she lowered her glass with a resounding bang onto the table in front of you and put her hand to her breast, the ringed fingers splayed as though to steady a beating heart. "And have you ever met one who thought of anything else? Have you ever met a man who did not want to know as soon as he had caught his breath what you thought of its size? Who bloody cares is what I'd like to know. Measuring tapes carried in one's handbag one would need to keep them happy. What a woman wants ..." she said, dealing out each syllable deliberately like cars laid on a counter: "is a little ... T ... L ... C, am I right? Tender ... loving ... care.... And what do we get?" she cocked one brow with alarming agility.

What?

"Vital statistics! And none too vital at that."

Deprived of the ballast of her glass she appeared dangerously unstable: "Do you mind ..." she said, perhaps in recognition of the fact, "do you mind if I join you?" and tilting forward she collapsed abruptly into the armchair next to yours.

Can't live with them, can't live without them. That indeed was just about the size of it. Appalling how these clichés were gradually creeping up on you, posing as sudden insight. True love never runs ... no fool like an old ... love is blind ... attraction of opposites, etcetera, The whole rag-bag taking over. Making a laughing stock of experience.

"If it were not for an in ... in ... erad ... icably ... trusting dish ... position ... I would not be lodged here tonight. A lifetime of misplaced trust. Yes ...," her voice seemed to slither between invisible obstacles, one moment bumping to a halt, in the next, gusting recklessly forward. "That is the story of my life. A sorry tale. What is yours...."

"Much the same in reverse, I suppose," you answered wearily.

"Ah, then ... no need to explain. Ex ... ploitation of trust ... you are familiar. One lives and does not learn. Once trusting always trusting, am I right?" She swung her head with a jolt in your direction to regard you with a wavering glance: "Are you trusting? ... I think not.... You look to me the thoughtful type ... look before you leap and all that. Very commendable, very ... only trouble is ... who is there left to leap? If you see what I mean?"

Yes you knew what she meant. You leaned back involuntarily from the reek of vodka. It would be vodka, this kind; ex-country petty bourgeois always drank it. Began, on the upward climb, thinking it ladylike – all fizz and lemon – too late very soon to change. Yourself now ... well that was different ... strictly for emergencies. Mind you, you thought, for all the battering she was still an attractive woman. Well preserved as she would say, well rounded rather than fat. The full lips sagging a little but the brown eyes had a look of rueful sensuality.

"A sense of timing ... next to godliness, don't you think?"

Indeed, indeed. How Alanah would agree with her. Lousy timing that was forever your problem. What had got you into this mess. If only you had held your tongue. With your stupid literal mind. Would you never learn? People who asked for the truth never wanted to hear it. If only you had waited. You would be with her now. In Byron's house, in the attic room, the brass bed almost touching the windowsill. Or standing in the garden, the rain by now a soft drizzle, listening to the river's swollen voice. Holding hands like first lovers, delaying the moment. . . . And then. Oh no ... get off this track quickly or you'd be in trouble again. . . .

"May I invite you to join me in a small restorative?"

"Oh alright ... fuck it ... why not!"

"Exactly ... fuck it why not. If the little boy with the tight buttocks would just pass this way again. Forgive me if I do not stand up. . . ."

As obtuse and callous as any man when it came down to it, she had said. If you had even the slightest grain of consideration, you would have waited, waited to do it, waited to tell her, waited at least until she was over Richard. That was what she meant of course. That was the real reason behind her anger tonight. Not your sleeping with S. at all. Why hadn't you seen it before? Obtuse again she would say. But it wasn't for the want of trying. You had worn yourself out for six months with sympathy and concern. Emptied yourself to be as grief stricken as she was. What more could she expect? If you were a man of course, it would be sufficient to try, to show willing in a clumsy, masculine way. But women had to get it right. A woman was expected to succeed in the business of comfort.

"Consideration . . ." she asked with surprising pertinence, "is there anything more important I ask you?"

"Oh it may be important," you heard yourself answer, "but it isn't as easy as it sounds, is it? I mean you can consider every bloody thing in sight and still miss the one thing you were expected to consider. . . ."

"Indeed . . . never easy. Miss the one thing you were expected to consider. The essence eludes . . . time and time again. I comprehend . . . you have your troubles . . . I have mine. Companion in misfortune. Do not interrupt . . . please continue. . . ."

And you did. You heard yourself begin on the whole woeful mess. Well you needed to tell someone and why not her? After all she was far beyond registering anything said to her.

"Her brother, you see . . ." you were saying, hearing your own voice rather muffled as if through a poor telephone connection. "I didn't understand how it affected her. How could I? She couldn't understand herself."

"How indeed! The essence eludes . . . time and time again. Ah, here is the tight assed boy. Two double vodkas, no milk."

"But she expected me to understand. She expected me to know by instinct. Callous as any man she said. But how can you give something someone doesn't know how to ask for?"

"Exactly . . . bloody men . . . say no more. . . . The male of the species lacks above all else, I consider, consideration. I comprehend exactly. Not worth a mouse's fart. Cheers . . . chin chin . . . as it were."

"Her brother, you see, died. Her favourite brother you see he was, though I didn't know it. I don't think she knew herself until it was too late. . . ."

"Ah, favourite brother . . . ashes to ashes . . . death do us part . . . say no more. There is a time in the tide of men . . . there is a tide in the time of men . . . timing of the essence . . . please continue. . . ."

"Agh . . . its too long a story – I don't want to get into it. . . ." You hadn't understood how she felt. That was the root of your guilt. The inexplicable blood tie that you, an only child, couldn't hope to understand she said, as though that also was your fault. Some illusion of security, of trust in the basic order of things had vanished for her with his death, forever. You did understand that. You had tried to show it. You had gone with her almost every time. You couldn't stand hospitals since your own father. . . . But you went. Waiting in the bloody car for hours while she sat with him at night. It was a relief, yes a relief when it was finally over. A relief to her too (you knew that and that deepened your guilt). Well you had given every drop of comfort and consolation that was in you but you could not go on forever, could you? You couldn't go on feeling like a traitor every time she heard you laughing or when you came home from seeing a friend in the pub, a bit drunk and jolly. You couldn't keep up a long face for the rest of your life. She called you an insensitive shit. Maybe you were. . . .

"But oh god . . ." you said, your voice loud with exasperation, "were women to be endless fountains of sympathy, depthless outpourings of love and empathy? Could you never be tired or just plain bloody selfish without being accused of acting like a man. . . .? And it was for a man of course that she was grieving. Where did that leave you both?"

"Bravo . . . bravo . . . nail on the head. Well spoken. Where did that leave you . . . exactly!"

"That's where I failed you see . . . that is my crime. A woman's greatest fault. Lack of empathy. The inability to make myself as depressed as she is. . . ."

"I take your point . . . a woman's crime . . ." she raised her glass and finished half of it. You saw the crimson smear of lipstick left on the rim and on the surprisingly white enamel of her front teeth. "Men," she said, her head swayed on her neck like a flower on its stem, the continued effort of holding it upright seeming too much, ". . . lack the essence . . . of timing . . . brothers . . . husbands . . . where's the difference? . . . no comprehension, no timing . . . dying when you least expect it . . . husbands leaving for the milk . . . same old story . . . sorry tale. Am I right?"

"Probably . . . will you have another anyway . . . my turn. . . ."

"Another probably . . . when the tight assed boy returns . . . and now I will tell you a story . . . a story of . . ." her nodding head jolted upright again and she held it rigid for a moment while she stared with narrowed eyes across the room: "Who is that man . . . may I ask, lurking under the archway . . . regarding you in a familiar manner. . . ."

"Where?"

"See . . . by the rubber plant . . . looks to me executive class . . . dry champagne window seat . . . I am familiar you understand with the species . . . air hostess . . . you know . . . Alice Somers . . . previous existence . . . coffee tea or fly . . . like flies to the honey pot . . . you know. Who is he. . . .?"

"Oh him . . . no one. I was talking to him earlier in the bar . . . chatting me up."

"Ah, I comprehend . . . chatting up . . . chatting down . . . previous understanding . . . am I right? You may be excused."

"No, no," you said sinking deeper into your chair. "I've no intention of going over there again . . . I'm grand where I am thanks. . . ."

"Grand where you are. . . . Splendid. . . . I congratulate you. Most commendable. Will not answer bell . . . dry champagne window seat. Please ignore." Using both hands she straightened the skirt of her black cocktail dress, drawing it demurely over her knees, "But I was speaking, I think, of consideration. May I continue with my story on the subject . . .? A little fable of our time. . . . My late husband and I . . . that is to say my ex-unpunctual husband, my first and my last . . . were having breakfast one morning in the breakfast room . . . a well-appointed south facing room built on at considerable expense six months previously. Breakfast . . . one would have thought, an innocent kind of repast . . . would you not?"

"Oh yes," you replied, smiling, "I suppose it could be innocent, in some company. . . ."

"Exactly . . . innocent company . . . sun shining, good humour all round, lashings of toast, coffee and marmalade . . . air stewardess, experienced you know . . . when my late husband notices that we have run out of milk. My god, he says, we have run out of milk, I will just run round to the corner shop and bring back a bottle. Very well I say and some cigarettes while you're at it. . . . Marlborough, twenty it was then – forty now, but never Marlborough, after that. He went out for the milk and I being of a trusting disposition waited for the arrival of the milk. I drank black coffee and waited. And what happened? I waited and waited, milkless . . . first in the breakfast room, then in the lounge, then in the garden, eventually in the bedroom. I not only waited, I rang. The corner shop, the office, the guardai, the hospitals. Nothing. My late husband it seemed had vanished into the ether. Without trace, you understand. Next morning, drinking black coffee in the breakfast room a letter arrives. My late husband announcing his intention – carried out twenty four hours earlier – of leaving me for another woman. Very regretful, most appreciative of many years of service, always to count as a friend etc., but he had met the special one . . . the fated one, and felt compelled to surrender himself to destiny. I enjoyed that line at the time: 'compelled to surrender himself to destiny'. Fine ring to it, don't you think? And do you know what?"

"What?"

"I have not so much as touched it – from that day to this . . . not so much as one drop has passed these lips . . . not one. . . ."

"What?"

"Milk! Nauseous substance . . . the very smell of it – de trop. . . ."

"Well," you said, impressed, "that is quite some story. . . ."

"Some story indeed! A tale of the most blatant de . . . ro . . . gation of trust in my experience. Experience I re . . . gret to say, long and painfully well informed."

Her head, suddenly losing the battle, dropped forward with a thud against her chest, and a rattle of pendulous earrings. For a moment you thought she had passed out. But no, after a brief pause she raised it laboriously once more and considered your face with grave concentration. You thought you saw the glitter of tears on her cheeks, but decided it was more likely the beading of perspiration.

"I do not know about you," she enunciated sorrowfully, "who are perfectly fine as you are . . . but I . . . who am no better than the wreck of the Hesperes . . . am going to have another . . . bloody . . . drink! No milk!"

A little later when the young country barman had brought you over two more gentle restoratives, bloody vodkas, and you were, gingerly now, because of the strange numbness about your lips, taking the first sip, your companion noticed a figure standing at the entrance to the room: "That man – executive class – is regarding you again, I fear, from the archway. Would you care to press the bell for service . . . hostess you know can take care of these matters. . . ."

"No, no, just ignore him and he'll go away."

"Exactly the thing . . . goaway . . . goaway . . . flies you know . . . flies to the honey pot . . . please ignore . . . best policy . . . not worth a mouse's fart . . ." she raised her hand and tapped a dark wing of gleaming hair exploratively as though adjusting a wig: "But I have talked too much . . . as is my wont . . . why do you not now . . . embark on yours . . . by way of a change . . . light relief I fancy."

"Oh mine," you said dismissively, "unless you have the rest of the night we better not get started on mine. Just let's say it began with men in the usual way and after several episodes quite unlike yours it ended up with women."

"Women . . . say no more! There is nothing further I have to learn on the subject. Women I consider, after some consideration . . . fall – and fall is the operative word – into one of two categories. Either they are women of one's own age attempting to prove they still have it, or they are young girls in bobby socks attempting to prove they have developed it! Am I right? Of course," she continued, her delivery as if in need of winding, losing pace gradually, "if it . . . were not for the male of the species ... being so bloody gullible and infantile ... one would not have to worry about women, would one? But ... can not live with them ... can not live without them ... am I right or am I right?"

"No, no no," you heard yourself answer, your voice sounding strangely like hers, pedantic and solemn, "you're not understanding me. Men aren't my problem ... not for years. I've nothing to do with them, you see. It's women who are the cause of all my problems...."

"Exactly ... some of my best friends ... women. All very well in their way. Right time and place ... excellent companions for the daylight hours. But timing of the essence ... nine to five ... superlative ... but don't ask them home after six ... if you take my point?"

"Oh that wouldn't work for me. I live with one you see. I live with a woman, not a man...!"

"You live with a woman?" she repeated reflectively. "... live with, as in live with, as it were, is it? I take your point! Extremely sensible if I may say so ... extremely bloody sensible ... a thousand times better off without ... without ... whatever it is.... No waiting about ... the condition to which I expire!" she reached out her hand and beat it against your thigh in a gesture of encouragement or congratulation, "a thousand times better off ... tell me more...."

"Well, I don't know if it is that much better. I mean man or woman, the basics I suppose are much the same. Jealousy, misunderstanding, resentment, isn't it much the same? Past a certain point no one human being can really help another can they? We're all alone when it comes down to it...."

"Alone?" she said, raising the other eyebrow this time, which was quite a feat, you thought, "did you not give me to understand that you were living with a woman?"

"Yes, yes, but it doesn't solve everything does it? Some things it makes harder. There are no excuses left for one thing. I mean with a man and woman there are so many barriers ... whatever goes wrong you can put it down to the war of the sexes, natural antipathy. But with another woman, what can you say? You're face to face with yourself . . . that's it. No one else to blame. You can't even say 'bloody women' the way you say 'bloody men' because you're one yourself. . ." your voice trailed off in an exhausted sigh.

"Indeed . . . I take your point . . . you have your troubles . . . I have mine. Nothing from the sound of what you say, very gay . . . about it! *'Gay'* . . . I don't know why they use that word. Silly word. Makes it sound like a Maypole . . . lads and lassies . . . buds in May . . . that kind of thing. What was wrong with queer? I mean it *is* . . . queer . . . *extremely bloody queer* . . . if I may say so. . . ."

Queer? Nothing short of supernatural. Most of all the way it was lasting. Going on forever and no sign of let up. You waited, so used to endings and movings on, it would be a relief to get the waiting over. You woke each morning expecting to find it had happened at last, expecting to find yourself detached, wise, tender. You waited to grow close enough to tire or mellow. But time seemed only to embroil you deeper. You waited for the day when your body would stay cool at the sight of her, the smell, the sound of her; her voice, even from the far end of a telephone line. You waited patiently because this day must come as it always had. But not yet, not for an hour, not even tonight when she cursed you and shut the door in your face. Not tonight when you swore that you regretted the first time you laid eyes on her, not tonight when she called you a bitch and a hypocrite. No, not yet. You could not be parted yet. She was built into your flesh, her bones under your skin. You could not loose yourself without tearing yourself asunder. You could feel like scorch marks, the pain of her hands leaving your skin, of her eyes turning from you. Her luminous, passionate eyes. Where would you look if not into her eyes? Good god, you'd better stop this. You reached for your glass needing it urgently. But for some reason the distance between the table and your lips seemed to have lengthened.

"Have you ever loved someone," you asked her,

"so badly it would be a relief to stop? You know, loved them until you were sick with it, and you waited just to get it over? To be free of it?"

"A relief? . . . the man who went out for the milk . . . a relief? . . . . No . . . it was not a relief. An annoyance, a gratuitous insult . . . very shabby behaviour I thought. Not a relief. I cannot say I recall feeling relief. There is a time and a place for everything . . . and breakfast on a sunny morning in the breakfast room is neither . . . if you see what I mean."

"Yes, I never seem to get either of them right. Alanah says my timing is shitty."

"Allannahh . . . who is Allannahh . . . may I ask? Sounds like someone Maureen O'Hara would play in a shawl?"

"Alanah," you answered with deliberate dignity, "Alanah is the woman I live with . . . the woman I love!"

"Allannahhh . . . the woman you love . . . very commendable . . . very appropriately named . . . if I may say so . . . my congratulations." She offered you her hand, her face assuming an air of grave benignity. "And tell me . . . tiny inquiry . . . does she also . . . the woman you love . . . look like Maureen O'Hara . . . the auburn tresses. . .?

"No . . . no she doesn't. Not at all. More like Jeanne Moreau as it happens . . . the mouth you know."

"Ah . . . the french touch. . . . Jeanne Moreau . . . the jenesais what . . . very appropriately named! But tell me this . . . if she looks like Jeanne Moreau the woman you love . . . and sounds like Scarlett O'Hara . . . why are you not at home living with her at this very moment?"

"Oh god . . . I don't know. It's a mess. Nothing's that easy, is it?" you groaned. "We had a row you see, a ridiculous row and she went off. . . ."

"Ahh, . . . say no more . . . a case of cherchez le lait. . . . I comprehend . . . bloody milk. A sense of timing is of the essence. Does Scarlett O'Hara also, lack a sense of timing. . .?"

"No, I do. I never know when I'm well off. I shouldn't have told her. I shouldn't have told her tonight anyway ... I shouldn't have done it." You sighed with impatience, "I should just have come down and had a good time."

Her left eyebrow twitched as if about to assume the familiar acute angle, but no, it merely twitched.

"Told her what ... may I inquire?"

"Oh, I slept with another woman ... but it wasn't important ... well not *as* important, or important in a different way. Oh shit ... who knows what I mean. ... It was important, but not in the way I think she thought it was important, if you see. And it is not ... it is definitely not," you saw your index finger beat the air emphatically, "that I am bored or frustrated. That is not at all the case. I am fully satisfied, so satisfied ... it's nerve racking. ..."

"Exactly ... I comprehend. My late husband exactly ... man who left me for the milk ... could not complain of lack of satisfaction either ... did not complain ... no ... not on that score. Night after night ... mornings too, weekends ... slack period. I could not complain that he shirked on the job ... no ... never that. ... However, I would have preferred it ... if he had said something occasionally ... my name perhaps ... at critical moments or afterwards ... if only to show that he knew who I was. ... Or if he had done something different, you know, or at least ..." she had fetched a fresh pack of cigarettes from her handbag and was carefully unwinding the cellophane wrapping, strip by strip, "or at least the same things ... in a different order. But that," she sighed, "is the male of the species, I think, creatures of habit. ..."

"Yes, bad old, tedious habits!" you laughed, "But that isn't our problem ... nothing ever lasts long enough to form a habit. Something about it ... leads to extremes, somehow. ..."

Something in the nature of the thing, was it? that bred such fever and intensity. A degree of intimacy it might take a woman and man years to establish, flowered in a night. After one week so close strangers could not tell you apart, even old friends confusing your names. Everything seemed to move at three times the normal pace, like an old movie, reeling headlong to the final frame.... Oh Alanah ... was it happening already? Was this its commencement?

"Extremes ... what kind of extremes ... may I ask? Does Scarlett O'Hara not say your name at critical moments?"

"Oh yes ... she does ... all sorts of moments, critical and otherwise...." Yes. You could hear it now, your name said in all her voices. In the morning, husky from sleep, calling for the first cup of black coffee, tender, imperious. And what could touch that first time; the first morning in your house, when you heard her call you ... the new confidence in the tone, ringing down the stairs, summoning you to the bedside, as if she had lived there always. Oh Alanah, of all the voices ... that one....

"Yes she says my name ... But it's not that. It's not the sleeping with someone else that matters.... I mean that's happened before. We've dealt with it ... we've got over it you know, we've always been able to talk things out before, you see ... but this time ... well, it's just the timing of it. She can't forgive me the timing of it...."

"Exactly ... that is it ... of the essence...."

"It's been a bad time for her for months you see," you had picked up your companion's empty cigarette packet and were using it to drum the glass table top, "Well, I told you about her brother ... her favourite brother who died. Cancer of the lung, actually. Never smoked a day in his life, poor bastard...."

"Ah ... no smoke without fire ... they say...."

"Yes, that's it ... burnt himself out. Lived ten years in the space of one. She used to say he'd be dead before thirty, joking of course. He made it to thirty two. Just goes to show ... you can't win, can you?"

"Can't win ... exactly ... not so much as a lottery ticket! Every morning post office ... different post office every morning. Pay your pound ,.. scratch scratch ... beating heart, and what? Nothing. Can't win ... emphatically! Say no more...."

"And she can't come to terms with it, and I can't help. I'm so tired of trying, you know, trying to be as miserable as she is and I simply can not go on with it.

That's why I went to bed with someone else . . . to prove to myself that I was still alive. . . ."

"I comprehend totally . . . all clear. . . . *You,*" she said decisively, "cannot go on being as miserable as Scarlett O'Hara, and *she* cannot go on being as miserable as the favourite brother who did not smoke . . . and I . . . cannot go on being as miserable as I myself have been . . . where does that leave us all?"

"The matter in a nutshell. . . ."

"Some nut . . . some shell." Her head waved sadly from side to side, her eyes closed for a moment but only for a moment, "Can't win," she said reviving again, "but you, my friend, at least are in the draw . . . so to speak . . . that is to say, you possess a ticket, am I right? or know of its whereabouts . . . if you take my point? I think, all in all you should return to the woman you live with . . . with the Jeanne Moreau mouth . . . the woman you love. A fine actress, I might say . . . not Marilyn Monroe of course, but an ad . . . mir . . . able actress nonetheless . . . of a different stripe. . . ."

"But I can't go home . . . she's locked me out. I can't wake her up at this time of night, can I?"

"Yes, timing . . . I take your point . . . of the essence. But why may I ask has she locked you out? I thought women might be more original . . . nothing very gay about it . . . as far as I can see. . . . Incidentally . . . why do they use that expression? *What* have they got against queer? Extremely queer, the whole thing. . . ."

"Yes, queer beyond understanding. . . ."

"But if women are going to lock one another out, sleep with other women," she said with some irritation, "and generally disport themselves like the male of the species . . . what is the point? What is the point of being different if it's all the same?"

"But it's not the same you see," your earnestness matching hers, "it's all different . . . different from one day to the next, from one minute to the next . . . there's no script . . . no costumes . . . no stage directions . . . it's all ad libbing . . . from start to finish."

"Ad libbing, I take your point. Highly commendable . . . timing of the essence. Do you think I would be good at it . . . this . . . no costumes . . . play it by ear as it were ... my late husband always said I had a good ear, if nothing else you know.... But what was my point...? Ah yes ... would I be able for this adlibbing? ... not very gay of course." She subsided for a moment. "Is it, may I ask a pre-requisite ... levity ... of your order? or merely an ass ... pir ... ation?"

"Oh who knows," you laughed raucously, "a consequence, let's hope.... Anyhow we don't use that word you know. That's the men's expression. We say lesbian...."

"Ah, Lesbian ... the greek isles ... poetry and the lyre, blue skies, azure seas, phillosophhhhy ... tragedians ... not quite my line either, I fear...."

"Who knows," you answered idly, "never too late to try...."

"Never too late ... very commendable ... very desirable ... but where would one begin, I wonder ... one who was not an in ... itiate, if you see what I mean? I have often wondered where they begin ... where anything begins.... Tell me," she asked with a new vigour. It seemed to you the more she drank the more coherent she became. "Where do you find these women you sleep with ... when you are not sleeping with Scarlett O'Hara ... where do you come across them, may I ask?"

"Oh here and there, bookshops, parties, bus-stops, pubs, conferences ... you know, the usual way...."

"Conferences? Sounds like the male of the species? Conferences of what may I ask?"

"This and that ... political stuff ... women's rights. Did you hear about the one at the university this weekend, we came down especially for it. Alanah was speaking, you see."

"Of what was she speaking ... the Jeanne Moreau mouth...?"

"Battered women, the need for more money for the refuges...."

"Battered women? Nothing very gay about it?"

"Battered by *men*, I mean. *Wives* battered in their own homes, you know. It wasn't a lesbian conference...."

"Pardon me if I am in error ... but did you not give

me to understand that you met at conferences the women you slept with ... when you are not sleeping with Scarlett O'Hara?... Are these not lesbians of the greek isles?"

"Yes, some of the time, most of the time, but it's only an example you know. I mean there is nothing special about conferences, at least not officially.... It could happen anywhere...."

"I see. Anywhere. Could it happen here ... par example...?"

"What?"

"Might you find one of the women you sleep with when you are not sleeping with Scarlett ... here ... par example?"

"I suppose you might.... If there was a woman here who felt the same way."

"How would you know?"

"What?"

"If she felt the same way? How would you know ... if you were not at a conference or a bus-stop or a bookshop ... the usual way...."

"Hard to say.... You get talking I suppose and then the way someone looks you know ... the way they look at you ... the things they say. The usual thing...."

"The usual thing...? And what pray ... is the usual?" She plucked with uncertain fingers at what might well have been an imaginary tobacco flake on her lower lip, "I met my husband ... par example ... my late husband ... on a London escalator. He ... was going up ... I down. Like the grand Old Duke, you know ... we met ... neither half way up or down. An augury, do you think, of things to come?" she looked at you, a question in the brown rueful eyes, "Was that, would you consider, the usual thing?"

"Hmmm, usual...?" you pondered, "a bit queer alright...."

"Pre ... cise ... ly ... a bit queer. But is it queer enough?"

"Queer enough for what?"

"Exactly ... queer enough for what? For whom? I take your point. But tell me please ... when you first met Scarlett O'Hara was it the usual thing? Did you notice her resemblance to Jeanne Moreau insttt . . . in . . . stant . . . ly. . . ."

"Yes, actually as soon as she spoke . . . and her eyes too – she has these big dark burning eyes you see. . . ."

"I see . . . and where did you first see them?. . ."

"We met in a refuge. . . ."

"Refuge?"

"A refuge for battered women. . . ."

"Jeanne Moreau . . . in a refuge for battered women? Not the usual thing . . . de . . . finitely . . . not the usual. And was it love . . . as they put it . . . at first sight?"

"Oh yes . . . first sight. Almost the very first instant. She was in the kitchen of the refuge, sitting at the table comforting one of the women who had just arrived. Alanah was talking to her and filling me in on the details, as she went. I tried to listen. I tried to concentrate . . . I mean the woman was in the most terrible mess; bruised and head bleeding, but I was so enthralled by Alanah, amazed, by her eyes, you know, she has these great eyes . . . and her mouth – *the* mouth – and then I looked at her shirt. Well she was wearing a black shirt, it was a hot day . . . a hot day in the kitchen and the top buttons of the shirt were undone. . . . I could see the line of her breast, you know, the cleavage showing at the neck of her shirt . . . she was wearing a plain gold chain, it was lying flat on her skin, this beautiful brown skin. Well, I couldn't take my eyes off her. . . . I had this almost unstoppable desire to reach out and put my hand under her breast, just like that, as she talked to this unfortunate housewife, who'd had her teeth kicked in. . . ."

"Ah, yes . . . I comprehend . . . overwhelming . . . the breast . . . first source of solace . . . maternal longing . . . very touching . . . the un . . . fortunate housewife . . . her sorry tale, excluded. . . ."

"Yes, she was excluded alright. Then when Alanah went upstairs I followed her. Didn't stop to think . . . just followed her. And there on the stairs . . . well . . . I put my arms around her from behind you know and she turned, she turned to face me smiling and we kissed right there and then, kissed on the mouth. . . ."

"Very commendable . . . very passionate . . . the jenesais quoi . . . the french touch . . ." Alice beamed her approval, "very considerate. . . . Then what?"

"That was it more or less . . . reckless passion . . . months of it . . . until her brother . . . until tonight."

"Ah, yes . . . the brother . . . very regrettable. . . . If I were you . . . if, that is to say, Rhett Butler kissed me on the stairs as Scarlett O'Hara kissed you I would return to him . . . to her . . . post haste. . . . A woman of such extraordinary attributes. . . . I would return and seek solace. The love of a daughter . . . *two* daughters . . . *two* mothers . . . extremely considerate. . . . Return I say. . . ."

"But she's locked me out . . . I told you!"

"Ah, yes . . . the lockout . . . a disappointment . . . unoriginal . . . however you might telephone . . . essay a re . . . a re . . . a re con ciliation, that's it!"

"Too late . . . asleep now . . ." you groaned almost asleep yourself, slumped on your seat, head lolling.

"Too late? Surely not? I thought you told me . . . never too late?"

"Well this time it is . . . *too* bloody late."

"Ah yes . . . say no more . . . sorry tale . . . companions in misfortune. . . Both lodged here involuntarily. I waiting at the prearranged place and time . . . stood up . . . you perfectly fine, as you say you are . . . locked out. Unforgiven though repentant. A sorry tale. This I believe," she said, with a vague gesture of dismissal: "is what they term 'la vie'. . . . We had better get used to it. . . . Another drink might do the trick, perhaps. . .?"

"It might, it might. . . ."

"However . . . I consider . . . better a thousand times . . . a thousand . . . *locked* out than *stood up* . . . I must stand up . . . in the near future . . . I must stand up . . . draw to a close. Or you . . . stand up and telephone . . . rec . . . rec . . . rec reconciliation . . . what do you say?"

"Too late, too late, too late. Everything too late until tomorrow. . . ."

"Ahhh . . . tomorrow and tomorrow . . . fret our little hour upon the stage . . . sweet sorrow! We must console each other as best we may . . . my friend . . . my good friend ... companion in misfortune ..." she put her hand on your knee, resting it there a moment, "the spirit of Piaf ... fortitude. ... Judy Garland ... somewhere over the rainbow ... jeneregrette," she closed her eyes and threw back her head. For an instant you thought she was about to sing. But no, she remained silent. Had she fallen asleep perhaps? Not that either, after a brief interim she lowered her head and eyes wide open, commiserating, rueful, she patted your thigh again. "Make it through the night ... nil desperandum.... 'Cheers' my good friend," she was lifting her glass to her mouth when she caught sight of a new arrival across the room. "Ah look," she said, her hand in front of her mouth, her speech sidelong, "who is that ... just come in ... skunking behind ... I mean skulking behind the rubber plant ... is it who I think it is ... is it? I think she is who I think it is ... is it Joan O'What's her name from the television ... O'Hara, that's it...."

"O'Malley."

"O'Malley what?"

"Her name's O'Malley, not O'Hara...."

"Ah yes ... not Scarlett. I comprehend ... but scarlet woman nonetheless ... am I right? She looks larger off the box ... mind you. Very large woman for such a small box, average sitting room. Sta ... statchew ... statuesque, you might say.... She is regarding you, I think. An introduction in order, perhaps?"

"No no. Hardly knows me."

"You know her perhaps?"

"Ahh ... more or less." Of course she would be here. You should have known it. The only place she would stay in town. "She was down for the conference," you see, "this weekend."

"Ah yes, the conference, where you meet the women you sleep with in the usual way. I understand, but tell me this ..." she paused, and holding her glass to her face, as though for camouflage, she peered cautiously over its rim: "Ah, but look ... who is that beside her ... you see ... in the black suit and polo neck.... I think I recognise a holy priest ... am I right

...minister of the church ...in fact ...I think I rec ... cognise ... the oneandonly Father Leering! The dancing priest, am I right or am I right? very festive...."

"You know ... I think you *are* right...."

"Companions in disstress perhaps...? not the usual thing?"

"Yes, he was probably hanging around the conference too ... his kind of scene – to be seen you know...."

"Very peculiar ... all these people hanging in the conference ... male of the species I thought ... or lesbians of the greek isles you say ... why a dancing priest ...? very peculiar ... but tell me this ..." she took a surreptitious swig of her vodka before returning the glass to its station in front of her face: "tell me ... Joan O'Hara ... off the box ... male of the species? usual thing?"

"Oh not at all ... quite femme I think, as it happens...."

"Femme... what is that? as it happens.... But does it happen that is precisely what I wish to know ... off the box you understand...?"

"Do you mean is she gay ... oh yes, since the ark! Likes to keep it quiet though."

"Exactly ... hushhush ... very ... state secret ... please do not inquire ... but why? when the dog in the street, if you take my point ... even the dogs ... the world and his wife ... cognizant as it were?"

"She just doesn't like to come out in public with it I suppose...."

"In public ... why not ... off the box what is the problem ... very queer ... very queer on the box ... very large woman for such a small box.... From what – from whom is she hiding ... skunking behind rubber plants ... the dancing priest unlikely alibi...."

"Well I don't know if she is hiding exactly ... well yes ... she is ... in general I mean ... but it's not at all easy you know, you can still get the sack over night, lose your friends, your reputation, all that still operates ... break your mother's heart...."

"Break your mother's heart ... ah yes ... the

mothers of Eireann . . . a fragile species . . . but in this case a very large mother . . . I imagine . . . a very large heart surely? And considering her position . . . that is to say. . ." a sudden impatience had entered her voice, she kept her eyes fixed balefully on the half visible couple across the room, "her height on the perch . . . what is she afraid of? I mean to say who givesadamn. . .? who cares after all apart from the Mammy . . . that's what I'd like to know? I mean on the box not in order perhaps . . . but off it . . . gay or half dead off the box . . . never watch it myself . . . sitting room wrongly proportioned . . . breakfast room another story, sorry tale. . . . But off the box why so hush shush when the very dogs in the street. . .?"

"As I said she's got her living to think of . . . you'd be surprised how small minded people can be. . . ."

"Exactly . . . small minds . . . small box say no more. I take your point. However, that is what I say . . . however, nonetheless, notwithstanding, that said, my point is . . ." she spoke now with a distinct testiness, a disdainful arch to her upper lip, "if I were she . . . that is to say if I were not me . . . that is to say if I were queer or at least more queer than I at present manage . . . I would not I think . . . skunk . . . that is to say skulk . . . no . . . head high . . . caution to the winds, I think. Who bloodycares? Put it in the papers . . . mind their own bloodybusiness . . . social and personal. . . . Yes no creeping about, not my style, skunking, or yours I think? Certainly not Scarlett's style, am I right? In the home for battered women when you embraced on the stairs, caution to the winds . . . no skunking am I right? Jeanne Moreau would not stoop to caution I imagine?" she demanded, throwing back her head.

"No, too reckless for her own good. . . ."

"Ah look . . . the dancing priest. Father Leering coming this way I think . . . no consideration . . . sense of timing . . . ladies would you care to etc. . . . who cares . . . statistics of no consequence. . . . Ah but no . . . averted . . . re-routed . . . call of nature only, I believe . . . please continue. . . ."

"Well you're right of course, life is far too short for all this secrecy. I mean there's little enough passion in the world without hiding it when you've got it."

"Exactly . . . my point . . . when youvegotit . . . flaunt it! Bravo . . . only policy." Her hand groped behind her for the black leather bag, battered though voluminous which she had wedged for safekeeping between her hips and the seat back, when a fresh movement across the room caught her eye. "Ah look . . . executive class previous understanding approaching again I fear, please do not disturb . . . oh no, I stand corrected . . . re-routed I believe . . . now approaching rubber plant . . . vacancy at window seat . . . dancing priest temporarily engaged. Look – very small man for such a large woman, circling before landing permission granted, I think. . . ."

"Will you have another?" you asked.

"No thank you . . . I have now I think sufficient for my needs. . . . I think perhaps I will retire shortly, tight assed boy gone home . . . refreshment trolley stationary. Tell me please . . . if you wish to retire . . . will not detain further . . . cabin lights dimmed you know . . . blankets available on request."

"I can't retire, I told you," you said gruffly.

"Oh yes, very unoriginal. . . ."

"I'll probably have to check in here. Cost me half a week's wages."

"Cost? We must not count the cost surely? Not very gay! Knit up the ravelled sleeve whatever the cost . . . don't you think?"

"Yes but I have to count the cost . . . I may not have enough on me, and they'll want it in advance to – have to sleep somewhere don't I?"

"Indeed . . . I concur . . . must sleep somewhere . . . comes to us all. . . . Tell you what . . . may I propose . . . if not with Scarlett. . . . Why not with me? Yes! Vacancy in the bridal suite you know . . . stood up at the pre-arranged place. Companions in distress, I think . . . sweet solace. . .?"

"Stay with you? In your room, you mean?"

"Yes why not with me? Exactly. . . ." a cloud of smoke exhaled from the corner of her mouth blew into your eyes, "not very gay of course but I think," she fanned the air back and forth with a brisk motion of her hand, "I think, perhaps, I could manage queer...."

"Well ... that's very kind but ... I don't want to be any bother...."

"No bother. Say no more. Case settled. 102 ... no hassle. Phone Jeanne on the morrow ... knit up ravelled sleeve...." She rested her hand lightly on your wrist. Her eyes turned to you, the focus steady for a moment. Lovely eyes now that you looked into them, dark and remorseful, supplicating, "The best of friends ... am I right? All settled ... until tomorrow?"

"Tomorrow ..." you said contemplating her face, the fine skin wrinkled under the eyes, the sensuous mouth grown sad at the corners, "that's what we all tell ourselves, isn't it?"

"Isn't what?"

"We all think tomorrow will sort everything out ... postpone it all until tomorrow...."

"Exactly ... I take your point ... never put off tonight what you can do again tomorrow...."

"Yes, but we wouldn't make such a mess of things would we if we didn't believe in it ..." something in her words or was it the expression in her eyes had brought on a new bout of dejection, "we're all in thrall to tomorrow...."

"In thrall?" Alice asked dubiously.

"Yes. I mean we walk out on people. Slam the door in their face. We don't wait to explain or apologise because we think – oh well, there's always tomorrow ... we'll work it out tomorrow."

"Exactly my point. Tomorrow ... *indispensable*...."

"Yes, but sometimes there is no tomorrow, is there?"

"No tomorrow? Most inconvenient.... Unreliable. Not a very festive consideration, surely?"

"No, it's not, is it?" you chewed at a slice of stale lemon fished from your glass: "but sometimes you can't help thinking it. Do you know what Alanah's last words were to her brother in the hospital ... very last words?"

"Ah the brother . . . I remember him well. No fire without smoke. But let us not return to the dead brother . . . insalutary . . . I think . . ."

"As she was leaving him," you persisted, "On the last night . . . though she didn't know it of course. He was sitting up in bed, smiling. He called something she didn't catch. She was at the door, already late, so she just smiled back, waved and said, 'see you tomorrrow.' See you tomorrow – Can you imagine that?"

"Certainly I can imagine that. See you tomorrow – very sensible attitude. . . ."

"But she didn't, did she?"

"But she didn't did she what?"

"She didn't see him. That's the point. There was no tomorrow," you said with rising anger, "he was dead tomorrow, wasn't he?"

"Dead tomorrow?" Alice was incredulous, "*most* inadvisable . . . downright . . . irresponsible. . .!"

"Afterwards . . . afterwards . . ." you went on, your head fallen, your arms wrapped around you, suddenly cold, "whenever she talked about him that was what hurt her. She had only to think of those words, to remember that smile, that wave, to start weeping all over again. It broke her heart." You felt ready to cry yourself. Overcome by a wave of gloom and self-pity. What a lousy miserable life it was, groping in darkness, battering each other in fear and incomprehension, lured on by the hope of tomorrow, the light at the end of the tunnel that never came. "What's the point of it?" you said with sudden savagery. "What's the point of loving people who die? Loving people you might never see again?"

"Never see again . . . never again . . . I see what you mean. Like the man who went out for the milk. Stood up by mortality. Very dismal. Most dispiriting reflection. I see what you mean, indeed." Alice shook her head slowly from side to side. "But I do not wish to sink, let us not sink into the dumps. Drown in the doldrums. No, not into the dumps tonight. We must rise above it, rise my good friend, companion in distress. We must take arms against a sea of troubles, that is it, a sea of troubles ..." she pointed an elbow towards you and made as if to stand, "would you take my arm? A little assistance gratefully received." There was in her smoke filled voice a tenderness and in her smile a jaunty defiance that cheered you again, did you good. "Only live twice you know ..." she added.

Oh why the hell not? Where else could you possibly go? She couldn't be any more trouble. Bound to go out like a light the second she hit the pillow. And you could not stay here once she had gone. You couldn't walk the streets. Maybe you should have called S? She at least would have been pleased to see you. But now?

Alice had taken a mirror and lipstick from her bag. With a remarkably steady hand she swept two broad ribbons of colour over her lips. "Oh look – " she said, with new interest in the far corner of the room, "Look – Joan and executive class are making friends ... very peculiar. Drink taken I think. Dry champagne window seat you know." The business man was leaning towards Joan O'Malley's shoulder whispering in her ear. Something that brought a snort of laughter. "What is he saying?"

"Talking about his wife ... marvellous woman ... but something somehow missing. ..."

"Missing ... I comprehend ... the missing wife. Miss O'Hara, however will compensate, I fancy...." She gave a broad wink. "Am I right?"

"I have no idea!" you laughed.

"Well well. Time and a place." She opened her bag, replaced the mirror and lipstick and closed it again. "Never too late, I think?" She patted her hair and straightened her dress about her hips. "Shall we?" she asked, offering you her hand. You felt her fingers closing over yours, the rings pressing into your flesh, her clasp warm and confiding. She swayed as she neared the upright position. You tightened your grip and stepped forward.

"I think I recall ... short journey." she said.

Finally in motion you were surprised by how swift her progress was. She cleaved an unwavering path across the centre of the room. Speed perhaps necessary to stay on target. As you neared the far end where Joan O'Malley and the business man sat behind the rubber plant, Alice inclined her head, raised her hand and with a pert waggling of fingers called, "Caution to the winds!" and sailed on.

You halted at the lift. With your free hand you reached out to press the switch.

"Which floor?" you asked.

Alice shook her head.

"No, no. No mechanical elevation. Tonight I wish to stay on terra firma . . . such as it is. The stairs I believe this way. Come!"

As you moved on, she swayed against you. You caught the scent of Chanel number five, and rouge was it or lipstick? two fragrances you had forgotten the existence of, striking you with something like nostalgia.

"First floor." she said. "no hassle."

Your hand on the bannister, as you mounted the first step, you heard a voice behind you. You turned. She was standing in the hallway wearing a dark trenchcoat, the collar turned up over the green tee-shirt, her blonde hair dripping about her face and neck, her cheeks pallid. God, had she come all this way in a downpour, at this hour?

"I thought I might find you here. . . ." she said.

You felt surprise. Pleasure. And absurdly guilty. Yes . . . guilty. Why? As though caught in the act.

"Alanah!"

"But of course . . ." with the superb poise of a society hostess, Alice swung slowly round, a brilliant smile blossoming on her lips. "Ah . . . a sense of timing. . . . Flawless! May I congratulate you?" with a sweeping motion she extended her right hand to the astonished woman waiting at the foot of the stairs. "Scarlett O'Hara . . . I presume?" she said. "I would know you anywhere. . . . The mouth you know. . . !"

Alanah looked slowly from you to Alice and back again, a livid colour appearing in the hollows of her cheeks.

"Am I interrupting something?"

"No . . . we were just . . . or I was. . . ."

"No interruption . . . never that!" Alice's tone was suave. "A small restorative, merely . . . knit up the ravelled sleeve . . . you know. May we . . . may I . . . invite you to join us, perhaps?"

Alanah regarded you harshly. "A bit late for that, don't you think?" she said.

"Oh!" The dismayed and injured look that came onto Alice's face was childlike in its suddenness. "Scarlett! You disappoint . . . a time and a place, I thought?" She took one almost unfaltering step forward, her open palm still outstretched. "Never too late . . . Scarlett . . . surely?" her eyes brightening once more, dark with appeal, "Never too late. . . . Am I right . . . or am I right?"

SUIT, GOODBYE

Helen Smith

I fumbled around in the back of the wardrobe and there was the suit. I pulled it out, and for a moment I saw it new. Off the peg, and the assistants' eyes boring into my back, but it was worth their smirks to have it. Navy with a small white thread, wide lapels and good, full flares that would kick elegantly over the front of my patent loafers.

Under Susan's inspection the material was rubbed and stretched, the flares ludicrous, lapels ugly.

I took the suit off her and folded it again. We'd agreed on a clean sweep.

"Very butch," said Susan. The exact same words that Bren had used when I'd walked into the Merry Maid wearing the suit for the first time. Only in Bren's voice had been approval, warm and flattering. John was sitting next to her, feeding pork scratchings to his poodle.

"Isn't she, John?" said Bren, and John looked up and widened his eyes and said I looked groovy, and where did I get my tie. It was the silk one I'd got in Paris.

"Cheers queers," said Bren, and we drank to her toast. Good beer, Shipstones.

I got the tie out to show Susan the total effect, but she wasn't going to be impressed.

"It is a bit wide," I said, and she said, "Yes," and added, "Real silk, though," as if she'd forgotten.

"Bren liked my suit," I said. Good old Bren. Built like a barrel, then and now, she's not changed. You'd see her still in the Merry Maid, next to the bar along the bench with a view of the door, if they hadn't messed the place around, plush chairs and wallpaper instead of the old red rexine and pale blue gloss. Bren doesn't mind, she thinks I'm daft to miss it. At least she doesn't change. Shirt sleeves rolled up neatly over her solid arms, strong hands around her glass. Brown trousers she used to favour, and does still.

"Bren would," Susan said.

John and I were bitching about Vee and Barbara that night. Bren doesn't join in that sort of thing. She nudged us when they came in and then me and John looked right hypocrites saying hello as nice as pie. They came and sat with us.

Our table filled up, a couple of new girls at the bottom looking awkward. John talked loudly for their benefit and made them laugh. He was good at breaking the ice, but you had to be in the mood. I sat back and watched the comings and goings. My suit was making me feel good, the jacket lining slippy over the crisp shirt, the shirt smooth over me. It made me feel taller and better looking. I was showing off, holding my cigarette just so, my foot up on the bar of the stool. I was full of myself and full of life, glad to be what I was and where I was.

We'd had a good evening around our table. Vee and Barbara had been on good form. Someone started dancing, long after closing, we'd all been locked in, and drunk as we were the idea caught on. Lil stood behind the bar dunking glasses and looking benevolent while everyone started asking everyone to dance.

Barbara asked Bren.

Bren's five nothing. Barbara's tall and she had great high heels on. When they stood up together it was Match of the Day between Forest and Basford Athletic. Bren looked up at the six feet of red satin dress and was inspired. She pushed me off my stool, climbed up on it, pulled Barbara to her and the two of them danced cheek to cheek as nice as could be.

A good night. Eventually Bren and I got set to go. I nipped into the toilet, Bren was waiting outside the yard gate for me. I stopped to chat with someone and by the time we realised there was something wrong it was all over. Bren was lying on the cold stone, curled up around herself, around the places the boots had gone in. The street was empty. Shouting and the sounds of derision echoed from some alley further down. I put my jacket around Bren and said stupid things while we waited for help. She spat a lot of blood, and had her jaw wired for ten weeks while it mended.

It was that summer that Susan's lot started coming down the Maid. Young they were, little round glasses and big boots and full of themselves. They were a breath of fresh air that blew chilly for some when it came out what they thought of us. They expected a lot from life, more than we did. They took everything apart to see how it worked so that they could put it back together different. They thought we should be put back different too.

"Straight lesbians" they called us, though not to our faces. Meaning? The old butch and femme thing. Butch fancying femme and femme pushing the hoover. That sort of stuff. They'd giggle about dildos if they were drunk, be indignant at any suggestion of a lesbian using one, if they were sober. And then they'd look over at us. Did we wear y-fronts? They'd not dare to ask us.

Then one night when Susan and her mate came in they sat at our table. We carried on as usual, John camping his way through the evening. Then Vee and Barbara arrived.

"Now Barbara," said John, "you'll have to watch that. If you go butch Vee won't know where to put herself." Barbara was wearing trousers, bright, dressy things, but trousers.

We all laughed. We were interrupted by this voice from down the end. "Can't she wear what she wants?"

Bren looked up and then looked quickly down into her beer. I did the same.

Barbara took it on though and her easy tone made us look up. "Are you talking to me duck?" she asked Susan, nicely. "Of course I wear what I want. And," she jabbed at John's shoulder, "what an old queen like you knows about fashion could be written on the back of a button."

John grabbed Barbara's hand and kissed it. But the voice kept coming. "Lesbians shouldn't have to copy what goes on out there. Femmes copying straight women and butches copying men and putting women down."

"No," said Barbara and looked at Vee. "It's not like that. Vee doesn't put me down." We grinned. Impossible to imagine Vee putting anyone down. And Vee chipped in. "It's not her that does the housework, you know." More grins. Queen Barbara touching housework!

"Then what's the point of being butch or femme, or trying to be like a man?"

"I don't want to be like a man," said Bren.

John said, "Oh, I do," and everyone laughed. Everyone but me.

I could hear them all joking and arguing together. Barbara was teasing Susan about her boots, weren't they rather butch, and Susan said something about dykes and role playing and John told Bren what a dyke was.

But I was seething. I only realised how angry I was when I started talking and couldn't get my words out right. I knew what I wanted to say. About being proud to love women and proud to be different. About Bren being beaten up and those thugs knowing to beat her up because of the way she looked. That as far as I was concerned being a lesbian and being butch were one and the same thing.

In the end I had to go out in the yard. Bren came out after me, brought my jacket out and took me home and I gave her earache about the things Susan had been saying until I ran out of steam.

I kept bumping into Susan after that. She let on the first time which surprised me and always acted friendly, which had me trying to think up clever responses. One evening she handed me this magazine, folded open. "I thought you'd be interested," she said, "Something I wrote."

"All by yourself?" I said. She reached out a hand to take the magazine back, but I took it to my seat and read it.

It was called "The Visible Lesbian", and underneath was written "Layers of Meaning in the Butch Identity". I took my time reading it, and it seemed to me that she'd caught a lot of the things I'd tried to say that time I was angry and she'd put them down on paper in a pretty fancy way. She mentioned women only space several times, that would be the Maid, more or less, and patriarchal violence, that was about Bren being beaten up. And non-feminist lesbians. Guess who.

I took it back to her when I'd finished and I had to think of something complimentary to say. She was looking nervous, as if she cared what I thought.

Somehow we got talking. I'd stopped trying to be smart. And then it was the end of the evening and somehow we were back at my place together.

We carried on talking. For months. I'd never talked so much in my life. In bed, out of bed, we talked non-stop.

That's a good few years ago now. We ended up living together. The talking slowed down.

Susan and I are very happy together. We are. But just lately we've been talking things over. Things have been a bit touch and go, so we've taken to talking.

Susan asked me when had been the best time in our relationship, for me.

When she'd agreed to live with me, that had been pretty good, there had been plenty of good times, but all in all those early days had been the most exciting.

"How about you," I said, and her answer came up much the same. Then Susan started talking about her boots. The ones she used to wear when I first knew her.

I knew exactly what they looked like because she

still had them. All her lot used to wear them, either blue and white, or red and white, I'd call them the Boot Girls to be aggravating. Doc Marten soles, worn smooth, great round toes and dirty red laces, they were in a bag at the back of the wardrobe.

Susan was talking about what those old boots meant to her and why she'd kept them. She'd never said before. They were her boots for fighting the Revolution in. I hadn't heard that word said in a long time. It used to be said all the time, because it wasn't meant to be far off. Anyway, part of Susan's revolution was going to be running across the rooftops, doing some heroic deed, on her feet the red and white boots.

"Stop laughing at me," she said, so I tried. "It's not just daft things," she went on, "Those boots were getting my articles printed, and talking about stuff at conferences as if we were the first ones that had ever had those ideas. And I'm really happy with my life now," she said, and tailed off before she got to the but.

"It's like your suit," she said.

I had to think about why I'd hung onto my suit all these years. Then Susan made me tell her about it, and I sounded daft too, but the feelings were all right. About being a fighter then, being proud of myself, proud to be a lesbian.

"Has that changed?" Susan asked anxiously.

"Yes. No." I said. "We've just got old. Or respectable. We're not real fighters anymore."

"Not that we were then," said Susan, and I thought of Bren on the pavement and decided she was perhaps right to be harsh.

"Still, we're surviving the 80s," I said.

"That's it though," said Susan. "We're surviving, but we're not happy with it. Both of us are holding onto the past and when did you last feel excited about the future?"

"Too scared I'll see her still in it," I grumbled.

"Well, sod that," said Susan. "Let's do something."

We talked about doing something all night. We always could talk. And the most concrete thing we decided to do was neither here nor there really.

We got the stuff out the wardrobe. My suit, Susan's

boots. Susan's face was like a kid's, half sulky and half tearful.

"You can keep them, Susan," I said. "You don't need to throw them out if you don't want to."

"It's all right," she said, "just saying goodbye."

We took the suit, and the boots, out to the dustbin. The sky was just starting to get light. First time I've been up that late in years. We put the lid down on the past and looked at each other. Really looked at each other, and moved into each other's arms. Then we went to bed.

First time we'd done that in a long time too. So that was our promise to the future.

Afterword
THE WORD AND THE WORLD

Patricia Duncker

France, January, 1990

To:
Lilian Mohin, Director
Onlywomen Press
38 Mount Pleasant
London WC1X OAP

My Dear Lilian,

Well, here is the collection I want to propose to you with all my comments and editorial suggestions. I had a vast number of stories to read, often several from each writer, which meant I could read very different work by the same woman. I wanted to put together a range of styles, modes, voices, reflecting our strengths and our differences, a collection of work by published and unpublished Lesbian writers, a collection of chequered, various, differing meanings. Here are the stories I chose.

Not every word here is easy or comfortable to read. Some are properly controversial. Which is as it should be. Like every editor I had to keep two constants in my mind: the quality and uniqueness of each individual piece of writing and the overall shape of the book. I wanted to privilege writing that took risks. And writing that seemed to spring from directly Lesbian perceptions and interpretations; writing that illuminated our existence, making us the centre, not the rim of the world. And, of course, among ourselves, we too often reproduce the including and excluding circles of the society we inhabit.

One of my editorial priorities was to find and encourage work that contributed to the dismantling of the racist structures that are a creeping fungus in all our communities. Lesbians have always been involved in this crucial political work, and here, in this book, our writing should be part of that struggle for change. Words change women's minds, change women's worlds. But this doesn't mean that Blacklesbian writers should be the only women involved in unpicking an evil that surrounds us, and perpetually surfaces in our daily lives. Breaking that evil into shards means interrogating everything we are, everything we do, and every word we write. We need to ask ourselves hard questions, and to interrogate our texts, to demand accounts from our representations and from our lived experience, from our words and our worlds. Who are our lovers and friends? Who is on our side? Who fights for us? It is here that the Utopian impulse in Lesbian writing – the imagining of Lesbian communities – becomes crucial. I want to read writing that projects the world in which I want to live. That world doesn't yet exist. We must write it into being, and then insist on living within our own words. We can never re-create our lives in the flesh, unless we have argued, theorised, imagined and desired the world we want to inhabit. And that means that we will also engage, critically, angrily, joyfully, with the world that is not of our making. We write our stories with a double vision: a vision of that which is and a vision of what we desire. And we write with a passion that gives no place to despair. For we may well have to defend both our words and our worlds with our lives.

And so I have insisted on an anti-racist politics of writing for *In And Out Of Time*. Here are some of our beginnings, some of our work in putting that politics into practice. The love between Ella, a Blackwoman, and her white lover, is celebrated, honoured and mourned in Char March's "The Runners"; Naomi in Tina Kendall's narrative reaches across the unseeing white world to change another Blackwoman's life; Blacks, Asians, whites, gaze at one another uneasily in the South African gay underworld described in Claire

Macquet's "Gypsophila"; Shabnam in Daljit Kaur's "Diwali Mubarak" ponders on how to choose her way of telling her parents she is Lesbian, how to come out on her own terms, which may not be those of her white lover. Most devastating is Shameem Kabir's analysis of a racism within passion and sexual intimacy: the refusal to grapple with difference in the failure of love between the two singers, Smita and Ginnie. The white woman seeks sameness, an ease of being, not the prickly difficulty of the woman who is other than herself. This is the racism of complacency, an ignorance in the heart. I value all the writing in this book because here we are saying the things that are difficult to say in the world that is not of our making. And it is here that we can re-make the world.

One of the things that we have always found difficult to say is who we are. Many of us find it hard to say that we are Lesbians. The meaning of the sign Lesbian is disputed territory, even among ourselves. For some of us it is hard to write under the names we inhabit in the world. We fear for our jobs, our children, even our lives. Onlywomen Press insists on a political world-view that has been conveniently talked out of fashion in heterosexual cultural criticism. For us, there has to be a direct link between the flesh and the word, a living connection between the woman who loves, the woman who lives, and the woman who writes. Otherwise we would have no reason not to publish writing by straight women, or writing by men. I am not concerned with the question of what constitutes Lesbian writing, but with what we, as Lesbians, are writing now. For we have not always written in the same modes or styles, our writing is shaped by our different histories, cultures, political imperatives. Those of us who will not actually be imprisoned or murdered for writing Lesbian fiction no longer have to disguise our Lesbian characters as men. Or re-form heterosexual desire to conceal and yet reveal our meanings. We need not be doomed, damned and dead by the end of the tale. But what would our writing be like without the violence of the heterosexual society around us? That we do not yet know.

There are no closet stories in this book. That is to say, there are no stories which suggest that the closet is either a profitable, wise or safe place to be. But two of the writers are not able to write under their own names, for different reasons. All of us, at some time in our lives, use masks and disguises in the straight world. We sometimes persuade ourselves that it is for our own safety, but in fact it is only safe to do so if we have enough confidence and self-awareness to put on our disguises like costumes, and props; to use them to play games, to subvert and to outwit the world. If we are forced to adopt our masks out of fear we run the risk that the masks will be our masters, that the mask becomes the face. How can we be honest to each other in a world that forces us to tell lies? Here we need to find the balance, between courage, cunning and integrity, every day of our lives.

The practice of using pseudonyms has a long and strange history. Women writers often used masculine or sexually ambiguous names in order to be taken seriously by the world of literary men. Currer Bell and George Eliot were more adventurous in their lives than in their words. Some celebrated Lesbian writers never needed to use pseudonyms because they had the money and the class to protect themselves. Radclyffe Hall is a case in point. But there are other Lesbian writers who have felt too vulnerable to take the risks of freedom. Rosemary Manning published *A Time and A Time* as Sarah Davys in 1971. This book was an autobiography which discussed her Lesbianism and the pressures which led to her attempted suicide. Interestingly, both her pseudonym and her suicide attempt were the result of what she describes as 'the habit of secrecy'. Manning came out on an ITV programme in 1980 and re-published her book under her own name in 1986. By this time Manning was seventy and had retired from the teaching profession. She was no longer dependent on heterosexual opinion for her income. She had nothing to lose. In the opening chapter of her last book, *A Corridor of Mirrors* (The Women's Press, 1987), she has this to say about coming out:

> Coming out gives one the chance to be honest;
> indeed, it imposes the burden of honesty and it
> is a heavy burden to take up. The years of dis-
> honesty had formed a hard shell and I con-
> tinually found myself moving back under its
> protection, as a prisoner sometimes comes to
> love his gaoler. ... At last my sexual pro-
> clivities, which I had had to suppress for so
> long, were out in the open. This was significant
> to me not so much as a truth revealed to the
> world but as an inner tension relaxed, a decep-
> tion laid aside.

We live now in difficult times. We have always lived in difficult times. We have won nothing that we have not fought to win. Manning's coming out was not a solitary statement, but part of a collective refusal to live within lies. Each time a Lesbian woman insists on the truth without fear, she gives another woman the courage to live her life more honestly, and with greater courage.

I had several contributions from a Lesbian writers' group. All their work was interesting and two of the women are published here. Most of the contributors to this volume have, at some time or another, been involved in various writers' groups. I know that Onlywomen Press itself grew out of a writers' group which the founding women had joined because of their involvement in the Women's Liberation Movement. The politics of the press are, and always have been, based on the insight that making our own meanings is a crucial part of our long revolution. The making of meaning is not something that any one of us can undertake on her own; it is a collective project. We need to challenge and encourage each other, disturb our preconceptions, prejudices, assumptions, re-make our words. All writing is craft. Each piece of writing needs to be chipped, shaped and polished. But no conventional literary form ever fits our thinking like a second skin. Our written edges are often jagged and angry. We need each other's perceptions and criticisms. For it is the most difficult thing in the world to write with elegance, force and accuracy; to be precise about feeling, about the implications of betrayal, about passion, joy, pain.

And yes, there is a thread running through this chain of different fictions. That thread is time, our time, Lesbian time, the history of Lesbian lives, with all our disjunctions, discontinuities, gaps, and secret traditions. The landscape of our writing is as varied as the earth. And we begin where we always have to begin, with what we want, who we desire, where we are, who we are. The coming-out stories in this volume express different times, different worlds. There is South Africa of the 1960s in Claire Macquet's "Gypsophila", the hidden gay life of the Pro where a Black man in a coral necklace drinks at the same bar as the butch Indian dykes, the old Boer, Beatrice, with his basket of vegetables and passion for brickies, the ambiguous Diana, the white woman who voices her political opinions in a measured public school voice. Macquet describes the doomed, racist order which gave the white gays a 'gangster protection'. It is an order whose destruction we are now witnessing, torn down at last by the courage of Black people, who are taking hold of their piece of the world. But that time is our time; we were there, we are there. Daljit Kaur's sharp coming-out Diwali comedy, set in contemporary domestic British life, poses the question of language and culture. Where should Shabnam look for the words in her parent's culture to match her own understanding of herself as Lesbian? We still dream of a common language with our ethnic communities. Sometimes I am obstinately optimistic that we can find the words to disarm, persuade, convince, those that we love – even though there are whole worlds between us. But sometimes I am not so sanguine.

Naomi, the heroine of Tina Kendall's narrative, never speaks. Instead, she reaches past a queue of unwitting whites towards the other who is also herself, the other Blackwoman. The effect of her gesture causes a revolution in the life of the Blackwoman to whom she can say nothing; to whom she can give no words, yet to whom she gives another world. Coming out is a process, not a moment. Coming out is a continuing relationship to the world. The person who puts up the most resistance, as all of us know, is often neither parent, nor boss, nor friend, nor even the woman we love, but ourselves.

Two stories which deal, head-on, with the violence that exists between women and men are Cherry Potts' *Penelope Is No Longer Waiting* and Caroline Halliday's *The Wedding Stone*. Both these stories take marriage as their theme. And both writers view marriage as not simply a limitation in women's lives, but as a violence to our integrity. I think it's no coincidence that both are elegant, stylised narratives; prose that is both poetic and remote, yet as powerful and close as the assassin's knife at the throat. We live within reach of the menaces of men; but they too live within our grasp. They fear us, and they have good reason to do so. When we cease to be their wives, cease to be their slaves, cease to wait.

At the core of the book are the stories which analyse, with meticulous passion, the love we have for one another, the pain we cause, the ways in which we betray our lovers and ourselves, the ways we abuse or celebrate the women we love, the women we admire, fear, desire. I found that, throughout the summer, as I read on, the pairs of women in these stories, the named and the unnamed, the silent and the speaking, became the threads in my mind. They became part of me: Agnes O'Reardon and Gardenia Watts in Valerie Potter's fantastic dance, Marjolein and the narrator in *The Great Tropical Hardwood Walkout* facing the departure of their protesting furniture, Jackie, the gymmistress, and the other teacher who sees her across the staff-room, the unnamed neighbours in Rebecca O'Rourke's sassy squib, *You Can't Say That*. Smita and Ginnie, the singers in Shameem Kabir's powerful jigsaw of destructive desire and the defeat of love, give time a musical meaning; the moments of division, dissolution and discord, and the moments of harmony, strength and triumphant sexual joy.

There is some fine, explicit sexual writing in this book. And it is written into the script as part of, not all of who we are, how we love. No one makes love in a void. Every gesture, every kiss, every touch is encircled by the culture and the political community out of which we come. But we don't have to make love to each other within the fixed rituals of any prescribed patterns of courtship, any patterns determined elsewhere. Our passion can crack open the world, change the world. Our bodies lean across the limits set by our particular circumstances, our fears, our inhibitions and bad memories, to touch one another. But we love, make love, and write love within history, in time. We must know these parameters. And how to break them.

There has been increasing interest in our communities in sexually explicit and erotic writing, in fantasy, and in pornography. All of which has left me with a peculiar sensation that not only the Lesbian body, but also the Lesbian imagination is in chains. I want sexual writing that actually transgresses rather than reproduces the conventional limits of what is considered erotic by the heterosexual world. Which means finding new words and new ways of writing love. Breaking the limits placed on love is the process described in Aspen's *Another Garden*, as the two lovers, Tess and Jane, discover a different kind of eroticism in response to the sinister and debilitating illness which seizes Tess, an illness that is terrifyingly described.

I want to read writing that takes risks, writing that asks difficult questions, writing that is unafraid. Alison Ward's "Below Zero", a haunting, frightening narrative, takes on the possibility that there may be no meanings, that the only value we can attribute to all things, even to ourselves, is that we exist. That we are precious because we are. Ward proposes an existential dimension to Lesbian passion, but in "Below Zero" love is frozen into death. When we talked about this piece of writing you remembered the Arctic flowers, the miracle of life and colour on the edge of the waste. You saw us, the Lesbians, as the Arctic flowers, not only surviving, but flowering into beauty in a dead world. And I remembered the cold, and the cold giant limbs of the dinosaur. For my understanding of Lesbian time, our points of reference, now stretches back beyond history into an Antarctic void, inhabited by the ghosts of dinosaurs – and the passions of living women. That fragile passion between us is of infinite value. For the time inevitably comes, when we too cease to be. You said: but our words remain. And that's true. Sometimes no more than the bare threads of our lives survive in history. But we are there for the women who search for us, like the Arctic flowers.

There is an ambitious range of fictional writing styles here; from straightforward realism, the classical short story based on two or three plausible characters, with a scorpion sting in the tail, myths re-imagined, a sequence of lyrical tableaux, a brief thriller with fast action and plenty of strong verbs, meditations, Lesbian surrealism, and, as in "Below Zero" and "The Secret of Chantal Grey", original, disturbing use of first person narrative. These stories refuse to pretend that we are always open or honest with each other. We are often neither generous nor loving. Our inner lives are often confused, troubled or sinister in their opacity.

The explicitly political feminist narratives in this book written in opposition to the state and the patriarchy are set both in and out of historical time. Char March imagines Britain as a police state where Lesbian women form an underground guerrilla force; Shelly Anderson re-imagines ancient Greece and the woman who wrote us into the finest lyric poetry of her time. And of course, as in all political fantasy writing, March and Anderson are addressing contemporary reality, reminding us who is the enemy. Phaae of Crete sees the women of Lesbos as gossiping, trivial and vain, reflecting the inevitable dynamics of every small, inward-looking community. But the Amazon reminds her: "Before you shoot, choose your mark well. It's not the Lesbians you have your quarrel with." It's easy to forget that our real enemies are not among each other, especially when we feel that we have been betrayed, mistreated, or abandoned. With "Saccharin Cyanide" and "Scarlett O'Hara" we are in the world of contemporary feminism, the alternative world where our social lives take place in the Women's Centre, where we go to conferences, defend the women who have no one else to defend them, our minds filled mainly with the internal politics of the women's movement. The conference that is the backdrop to the bar in Mary Dorcey's "Scarlett O'Hara" is engaged upon the reassessment of feminism after twenty years. And the narrator is engaged with a reassessment of herself. But how are we to read Alice, the straight woman whose interrogation gradually clarifies the narrator's desperate muddle? It is Alice who has the courage to take risks, Alice who snaps her fingers at the famous closet personality of feminism; Alice who cries, "Caution to the winds!" as she sweeps off up the staircase towards her first experience of Lesbian love. And it is Alice who gives the two women lovers back to each other, to remake their love if they choose. Alice reminded me that there is a potential Lesbian in every woman.

Men's violence against us is never absent, never far from the surface of our fictions. But it is as if we cannot look that violence in the face for too long. Anna Livia shifts the ground from beneath our uneasy complacency. One of the butch dykes in Helen Smith's poignant outline of our moment in history, "Suit, Goodbye", pays the price for being out in the public space. But Smith's portrait of her lovers, the unnamed narrator and the young, political Lesbian, Susan, in her revolutionary boots, is as optimistic in impulse as is Mary Dorcey's image of Alice. Here are two Lesbians, with apparently nothing whatever in common beyond the fact that they are both Lesbians, who fall in love by talking to each other. The narrator's pride in being what Susan contentiously describes as a 'straight' Lesbian, is based on desire, the proud desire to love women in the flesh. Susan wants to talk about what that means; to turn flesh into words. On the night that they throw out the butch suit and the revolutionary boots, they talk right through till dawn, and then go to bed and make love. The words become flesh. And this is where we begin the future again, in anticipation of our future time, with the knowledge that our passion has a utopian energy, that we can subvert the whole world. It is here that we begin: talking politics, making love.

Being a writer also means being a reader. And, all last summer, this is who I have been; the reader, passionately engaged, and implicated in what she reads. The writing and the reading were entwined in my letters to you, in all the discussions we had, whenever we disagreed, whenever we were passionately in agreement. But the writer and the reader also need the publisher. You and I, and many of the women in this book, have been all three things. We will never write well, nor do ourselves justice, if we are not committed to rigorous critical reading, both of our own work and the work of other women. Nor will our words survive if we do not have our own publishing houses, our own means of communication and our own methods for distributing and selling our books. Onlywomen Press is the only British publisher explicitly committed to Radical Feminist Lesbianism and Radical Lesbian writing. Without the Press, this book would not exist.

I am perpetually haunted by our strength and our fragility. We must earn our own livings; we must inhabit this world. Even while we create our own. I have an enormous collection of books, pamphlets and ephemera from the 1970s and the 1980s, our words from all our years in the Women's Liberation Movement. I guard them carefully, knowing that these are the words of our worlds, our meanings. How am I – how are we to live in one world while desiring another? I don't wish to be a comfortable citizen in a racist, sexist and Lesbian-hating world. I don't wish to be integrated into a society which is based on hostility to my values, my priorities and my political concerns. And so I want writing that is subversive in this world, but that expresses the words of the world I desire. The virtues of insolence, the refusal to conform to heterosexual cliché, are the hallmarks of Lesbian writing. And they are also our strengths as Lesbians. We can rewrite the world – one word at a time. In this book we are making our own meanings. Triumphantly.

As always – very much love,
Patricia.

CONTRIBUTORS' NOTES

Alison Ward: Born in Hong Kong, has kept on the move ever since – lived in Kenya, Germany, France and various parts of England – studied first music, then accountancy, in London – and for the time being has returned there, to live and work in the Docklands. She has written one novel, *The Glass Boat* (1984), and is currently working on a set of plays for video.

Anna Livia: is 34, author of 4 novels and 2 collections of short stories, the latest of which are *Minimax* about the lesbian vampire Natalie Clifton Barnet, and *Saccharin Cyanide*, after the story printed here. She is currently translating a French detective novel and running a university database. She is co-writing an epistolary novel set in Venice and planning a comedy of stereotypes based on her short story, "Angel Alice".

Aspen: "Another Garden" is not autobiographical, though it is informed by my experience of chronic illness.

Berta R. Freistadt: lives in a basement in London and dreams of the sea. Other dreams include earning a living by writing, doing nothing all day, finding time to write a novel. She has had plays, stories and poetry published in several anthologies – this is the first time she has been published by Onlywomen. No one is more surprised than she is – and delighted.

Caroline Halliday: is a white lesbian, born in 1947 in London. She works as a freelance consultant on management training courses, and teaches lesbian creative writing. Her poetry has appeared in a number of anthologies, including *Naming The Waves* (1988), *The New British Poetry* (1988), and in her own collection, *Some Truth, Some Change* (1983). She combines writing with being a co-parent; her daughter lives with her half the week.

Char March: I grew up in Central Scotland and now live in West Yorkshire. I *much* prefer writing stories and poems rather than bloody painful Contributors' Notes! Aside from enjoying reading her stories and novels I'm not connected to Caeia March. I am in an ACE lesbian writing group, based in Manchester, called "The Outlanders". We perform our work to packed audiences of screaming fans upon occasion. I'm really pleased with "The Runners".

Cherry Potts: I have been writing / telling stories for as long as I can remember. I have been middle aged all my life, and when I catch up with myself I shall start looking forward to retiring. I currently live in London in passionate domesticity with my lover and two cats.

Claire Macquet: I was born in South Africa in 1941, into a Catholic, white, working-class family. I became a dyke and a communist in my teens, and (on both accounts) left for Britain after the mass arrests of the early 60s. I discovered Lesbian community and culture when Clause 28 brought me onto the streets; I have since written a dozen stories and am struggling with a novel. I write under my own name as part of my job, and need official permission to use my byline in any other publication. So I write, I hope with her blessing, under my grandmother's name.

Daljit Kaur: "Diwali Mubarak" is the first in a collection of stories about Shabnam and Christine, which I am currently working on with my lover Margaret. I started writing because as an Asian lesbian I was acutely aware of the lack of our presence in fiction. My writing has developed with the support of the Asian Women Writers Collective, who I wish to thank. Although the collective is London based I would encourage any Asian women scribblers to contact us!

Frances Gapper: I am 32 and would like to move

out of London before I get much older. I write when I can, around the edges of work, etc. My novel, *Saints and Adventurers*, was published by The Women's Press in 1988. I live with my lover, Helen.

Helen Smith: is 35 and lives in Manchester but came out in Nottingham in the mid 70s. Despite her poor memory she has a streak of nostalgia a mile wide. One of the best things about her present is membership of the writers group, "The Outlanders", and her ambition to complete a novel eventually, gives the future a look-in too.

Margaret Melvin: is not my real name. She was born last year when I needed a public front to organise a Fringe reading for my lesbian writing group, Northern Dykes, which I have been attending for the last three years. This is Margaret Melvin's first publication. Her alter ego is 47, has written poems, short stories, songs and community plays, wants to get work as a Writer in Public and/or a Community Writer, is not out to her family or as a working writer, and reckons with Section 28 rampaging in Edinburgh she cannot at present take the risk.

Mary Dorcey: born and brought up in County Dublin, Ireland, she's travelled widely and lived in France, England, Japan and the U.S.A. Active in the women's movement since 1972, she was a founder member of Irishwomen United and the first Irish Gay Rights group. Her published work includes *Kindling* (poetry collection), Onlywomen, 1982; *A Noise From the Woodshed* (short stories), Onlywomen, 1989 as well as contributions to the anthologies: *Bread and Roses* (Virago), *In the Pink* (The Women's Press), *Girls Next Door* (The Women's Press), *Beautiful Barbarians* (Onlywomen), *The Spare Rib Health Anthology* (Pandora), *Mad and Bad Faeries* (Attic Press), *Naming the Waves* (Virago), *Ain't I a Woman* (Virago), *The Pied Piper* (Onlywomen), *New Angles* (Oxford University Press), *Wildish Things* (Attic Press).

Patricia Duncker: I was born in Jamaica in 1951. My father is West Indian, my mother English. I write fiction and political criticism. My work has been published in various academic or feminist journals and in *The Pied Piper* (Onlywomen, 1989). My book on contemporary feminist fiction, *Sisters and Strangers*, will be published by Basil Blackwell. I always knew what kind of work goes into writing fiction, and now I realise the labour needed to produce the book itself. I'm very proud to have worked with all the women who have written and produced *In And Out Of Time*. Bravo.

Rebecca O'Rourke: began writing seriously with the encouragement and inspiration of the Federation of Worker Writers and Community Publishers. She has published a novel, *Jumping the Cracks* (Virago, 1987) and has a story in the collection, *Reader, I Murdered Him* (Ed, Jen Green, The Women's Press, 1989). She also writes criticism, most recently, *Reflecting on The Well of Loneliness* (Routledge, 1989). She lives in London and in addition to writing, works as an adult education tutor.

Shameem Kabir: I was born in 1954, and wanted to write from an early age. I have a degree in English, and I currently work in television. Passions include being a lesbian feminist, women's books, and music. And of course writing. Because I write primarily for myself, this has allowed me to take risks and to experiment. "In And Out Of Time" was my first attempt at a short story. Although I would like to make a living as a songwriter, my ambition is to "find my form" as a writer. That novel, for instance.

Shelley Anderson: Since I left the US Army over ten years ago as a conscientious objector, I have worked in the peace movement. For the last two years I have also been involved with the International Lesbian Information Service, as I believe passionately in lesbians and in internationalism. I love to travel, and had the good fortune to spend one night near Eressos, legendary birth place of Sappho, where I was given the plot of "Someone In Some Future Time" in a dream. I think the Black American poet and activist June Jordan said it all when she wrote that we must become a menace to our enemies.

Tina Kendall: I am caught up at present in a double life spent partly in rural France, partly in the industrial north of England. The contrasts and conflicts which all this movement creates, refresh me and keep me on my toes. I write, teach, translate, and take care of our children. I could do with a forty-eight hour day and then maybe I could fit in some serious academic research and film-directing on top of everything else!

Valerie Potter: I was born in 1954 in Tenterden, Kent. I spent my childhood in Nigeria and then Jamaica as my father worked for the Overseas Education Department. Over the years I have worked in a number of occupations: as a dental nurse, a junior matron in a boys' prep school, a fish packer on the Hull docks, a marketing administrator for a wine and spirits firm. I am currently working as a library assistant. Two years ago I finished a degree in "History of Ideas" at Middlesex Polytechnic. I have a love–hate relationship with the Women's Movement and I am very proud to be a dyke.

MORE RADICAL FEMINIST LESBIAN BOOKS
from ONLYWOMEN PRESS

FICTION

STEALING TIME
Nicky Edwards
Squatters in decaying London plot against the credit card economy in a not so distant future. One deliberately dangerous adolescent finds even their methods tame. Both an exciting adventure and a novel of ideas that brings today's vicious politics to their illogical conclusion while offering a rascally hope for the future.
£4.95   ISBN 0-906500-31-1

SACCHARIN CYANIDE: short stories
Anna Livia
Contemporary dyke dramas, lyrical science fiction fantasies, snappy advice and fables at once sexy and surprising. Written with a glittering grace of language, these new stories emphasise both Anna's gift for witty dialogue and her depth of perception about underlying emotional values.
£4.95   ISBN 0-906500-35-4

STRANGER THAN FISH: short stories
J.E. Hardy
Rich details of place and fully realised characters narrating: the turbulence of "coming out", the world weary knowledge of relationships with heretofore heterosexuals, the damage as well as the enduring love found within family ties.
£4.95   ISBN 0-906500-32-X

A NOISE FROM THE WOODSHED: short stories
Mary Dorcey
Specifically sensual, altogether humorous, feminist language presenting: escape from an "old age asylum"; expatriate Irish lesbians confronting English racism; heterosexual rural Ireland; "romance" in a variety of guises. *One of the "top twenty" in Feminist Book Fortnight '90.*
£4.95   ISBN 0-906500-30-3

RELATIVELY NORMA
Anna Livia
Anna Livia's first novel — about a London feminist coming out to her family in Australia
£3.95   ISBN 0–906500–10–9

INCIDENTS INVOLVING WARMTH: lesbian feminist love stories
Anna Livia
A collection which interprets love with bittersweet humour and wryly accurate observations — "dangerous dykes", devious grandmothers and very perceptive eleven year olds.
£3.95   ISBN 0–906500–21–4

BULLDOZER RISING
Anna Livia
Futuristic novel of bone chilling glee. In a hi-tech city where good citizens must die at 41, a secret congress of "old" women love, quarrel, plot survival and fight back.
£4.95   ISBN 0–906–500–27–3

ALTOGETHER ELSEWHERE
Anna Wilson
A novel about women as vigilantes: wage clerks, laundrette workers, mothers — black and white, lesbian and straight. Fiction which demands reflection.
"its language is taut and precise ... makes the pulse race."
City Limits

£3.95   ISBN 0–906500–18–4

CACTUS
Anna Wilson
Realism in Anna Wilson's lyrically graceful first novel about lesbians within the social pressures of contemporary England and those of twenty years ago.
£3.95   ISBN 0–906500–04–4

SATURDAY NIGHT IN THE PRIME OF LIFE
Dodici Azpadu
Tough, tightly written novel about lesbianism in the long term — as one of the characters says, "Queer begins at sixty."
£3.95   ISBN 0–906500–24–9

GOAT SONG
Dodici Azpadu
Urban, dyke street-life in a novel which looks at the excitement, the danger and, ultimately, the profound moral dignity of its characters.
£3.95   ISBN 0–906500–25–7

THE NEEDLE ON FULL: science fiction short stories
Caroline Forbes
More than dykes-in-space; stories that show us a range of all-too-probable futures, stories that crackle with wit and urgency.
£4.95   ISBN 0–906500–19–2

THE PIED PIPER: lesbian feminist fiction anthology (1989)
ed. by Anna Livia and Lilian Mohin
Work by 19 authors with landscapes that change as you move from one story to the next: medieval Britain, 19th century Jamaica, modern southern France, dyke bars in the U.S.A. and London. Between them they touch on many myths and issues: "passing", definitions of activism, definitions of love.
£4.95   ISBN 0–906500–29–X

THE REACH: lesbian feminist fiction anthology
ed. by Lilian Mohin and Sheila Shulman
The first in Britain and still being reprinted for its gripping writing, its wide range of subjects: family confrontations and connections, futuristic fantasies, struggles with anti-lesbianism, the exhilaration of love.
£3.95   ISBN 0–906500–15–X

THEORY

FOR LESBIANS ONLY: a Separatist Anthology
ed. by Sarah Lucia Hoagland & Julia Penelope
The world's first anthology of lesbian separatism. 608 pages documenting twenty years of both activism and scholarship. Novelists, poets, musicians, philosophers and rowdy dykes contribute here to a declaration of lesbian civilisation.
"something to cut through the late 1980s 'post-feminist' confusion like a hot knife through butter"
The Pink Paper
£8.95   ISBN 0–906500–28–1

LOVE YOUR ENEMY?
heterosexual feminism and political lesbianism
The debate as originally seen in letters to "WIRES".
"essential reading for anyone trying to work out how feminists view lesbianism" *Undercurrents*
£2.95   ISBN 0–906500–08–7

WOMEN AGAINST VIOLENCE AGAINST WOMEN
ed. by Sandra McNeill & dusty rhodes
Three sets of conference papers discussing pornography, rape and feminist action.
£4.95   ISBN 0–906500–16–8

BREACHING THE PEACE
Collection of essays from a Radical Feminist conference anti the women's peace movement.
£1.25   ISBN 0–906500–13–3

DOWN THERE
Sophie Laws
An illustrated guide to self-exam.
£1.50   ISBN 0–906500–05–2

WOMEN AND HONOR
Adrienne Rich
Prose from one of Lesbian Feminism's foremost poets.
"to extend the possibilities of truth between us. The possibility of life between us."
£0.75 (pamphlet)   ISBN 0–906500–02–8

POETRY

BECAUSE OF INDIA: selected poems and fables
Suniti Namjoshi
Work spanning 9 published books and accompanied by essays which situate these deft, precise poems in the time, place and sexual politics which surrounded their writing. A landmark publication. *One of the "top twenty" in Feminist Book Fortnight '90.*
"blending that which is uncompromisingly Indian in her with the best of the English satirical tradition ... demonstrates how effectively the personal may be fused with the political."   *SpareRib*
£4.95   ISBN 0–906500–33–8

PASSION IS EVERYWHERE APPROPRIATE
Caroline Griffin
Memorably rhythmic verse in the first full collection from a much anthologised poet. Poems that wring an exhilarating energy from the ordinary detail of contemporary British lesbian life.
"the journey towards oneself requires courage and honesty. Both qualities are here ... always earthed in the experience of feminist lesbianism"   *City Limits*
£3.95   ISBN 0-906500-34-6

LOVE, DEATH and the CHANGING of the SEASONS
Marilyn Hacker
A novel in verse. Sonnets recounting the heady start through to the rending conclusion of a one-year love affair.
"virtuoso displays of poetic craftsmanship"
Poetry Review
£4.95   ISBN 0-906500-26-5

BEAUTIFUL BARBARIANS: lesbian feminist poetry
ed. by Lilian Mohin
An anthology that concentrates, rather than collects; displaying the work of sixteen poets (with photos and biographical notes).
"juicy and contentious"   *Everywoman*
£4.95   ISBN 0-906500-23-0

ONE FOOT ON THE MOUNTAIN: British Feminist Poetry 1969-1979
ed. by Lilian Mohin
Not just the first — still the one that changes lives.
£4.95   ISBN 0-906500-01-X

DIFFERENT ENCLOSURES
Irena Klepfisz
Work from three collections by a major Jewish lesbian feminist poet.
£3.95   ISBN 0-906500-17-6

THE WORK OF A COMMON WOMAN
Judy Grahn
A poetry of love and activism, the heart of the women's liberation movement.
£3.95   ISBN 0-906500-20-6

Free catalogue from:
Onlywomen Press, 38 Mount Pleasant, London WC1X 0AP

If ordering books, please include 15% for packing and postage. Prices may change from those listed here. We endeavour to keep them as low as possible.